remember to forget

Never stop smiling!

Ashley

remember to forget

Revised and Expanded Edition

By Ashley Royer

BLINK

BLINK

Remember to Forget, Revised and Expanded Edition
Copyright © 2016 by Ashley Royer

This title is also available as a Blink ebook. Visit www.zondervan.com/ebooks.

Requests for information should be addressed to:
Blink, 3900 *Sparks Dr. SE, Grand Rapids, Michigan 49546*

ISBN 978-0-310-75171-7

Cover design: *Cindy Davis*
Cover photography: *Shutterstock*
Interior design: *Kait Lamphere*

Printed in the United States of America

16 17 18 19 20 21 22 23 24 25 26 /DCI/ 20 19 18 17 16 15 14 13 12 11 10 9 8 7 6 5 4 3 2 1

I'd like to thank everyone who has been with me through the writing of this book. Without your support, comments, and messages, I would not have made it this far. I love you all.

LEVI

When I was younger, I loved when it rained. I liked running outside and jumping in the puddles and splashing through the streets. If there was thunder and lightning, I would perch my five-year-old self onto the windowsill, face pressed against the glass, to look outside. I'd count the seconds between each boom and flash to see how far away the storm was.

Every other little kid at school would scribble smiling suns or clear blue skies, but when I drew pictures, I would always draw rain.

My mum questioned me every time I brought home drawings. I'd happily show her my art, proud of what I'd done. I didn't get why she constantly told me to draw sunshine. I liked the rain. I thought everybody liked the rain. I continued to draw storms, as backgrounds for smiling people holding balloons or maybe a picture of a dog. I wanted them to be happy like me, and rain made me happy.

I never really understood why I was so fascinated by it, I just *was*. My favorite part was looking for a rainbow afterward. I always wanted to find the end, but I obviously never did. But to young Levi, the end of the rainbow seemed close, like I could run out and catch it, like it was part of some scavenger hunt. The older I got, the sooner I'd end my search. Until one day, I just gave up and stopped trying, knowing I would never find the end.

That's the situation I'm in right now. I'm seventeen years old, no longer a young kid dreaming about where a rainbow could lead. I watch the rain from inside, but that's about it.

Most guys my age are out with girls or playing sports or doing who knows what. Not me. For the past few months, I've been trapped inside my body and mind, stuck in an inescapable void I created myself. I have no hopes of leaving, though attempts are always made. With each step away from the emptiness inside me, I'm pulled two steps back. There's no escape from myself or my thoughts.

I haven't seen the rainbow at the end of the storm in a long time. I'm beginning to wonder if there ever really was one.

Chapter One

Levi

"Levi, come out! We have to talk about this!" my mum says from outside my room. I'm sitting on the cold wood floor, my knees hugged to my chest as I lean on the door. I dig my teeth into my bottom lip, the harsh pain sinking in quickly. I bite deeper until the only thing I feel is the slight vibrations beneath my teeth.

"Please, just let me in," she begs. "This hurts me as much as it hurts you."

I take a deep breath and slowly stand, my hand wavering above the knob for a few seconds before I twist the lock. I walk over to my bed and wait for my mum to walk in, and when she does, she looks tired and upset. Her eyes appear heavy and her lips are turned into a frown. All of this seems to have aged her twenty years. She looks at me, and I look at her, neither of us saying anything. But she expects that from me.

"I don't want to do this to you, Levi. But it's the only choice we have left," she says, sitting down beside me. I don't look at her. I nervously crack my knuckles. She sighs. "Your flight leaves in two days. I wish I could come, but I can't." I stare blankly ahead. "This is what's best for us, for you. Your father and I"—she pauses, her voice cracking—"we just want you to be happy again."

And with that, I leave my room and run down the stairs and out the front door. I slam it behind me, and the cold rain instantly pelts my skin once I'm outside, but I don't care. I continue walking down the dark street. The street lights are the only source of any brightness. I kick a pebble that's in front of me and hear it splash into a puddle.

I hate this.

How could my parents do this to me? They want me to move from Australia to go live with my dad in Maine. Moving all the way to America to live with Dad doesn't seem like the solution to my many problems. I barely know him, and I'm entirely sure he doesn't know anything about me. I haven't seen him for three years. All I've gotten are some cards and presents on holidays.

He moved when I was fourteen years old. At the time, everything was perfect. Perfect family, perfect friends, perfect life. All I did was go to school, eat, sleep, and play video games. What could have been better? I wish I could go back to when everything was simple.

Nothing has been simple for a while.

My mum told me I'm leaving for many reasons. One being that I need a break from all the things I'm too familiar with. She also thinks I need new experiences. It all comes down to the fact I can't be around things that make me remember Delia. Mum wants me to forget, everyone wants me to forget. But how can I forget everything about the one person I really cared for? It's not like I can just remove her from my brain and everything will magically be okay.

I'll have to meet new people who know nothing about me. That could be a good thing, but it could also be a bad thing. Not to mention the new therapists and doctors who will have to learn everything about me. I don't want to go through that process again. All of the questions and answers, forms and tests—I hate it. I was finally comfortable with all of my doctors, and now I'll have to start all over.

I pull my hood over my head and stuff my hands far into my pockets as I continue to think. I sigh heavily, wishing that things were different. Somehow, someway, I want things back to how they once were. How did life get to be this terrible?

"Splendiferous," I say, the word rolling off my tongue. "Today is going to be splendiferous."

"You're splendiferous," Delia says, smiling. I look over at her and see her dimpled cheeks as she smiles. She bites her tongue a little; she always does when she smiles widely.

I blink quickly and rub my eyes furiously, trying to make the flashback stop. It's all so vivid in my mind, like it happened yesterday.

But it didn't. It happened six months ago. One hundred eighty-two days, to be exact.

It was the last time I saw her smile like that.

Every single day, I wish I didn't wake up. I wish things were different. I wish she was here with me, but she's not.

I sit on the curb, suddenly overcome with dizziness. This always happens when I think too much, usually about the incident. And I think about it a lot. The quietest people have the loudest minds, and mine is screaming for help, but my lips don't move.

I shake my head and place it in my hands, feeling the rain pound down on me. I stick my hand out and catch some falling water, watching it trickle through the small cracks between my fingers. I open up my cupped hand and watch the water drop to the ground, splashing once it hits the pavement. It's like feeling on top of the world, where nothing can touch you, but suddenly the world opens up beneath you and you fall quickly. Everything changes. You're suddenly at the bottom, watching everyone live life above you while you're stuck in a puddle.

That's what I feel like.

I wonder what it's like to not feel the rain on your skin or to not hear the sound of it falling. I wonder what it's like to take your final breath. I wonder about a lot of things.

Most of my time is spent wondering.

A car drives by, slowing to a stop in front of me. The lights blind me for a second, but I quickly adjust to the brightness and figure out who it is. The familiar chipped navy paint and the dent that looks like a ghost make the vehicle immediately recognizable.

11

"Get in the car," Caleb says once he rolls down the window. He always seems to know whenever I run out of the house or get into any sort of trouble. And he's always the one to come get me.

I roll my eyes and get inside, turning off the radio. As usual, Caleb has his music playing loudly. It annoys me how he can enjoy something so much.

I don't really like Caleb most of the time because he reminds me of things I don't want to remember, but he tolerates me, so I tolerate him. He seems to be the only one who can.

He looks over at me and sighs. "Had a fight with your mum again?"

I nod, not looking up at him.

"Did she tell you about moving?" he asks. I look up at him, confused. How did he find out before me? "She wanted to know what I thought about it all," he says. He always knows what I'm thinking, and I don't really understand how he does.

I ball my hands into fists, my knuckles turning white. Caleb knew and didn't tell me? I look over at him, my glare venomous.

"Look, Levi," he says, turning down the street, "I want my best friend back. And I know this whole thing sucks, but nothing has helped so far. This might, okay?"

I sigh and look out the window, watching the rain slide down the smooth glass. I wonder what it's like to be a raindrop. I bet they pretend to race down the windows. I wonder if their life only lasts a few seconds, and if they die once they hit the ground.

I wish I were a raindrop. I bet they don't worry.

Caleb continues to talk about stuff, but I zone out. I block out his talking all the time, and he knows that, but continues anyways. He never gives up. It drives me crazy.

Once again I find myself thinking of living in Maine. It's thousands of miles from Australia, where I've lived my whole life. I don't understand how moving so far away will help. If anything, it may make matters worse. Nothing will help me, it never will. They could send me to Mars, and I still wouldn't change. People can't be fixed once they're broken. They are like shattered glass, a bunch of tiny pieces that can't be taped back together. Invisible, sharp, and crushed. Even if I wanted to fix myself and put the pieces I have back together, I couldn't.

"Levi? Levi!" Caleb says, snapping me out of my thoughts. I look over at him, turning my neck sharply to show my annoyance. I glare at him fiercely and wait for him to start talking. "As I was saying," he says, "I think you should just go there and have no previous perceptions of it all. Just have an open mind, it'll be okay."

It'll be okay.

That's what everyone said six months ago, and they continue to say that. Do I seem like everything's okay? No. Nothing will ever be okay.

"And," Caleb adds, "Delia would want you to do this. She would want you to be happy."

I flinch at the mention of her name and bite my bottom lip nervously. All she ever wanted was for me to be happy, but look where I am now.

"Sorry, I didn't . . . You know . . . I'm sorry," Caleb says, fumbling with his words.

I look away from him again and try to forget, like I always do. Just try to forget what I always remember.

"What should we do?" Caleb asks quietly to change the subject. He taps his fingers against the steering wheel and bites his lip. "I know you don't want to go back home."

I shrug. He knew I would respond with that, but he asked anyway.

"What about some pizza? Are you hungry?" he asks me.

I shrug again.

"Okay, pizza it is."

We drive the rest of the way in silence; the only sound is the rain against the car and the tires rolling on the pavement. As loud as it may be, nothing is ever loud enough to drown out my thoughts. I will always be left with all of my thoughts deafening me.

13

Once we get to the pizza place, Caleb orders for both of us, like always. He knows exactly what I want: a large Coke and a pepperoni pizza. I sit at a high table and wait, watching him lean against the counter and fold the receipt neatly. His brow is furrowed as he waits, like something is bothering him.

I bet it's me. I'm a bother to everyone.

He sits across from me once the pizza is ready, picking up a slice full of cheese that stretches high until it breaks. He smiles and licks some sauce off of his thumb before taking a bite.

"Are you gonna eat any?" he asks with his mouth full, nodding to the pizza.

I reach for a slice, even though I'm not hungry. I rarely ever am.

"When do you leave?" Caleb asks.

I sip my soda and pull my phone out of my pocket and type something quickly. Caleb waits for my response and puts his pizza down.

A monotonous robotic voice comes out of my phone, reading what I had previously typed. "I leave in two days. How far away is Maine?"

Caleb bites his lip and thinks. "I dunno. Definitely really far, though."

I type again. "Isn't Maine cold?"

"Yeah," Caleb says. "Like your heart."

I roll my eyes and glare at him. He puts his hands up to defend himself.

"Anyways," the robotic voice reads, "I'm glad it will be cold. I hate this hot weather. Maybe I can freeze to death."

"You don't mean that," Caleb says.

I nod and raise my eyebrows at him.

I mean everything I say.

Or, to be exact, don't say.

Because the last time I talked was one hundred seventy-nine days ago.

Chapter Two

LEVI

Airports are consumed by hellos and good-byes, tight hugs and warm embraces. It's a place to leave what you know, or start somewhere new. There are hundreds of people with hundreds of stories. I am one of those stories amongst the sea of people. And right now, my story is just beginning at the same time it is ending.

"Levi," Caleb says shyly, looking down at his feet. "I know it's been rough for you. And I wish I could help. Just promise you'll try to make it work, all right? I miss the old Levi. When you come back, hopefully it'll be soon, and hopefully my *real* best friend will be back. I'll be waiting." He embraces me in an awkward hug, and I keep my arms down at my sides before slowly wrapping them around him. I hear him sigh as he lets go, and he tries to smile.

I can tell he's upset about me leaving, probably because he's worried. He shouldn't be worried about me. I'm not worth worrying about. I'm just a lost soul. I don't think the *real Levi* will ever be back.

My mum stands beside Caleb, trying not to cry. Her bottom lip is quivering as she watches us.

"I'll miss you so much," my mum tells me for the hundredth time as she hugs me tightly. She pulls away and keeps her hands on my shoulders. "It'll be fine, I promise. I wouldn't be sending you if I didn't think it would help. Your dad will be at the airport once you get there. Make sure you text me when you land so I know you're safe. Oh, and don't forget to take your pills. I've already told your dad to remind you. And make sure you eat on the plane—it's a long flight!" She rambles on and on about important things to do and remember, but I'm not listening.

I don't get why everyone is so worried and upset about me leaving. It's not like I ever did anything great. I don't get why they would want me to stay. They should be happy that I'm leaving, that they're finally able to get rid of me. I'm no longer their problem. All I am is a nuisance. I never do anything right, all I do is cause myself and others stress.

I notice that it's getting close to the time I need to board my flight. I pull away slightly and point to the screen in front of me showing the flight schedules, and my mum turns around to see what I'm referring to. "Your flight is boarding soon!" she says frantically. "Here's your bag. Do you have your phone? I feel like you're forgetting something!"

I raise my eyebrows and tap my foot impatiently.

"Right, right. It's time to leave or you'll miss the flight. Okay. I can't believe you're leaving! I love you." She hugs me once more, and for a second I think she'll never let go. But she does, and I start to head through security.

"Bye, Levi! Bring me a souvenir!" I hear Caleb call. I can tell he's trying to lighten the mood, but it's not helping.

I walk toward the security agent, and I know my mum has already started crying. I turn around and I was right; there are tears on her cheeks. I give her a thumbs-up and a small wave. She smiles and waves back. Caleb puts his arm around her shoulders and tries to console her. I guess he can be all right sometimes.

"Ticket, please?" the security guard says.

I show her my ticket, and she looks at it quickly. "Levi Harrison?" she reads.

I nod.

"All right. You're at Gate A8. Enjoy your flight."

After a flight that felt like it lasted fifty hours, I finally landed. I slept most of the way because I had nothing else to do. I could've watched a movie, but none of them interested me.

I search for my dad in the airport, but I can't see him yet. I look over the sea of people, scanning to find him.

"Levi?" I hear someone yell from behind me.

I turn around slowly and look around. My eyes land on my dad, who is standing a few feet away from me.

He's less tan than I remember, and he has less hair. He's wearing a black fleece jacket and jeans. I remember him always wearing T-shirts and shorts.

He smiles widely and shoves through the crowd of people.

"You've grown so much!" he says. "Your hair has grown too!" He chuckles at his own stupid remark.

I roll my eyes and rock back on my heels, unsure of what to do. He seems a little nervous.

"So, uh, how've you been?" he asks.

I start to walk through the crowd of people to get to the baggage claim, completely ignoring my dad.

I don't want to be here. This whole thing is pointless. I already want to get on another plane and head home. I'd even go to Alaska. Anywhere would be better than here.

"Well," he mumbles as he walks behind me. "Great start."

I don't think he realizes I can hear him, even though I'm only a few feet ahead. When you're as quiet as I am, you hear everything.

I watch the bags come out one by one and wait for my black suitcase to appear. My dad stands beside me, a little too close for comfort. My bag appears, and I quickly grab it.

"I guess this is where we're supposed to hug," he abruptly says. "You know, if you want." He puts his arms out for an embrace, but I don't move. I bite on the inside of my cheek and cross my arms over my chest.

"Right," he says glumly. He puts his arms down slowly and rubs behind his neck. He shuts his lips tightly together and takes in a deep breath. "Are you hungry? Tired? Anything you want?" he asks in an effort to reduce the awkwardness.

My stomach grumbles, even though I was unaware that I was hungry. I look around for a place to get food, and I notice a McDonald's. I walk toward it as I drag my suitcase with me.

My dad could at least offer to carry my suitcase. That would be a *kind* thing to do. I pretend that the suitcase is extremely heavy and struggle to drag it. In reality, it isn't heavy at all. It's quite light actually.

"Want me to carry that?" my dad finally asks. I smirk slyly to myself; my plan worked.

I continue to drag it along. All I wanted was for him to ask, not to do it. I don't need people catering to me. Plus, it proves that my dad is somewhat willing to help. The father I remember never would have offered to help with anything. Maybe he's changed. I highly doubt it, though.

I glare at my dad, who is now beside me, and quickly walk to McDonald's so we're no longer at the same pace. He scratches his head in a confused manner since I'm now carrying the suitcase with ease. I roll my eyes at his stupidity.

"Are you heading to McDonald's? Yeah, you definitely are. Do you need money?" my dad says from behind, running over to catch up to me again.

I ignore him and pull out my wallet. I take out a wrinkled piece of cash and try to flatten it.

"Levi, you can't—" my dad starts to say, but is cut off.

"Next," the lady at the cash register says. I walk up and she smiles. "Hi, what would you like?" I go to the notes on my phone and type in what I want to order. My dad taps my shoulder, but I ignore him. What's he so persistent about? Can't he wait?

I pass my phone across the counter, and she scrunches her eyebrows together. She reads what's on my phone and a wave of realization crosses her face.

"Oh, all right. Are you deaf?" she asks slowly, overexaggerating the way she moves her mouth.

This happens all the time. Lots of people mistake me for a deaf person, which is understandable. At first it bothered me, but now it happens so often that I don't care. I shake my head, and she scrunches her eyebrows again.

"Oh. Well, that will be six dollars and eleven cents."

I give her my money, and she tilts her head to the side.

"Sorry, this isn't American money. We can't accept it," she tells me, handing it back to me.

I feel my cheeks heat up, and I fumble with my wallet, even though all I have is Australian money. My dad pops up beside me with cash in hand.

"Here. Sorry about that," he tells the lady.

I glare at him and slap my hand down on the counter in frustration. He could have told me sooner, before I had to embarrass myself like that. I bite my bottom lip in frustration and head over to the pick-up counter. I purposely shove my dad's shoulder when I walk past him, causing him to bump into the person beside him. I hear him grunt before he follows me. He plasters a fake smile on his face to hide his annoyance, but I see right through him.

"That's a neat idea," my dad says when he walks over to me. "Do you do that often?" he asks, pointing to my phone.

I turn away from him and pretend to be interested in something, anything really. When you don't talk, you notice more. I find myself constantly watching others, simply because there's nothing else to do with my time. At least it takes my mind off things, even if it's just for a little while.

I watch a small child run to a man, who I assume is her dad, and he hugs her tightly. A couple is fighting at the ticket counter over something. A mother nervously sends her teenager onto a flight alone.

I almost forgot about my mum! I pull my phone out of my pocket, and there are multiple texts from her. I text her that I made it and everything's fine. She was probably worried the whole time.

"Order fifty-two!" someone shouts.

I look down at my receipt, which says I'm order fifty-two. I turn around to grab my food, but my dad has already picked it up.

"Where do you wanna sit? How about right there?" my dad asks, pointing to an empty table.

I snatch the paper bag out of his hand and grip it tightly. He looks at me then down at his hand then at the bag that I'm now holding. He furrows his eyebrows and exhales heavily before sitting down.

"How long have you had that?" my dad questions. He points to my lip ring.

I ignore him and bite into my burger and shove some fries into my mouth. My dad watches me closely, probably hoping I'll answer. But I don't.

"Doesn't seem like something your mother would allow. How is she?" How many questions is he going to ask?

I shrug, not wanting to communicate with anyone right now. But then again, I never want to interact with people.

My dad bounces his leg nervously, causing the whole table to shake. He can't seem to keep his gaze on me either. His eyes keep wandering nervously in every direction. The table continues to bounce, and it's getting on my nerves. I grip onto each side of the table and glare at him sharply.

"Sorry," he mumbles.

I continue to eat in complete silence. The only noise is from the multiple people in the airport. Once I'm done, I get up quickly and start to head out. My dad follows closely behind, running to catch up to me.

"I thought you'd be tired today and wouldn't want to do much, so we'll just head home. Is that okay with you?" my dad asks.

I don't respond and just follow my dad through the parking lot. We get into the car, and I lounge back in the leather seat, putting my feet up on the dashboard. The car smells like it's been cleaned recently. The strong aroma of cheap vanilla is floating in the air, and it instantly overpowers my senses. I scrunch my nose and put my sleeve up to my face in hopes of getting rid of the smell.

"Levi, your feet," my dad says quietly.

I look over at him then at my feet, but refuse to move them.

He sighs. "Levi, please get your feet off the dashboard."

I keep my feet where they are and put my hands behind my head to get more comfortable.

"For the last time, Levi, get your feet off of the dashboard," he says harshly, slamming his hands onto the steering wheel.

I roll my eyes and obediently take my feet off the dash because I know he won't start driving until I do.

"Thank you," he softly says. He takes some deep breaths and starts to drive.

We drive home in silence—not even the radio is on. I decide to look out the window the whole time and watch the new scenery. We pass lots of tall buildings and go over multiple bridges, some of which seem newer than others. Most of the ride is just highways, but once we get into town, there's a more comforting feel to every-thing, if you'd like to call it that. We pass a small ice cream shop with some kids outside, and a few restaurants with outdoor patios. Lots of people are walking outside, even though it's cold. Well, cold for me anyways. I guess they're used to it. I never knew it could be so cold in October.

We turn down a street that leads to a bunch of houses, and I'm guessing it's my dad's neighborhood. He seems like someone who would live in an apartment, considering it's only him, but he lives in a house. We pull into the driveway of an average blue house with a small garden in the front, and my dad smiles.

"This is your new home," he tells me with a forced smile. I stare back at him with no emotion on my face. *Home.* This will never be my home.

Home is a familiar place where someone feels comfortable. I have no idea where I am, and I'm living with a dad I haven't seen in years. This definitely isn't home.

I get out of the car and grab my bags from the trunk. I only have two suitcases, as the rest of my stuff is being shipped here.

I wait for my dad by the door since it's locked. He finally walks up the steps and unlocks the door, letting me in first. I take a few steps inside and stand awkwardly because I don't know where to go.

There are a few stairs heading up to the kitchen and a long hallway beside it. I can see a television and small black couch on the opposite side of the stairs, which I'm guessing is the living room.

My dad shuts the door loudly, which startles me. I almost forgot I was observing his house.

"Want me to show you your room?" he asks.

I continue to stare at the house, not giving him an answer. I feel like I'm on some movie set, but I haven't gotten the script yet.

"Okay, I'll take that as a yes," he mumbles. He heads up the stairs and down the hall, pointing out different rooms. "That's the bathroom. My room is right here. This is just a closet. And here is your room."

I open the door and look inside the room. It's not too big, but not too small, and it's pretty much empty. Near the windows there's a bed with a blue comforter and matching pillows. A small desk is in the far left corner with a digital clock on it.

"We can go get some more things, I just didn't know what you would like," my dad tells me. "If you want. I mean, we don't have to, it's just a thought since it's kind of empty and—"

I walk inside my room and shut the door in his face, cutting him off. I just need to be alone right now to think about everything that's happening.

"Well, uh, I guess I'll leave so you can set up. If you need anything, just call for me. Wait, um, just come and get me since you don't, you know . . . Okay. I'll go now," he says from outside my room.

I roll my eyes and plop onto the bed, causing the springs in the mattress to creak. I'm too long for the bed—it seems like it was made for a ten-year-old. Definitely not for someone who is six feet tall. I try to lie comfortably, but nothing works. I sigh and let my feet dangle off the edge.

My phone vibrates in my pocket, so I pull it out to see some texts from Caleb asking how everything is so far. I don't reply and put my phone back into my pocket. Exhaling, I decide that I should unpack my things. If I don't do it now, it'll never get done.

I place all my pills on the desk, arranging them into a weekly container. I read the containers for the hundredth time. Anxiety, depression, and mood swings. I sigh as I shut the lids. The white pills seem to haunt me every day. It's like they follow me everywhere. Without them, I can't be me, and with them I'm not me. It's like they've taken over my life.

Once I'm done with that, I put my clothes in the closet, which is way too large. It's almost as big as the room, and I don't see why it's necessary for a closet to be that big. I hang up all my shirts, which have become quite wrinkly from being in my suitcases, and fold up the remaining clothes to put them into drawers.

I sit down in the middle of my huge closet and lean back while I look up at everything. The carpet is plush beneath my fingers and it feels nice. I reach up and run my finger over the hems of my shirts, causing some of them to slip off the hangers. I leave them sitting on the ground in a pile because I'm too lazy to pick them up.

I swallow as I realize that this will be where I'll live for the next few months, maybe even a year. I'm not prepared to start all over again. Just thinking about it makes me nervous. I was perfectly content with what I had been doing—absolutely nothing. But I feel like that will soon change. I'm not sure I'm ready for change, and I don't think I ever will be.

I don't understand how moving here will help anything. I'm in a different country, where I don't know anything or anyone. If anything, I feel like living here will be even worse. I don't want to give Maine a chance, as I'm almost positive that nothing here will help, just like in Australia.

I lay down on the carpet, folding my arms beneath my head for a pillow. Jet lag has made me extremely tired, more tired than usual. The floor feels strangely comfortable, and I start to doze off. My eyelids become heavy, and before I know it, I drift off to sleep.

Chapter Three

LEVI

Good morning, Levi!" my dad cheerily exclaims when I walk into the kitchen. I raise my eyebrows at his sudden exuberance. I don't remember him like this. "Want some cereal? I have Lucky Charms. I remembered that they're your favorite."

Lucky Charms *was* my favorite. Now I hate it. Lucky Charms are too happy and cheerful for me.

"What are you eating?" I ask her.

"Marshmallows," she says, tossing a pink heart into her mouth.

"Is that from my Lucky Charms?" I sit down beside her and grab one from the bowl.

"Obviously. They're the best kind of marshmallows."

"Now what am I supposed to eat for breakfast?"

She shrugs and continues to eat.

I run my hand through my messy hair and sit down at the table. I cringe at the memories. My dad pours two bowls of cereal and brings them over to the table. He sits across from me and smiles.

"Did you sleep all right?" he asks.

I push the bowl of cereal away from me, which causes some milk to splash out of the bowl. He furrows his eyebrows in confusion, but continues to munch on his cereal. I tap my fingers on the table and sigh.

I'm annoyed that my dad is trying so hard. He doesn't even know me anymore. He knows the happy, fourteen-year-old Levi. Not the mute, depressed seventeen-year-old version. The past me isn't even close to the me at the present. Instead of trying to remember how I was, he should just forget all of that. I'm not the same Levi, and I never will be.

"Is there anything you want to do today?" my dad questions, breaking the silence. "Anything you want for your room?"

I shrug. I don't really want to go out with my dad. I'd rather get the things I need alone.

He puts his spoon in his cereal and looks up at me.

"Well, today I have football—they call it soccer here. I coach for one of the local teams. You're welcome to come if you want, maybe you could help out."

I roll my eyes. I used to play football—up until two years ago, actually. Universities already wanted to accept me, but it just wasn't my thing. I always did it to make my dad happy, but once he moved, there was really no point. When I was younger, he would make me practice every single day. I had to be the best player possible, and I was. But I hated every aspect of football. Nothing was fun about it—it was just something to do. It was also another thing for my dad to boss me around with.

My dad and I never had a great relationship. He was always too obsessed with football and work. He was a coach and a manager for one of the biggest teams in Australia. The only thing he ever talked to me about was football. He never asked me about my day, never took me out for ice cream. He only took me to football games. Until one day, when he decided it was all too much. He needed a break. That's when everything broke. The divorce, his moving to Maine, and Dad becoming distant. Most of it's a blur, mostly because I don't care. Or at least, I try not to let it bother me.

Once I've had enough of my dad and his cheeriness, I get up from the table and pour my uneaten cereal into the sink. My dad opens his mouth like he's about to say something, but closes it and purses his lips. Then he takes a deep breath and finally speaks.

"We'll leave for football in an hour."

I don't remember giving any sort of indication of wanting to go. He can't just assume that I automatically want to do whatever he says. I'm certainly not going to a football practice. That's the last place I want to be.

I stare at him with an emotionless glare, and he stares back. I don't stop until he looks away. Once he does, I turn sharply on my heels and head to my room.

I walk into my closet and slowly turn around, examining all my things. There's not much here, since most of my things are still in Australia. I sigh and grab my beanie and place it over my messy hair.

When I walk out of my room, my dad is still at the table. His head is in his hands, and he's barely moving. I can hear him sigh and mutter, "My son hates me. My own son actually hates me."

My dad is right for once.

I slam a door so he's aware that I'm here. He jumps a little in his chair and looks up.

"Oh, you're back," he says awkwardly.

I ignore him and go down the stairs two at a time, my feet clomping all the way down. I reach for the doorknob just as my dad reaches me.

"Levi, where are you going?" my dad asks.

I shrug and open the door, slipping out before he questions me again. I honestly don't know where I'm going. I just want to be somewhere.

"But I thought we were going to the football field!" I hear him shout as I shut the door.

I start to walk down the driveway, but hear footsteps behind me.

"Levi! We need to talk," I hear my dad yell. "Or, I need to talk. Whatever, you know what I mean!"

I turn around sharply and stop walking. I raise my eyebrows and wait for him to talk. He stays silent for a few seconds, both of us just staring at each other again.

"Come back inside."

I cross my arms over my chest, turn quickly, and continue to walk down the street. I'd rather be anywhere than in that house. I hate my dad, I hate this place, I hate everything.

"Levi! Please!" he begs.

I roll my eyes and continue.

"At least stop walking."

I don't stop. I walk farther away from him and turn down the street.

———

I wandered around town for a few hours. I mostly just walked down random streets, occasionally stopping to look at things. There's not much around here except for some shops and restaurants. Just a regular town.

I got home around four o'clock, but Dad wasn't home. Typical. He was never around, and that hasn't changed. And since I don't have any keys, I've been sitting on the front steps for over an hour. Life is just wonderful right now.

I pull a cigarette out of my pocket and light it, watching the tip spark before burning. I place it between my lips and take a deep breath. I tilt my head back and let the smoke out of my lungs, then watch it swirl until it vanishes into the air.

I didn't start smoking until recently, and I don't do it too often. It's more something to keep my mind off things, just for a little. It allows me to focus on something other than my sadness.

The neighborhood is quiet at this hour; only a few cars have driven by. I like the silence. I don't like the bitter cold, though. I definitely wasn't prepared for this.

I place my chin on my hand and continue smoking. I can see the neighbors across the street in one of their rooms. It looks like a dining room. There are two people sitting at a table with flowers in the middle. Both are laughing as if something wonderful happened. I wonder what it's like to be that happy.

"Hey," I hear someone call. I snap my head in the direction of the voice and see a boy about my age walking toward me. "Are you Levi?"

I furrow my eyebrows in confusion as he sits down beside me. How does he know who I am?

"I'm Aiden, nice to meet you." He holds out his hand for me to shake, but I just stare at it. I take in a breath of smoke and puff it in his face. "Alrighty then," he mumbles, coughing a little bit. He awkwardly places his hand in his lap and takes a deep breath over his shoulder to avoid my smoke. "So are you Levi? Or are you some random dude sitting outside this house?"

I get up and start to walk away, not wanting to interact with him.

"Hey, wait up!" Aiden calls, walking in my direction. "I have a spare key!"

I turn around and raise an eyebrow at Aiden. He pulls a key out of his pocket and holds it between his fingers. I try to snatch it from him, but he pulls it away before I get to it.

He turns his head and eyes me suspiciously. *"Are* you Levi?"

I roll my eyes and nod, holding out my hand for the key. He obediently gives it to me, and I walk toward the door to get away from him.

"Dude, at least stop smoking. I can't breathe with that in the air," he says, following me.

I toss the cigarette on the sidewalk and squish it beneath my shoe. I was done with it anyway.

"I work for your dad. You know, helping out with soccer and stuff. You probably call it football, like your dad does."

I scowl.

"I also live right down the street. He mentioned something about his son coming, so I'm guessing that's you. I never even knew he had a son until a few days ago."

Great to know my dad never mentioned me. Thanks, Dad. Nice to know you care. Seems *absolutely normal* to never mention having a son. That's logical.

I fumble with the key, it doesn't seem to fit very well in the lock. I shove the door with all my weight but it doesn't budge.

"The cold weather makes the doors hard to open. You're from somewhere warm, right? Isn't it, like, Australia? Here, let me do it," Aiden says, opening the door with ease.

I feel the urge to slap Aiden to get him to stop talking. I already genuinely dislike him. His extremely fake, goofy smile is getting on my nerves. I clench my teeth through my frustration.

"Hey, you all right? You don't talk much, do you?" Aiden continues to babble on about stupid things and follows me inside. I just want to be alone. No one seems to understand that.

He plops down on the couch, putting his feet on the coffee table. I continue standing, leaning against the wall with my arms crossed.

"So, Levi, how are you liking it here so far? Maine is pretty dull if you ask me. I want to move somewhere cool, like Australia or something."

I roll my eyes at his statement. Australia is most definitely not cool. It's where dreams go to die.

Maine seems to be where heat goes to turn into a bitter frost.

Aiden looks up at me, waiting for a response. I guess he hasn't found out I don't talk. Or he knows, but thinks I will actually engage in a conversation with him.

He clears his throat and taps his fingers against the couch. He looks up at the ceiling, then down at the floor.

"Your dad told me you're amazing at soccer. You should join the team at school. Though they're pretty bad. I'm even worse. But I don't care, I'm still part of the team, you know? Just getting to be on the field and everything. You could really help us out."

My dad has always had this hope that I'd go back to soccer. But I never will. Not now, not ever.

I pull out my phone and type quickly. I press speak, and Aiden furrows his eyebrows when he hears it.

"First things first," it reads, "I don't talk. Ever. I haven't spoken for six months. Don't expect me to. Don't ask stupid questions, because I won't answer them. You've asked more questions than my mind can handle. I feel like I've lost brain cells from your horrific grammar, you know?" Aiden bites his lip, realizing I'd just quoted him. "Secondly, yes, I'm Australian. Australia is not cool, but you're welcome to move there. I don't like you, and I don't like Australia. It's a perfect match. Third, I will never play football. Don't try to make me think differently. I hate it. Lastly, please leave before I explode from frustration."

Aiden looks down and cracks his knuckles. "I'm just trying to be friendly," he mumbles, getting up from the couch. "I guess I'll be leaving then. Have a nice night, Levi. I'll see you around."

He hangs his head as he walks toward the door. Just as he's about to leave, my dad walks in.

"Hey, Aiden!" he exclaims. He's more excited to see him than he was to see his own son after three years. "I see you've met Levi!"

"Yeah, he was locked out. I brought him in. But I'm leaving. I'll see you later," Aiden says quietly, darting out the door.

My dad places his bag on the bottom of the stairs and walks up to me.

"Aiden's nice, huh? He's a great guy."

I shrug and walk past my dad and into my room. My dad seems to care more about Aiden than me. Not that I care. Why would I care? It's not like I actually like my dad. I don't like Aiden either. I don't care about either of them.

He didn't even apologize for locking me out. I sat outside for so long, and he doesn't even acknowledge it. I hate him. I hate him. I *hate* him.

All I care about right now is going to sleep, so that's what I decide to do. It's not like there's anything else to do. Even though it's only seven thirty, I'm still on Australian time. My sleeping schedule is completely messed up.

After an endless few minutes of restlessly lying on my bed, I give up on getting comfortable. I'm way too tall for the tiny mattress. I go into the closet and get comfortable quickly.

I like the small, open space of silence. It feels large and loud. I don't feel trapped in here the same way I do everywhere else.

I enjoy being alone like this.

Chapter Four

LEVI

I step into an all-too-familiar atmosphere at ten in the morning. A few other people are waiting in chairs, not making a sound. A lady at the front desk types quickly, which is the only sound in the quiet room. I roll my eyes and walk.

I've only been in Maine for four days, and I'm already at the therapist.

"Hi, how can I help you?" the lady says cheerily. She looks up at me, then at my dad.

My dad answers all the questions while I lean against the counter. I yawn slowly, having only woken up a few minutes ago.

The lady—her name is June—hands me a clipboard with some papers attached. The usual questions that I'm sick of answering.

Do you feel as if you are different from other individuals?
Are you constantly tired?
Have you lost interest in everyday activities?

I scribble down my answers just as I hear my name called.

"Levi Harrison?" a woman with curly red hair asks, grinning widely.

I stand up and cringe. I already dislike her.

"Good luck, bud. Come get me if you need anything," my dad tells me.

Bud? What am I, five years old?

My dad's been trying. Maybe a little too much. The past four days, I've been ignoring him most of the time. I don't really want to be around him. I think he realizes that, but he still tries.

I look at him as if he's crazy, which he is. He smiles meekly, his eyebrows arched upward. I turn away and follow the doctor.

"Hello, Levi. Nice to meet you. I'm Candace, and I'll be your therapist, okay?" She reaches out her hand for me to shake, but instead of shaking it, I put the clipboard in her hand. I don't want to carry it anyway.

She nods her head as if saying yes and closes her lips into a straight line. She brings me into a room, which is like every other therapy room. There are some games in the corner, a notepad on the table, a couch against one wall. A picture that looks like it was done by a seven-year-old is on one of the plain, tan walls. Maybe it's a panda. Or possibly a whale? Maybe it's half and half. Would that be a whanda or a pandle?

"Hello? Levi?" Candace says, looking at me.

I must have zoned out while looking at the painting. That happens a lot. I think so much that I forget about my surroundings. I look over at Candace to see her smiling widely again. Her teeth are way too white. I bet she's whitened them more than the directions recommend.

"Okay, there you are. I thought I lost you for a second," Candace says, forcing a small laugh. "So, I'm going to start off by asking you a few questions, okay?"

Okay okay okay. Stop saying okay, okay?

"Here's a whiteboard. You can write down all of your answers and thoughts on the board. Are you ready?"

I shrug and prop my feet up on the small table. Candace peers down at my shoes and tries not to look disgusted, but I see right through her. The corner of her mouth twitches as she picks up her notepad.

"All right, question one. When did you stop talking?"

I don't answer. I stare at the milky whiteness of the board. There are some black smudges on it from previous markers. I rub my thumb over one of the stains, but it's of no help.

This question is the first thing every therapist asks me. Clearly, I stopped talking six months ago; it's written in my information. So why does she have to ask?

"Okay, next question then," she says, "Why did you stop talking?"

And there it is. The follow-up question. The question everyone wants to know the answer to. Only I know the real reason why I stopped. And I don't plan on sharing it.

I've been through eleven therapists in six months. None of them could figure me out because I never answered their stupid questions.

I've heard the therapists and doctors talk to my mom. I hear what they say about me. All I need is to change my outlook on life and get some medical help. I can be fixed. There will be a miracle. Don't give up.

My life isn't a Hallmark card or a quilted pillow. Stop telling me useless quotes you learned when you got your degree.

Candace asks more questions, none of which I answer. I just stare blankly at the board, never moving. I feel as if I might fall asleep. Sleeping would be nice. I wouldn't have to deal with Candace's fake perkiness.

Suddenly a girl appears in the doorway carrying a box of manila folders. She knocks lightly before walking in.

She smiles at me, and I turn my gaze away from her. I look up at the first thing I see, which is the whanda painting. I wonder who painted it. I wonder what it's really supposed to be. I fill my mind up with questions to avoid the thoughts creeping into my head, and to avoid this girl.

"Sorry to bother you, but June wants all of your patient records. She says we're missing some from the past month," the girl says, balancing the box on her knee.

"Oh, yes, of course. They are all in the top right drawer of my desk."

I look from the whanda to the girl, then back again. I bite my fingernails and bounce my leg without even realizing it.

"Found 'em," the girl says, putting them in her box. "Thank you."

"Would you mind shutting the door on your way out, Delilah?" Candace says.

I flinch at her name and freeze in my spot. I need an excuse to leave. I can't stay here any longer.

I uncap the marker and quickly write something down. Candace waits anxiously, a smile growing on her face. I lift up the board to show her what I've written.

I need to take a piss.

Her smile falters once she reads what I've written. She excuses me, and I quickly get up from the couch. In my frenzy to leave, I crash into the girl, who I now know as Delilah. Her box falls out of her hands and crashes to the floor. I glance quickly from her to the mess of folders on the floor before quickly running out.

My breathing quickens and the hallway seems to be too small. I need space. I need air. I need to get out of here.

I run down the hall in search of the bathroom and finally find it. I step inside one of the stalls and lean against the metal door.

I wait for my pulse to slow, and my breathing to go back to normal. *In through your nose, out through your mouth. Breathe, Levi. Relax.*

I shut my eyes and try to calm down. All I can picture is that girl. The way she smiled, how one dimple showed up on her left cheek. The way her brown hair just passed her shoulders. How her cheeks reddened when the box fell.

I pound my fists into the stall, causing it to rattle.

I thought it was *her.*

I thought she was back.

I thought I could have her again.

But it's not Delia. She'll never be back. I'll never see her again.

The sudden rush of anxiety leaves after a few minutes, and I'm left with anger and sadness, along with the familiar feeling of emptiness. I head back to Candace and see her waiting for me with the same smile.

Here we go again.

My whole life is surrounded by plastered smiles and forced sympathy.

I try to focus on Candace, but I can't.

All I can think about is that girl, and how much I hate her.

Chapter Five

DELILAH

"Aiden, you can't just take someone's coffee at Starbucks. That's stealing," I tell him as we sit on the curb, watching cars drive by. We do this a lot since there's not much in the way of entertainment around here. He counts the red cars, and I count the blue cars. Whoever counts the most, wins. But there's never a prize, so it's a pointless game. But we do it anyway.

"It's not stealing. It's selectively choosing who I'm going to be for the day. Today I am Tanya," he says, reading the scribbled name on the cup. "I believe I am a twenty-two-year-old with pink hair. Maybe even a nose ring. Oh, maybe a belly button piercing! I come from Miami, and I had a rough life as a kid. But now I work for this club downtown. Oh, and I have a boyfriend of two days, I'll probably dump him tomorrow."

I roll my eyes. Only Aiden would think of a life story for the name on his coffee cup.

"So, tell me, Tanya, what would you like to do today?"

"Well," Aiden says in a girly voice, "I vote for mani-pedis, and then we can go to the petting zoo to help endangered animals!"

I muster a laugh at Aiden's goofiness. "You're such a weirdo! Why do I associate myself with you?"

"Because you love me," he says dramatically, resting his head on my shoulder. I nudge him off and take a sip of his coffee. Or, rather, Tanya's coffee.

"Tanya has good taste."

Aiden smiles. "See, it's not such a bad idea after all."

I punch his shoulder lightly, and he rubs it as if it hurt.

I've known Aiden almost my whole life. He lives two houses down from me, so I see him all the time. He's like a brother, and has been there for me through everything. Every girl needs a guy best friend, even if he is a little strange.

Aiden tosses the coffee into the trash and helps me up from the curb.

"Hey, isn't that Mr. Harrison's car?" I ask, pointing to the car across the street.

"How many times do I have to tell you he doesn't like being called Mr. Harrison. His name is Anthony!" Aiden says, laughing.

I shrug. "Now I just do it to annoy you," I say, and give him a half smile.

"I bet they're in Starbucks," Aiden says.

"They? Who's they?" I ask. Does Mr. Harrison have a new friend? That may happen to be a girl? Maybe it's Tanya.

As if to answer my question, Mr. Harrison comes walking out of Starbucks with a vaguely familiar boy in front of him.

Well, I sure didn't expect that.

The boy has his head down as he drinks his coffee, but I see he has a lip ring. Where have I seen that lip ring before? He has a snapback on backward and is wearing a plain black T-shirt. Some stray pieces of blonde hair are sticking out from his hat. He has to be at least six feet tall, maybe even more. And his jeans are skinnier than mine.

I've definitely met this boy before. Boys like this are rare here. Everyone is always the same, but he is definitely different.

"Hey, guys!" Aiden says, waving.

"Hi! Delilah, have you met Levi?" Mr. Harrison asks as he approaches us.

Levi looks up, and he has a shocked expression on his face. His blue eyes look nervous for some reason.

A memory starts to rise, but I can't quite grab it.

"Nice to meet you. I'm Delilah," I say, smiling. "I live a few houses down from you."

Levi bites on his bottom lip, and his eyes wander around.

I remember those wandering eyes.

"Wait," I say. "You were with Candace when I walked in, right? I had the box of folders. You crashed into me." Of course I remember him. He knocked all the folders out of my hands and didn't even help me pick them up.

Suddenly, Levi tosses his coffee to the ground. The ice and coffee splash everywhere, including onto my feet. I guess I shouldn't have worn white sneakers today.

We all stare at the ground with shocked expressions, confused as to what just happened. The coffee drips off the curb, and there's a giant pile of ice on the sidewalk.

Levi casually walks across the street gets and into the car, completely ignoring the mess he caused. Just like he did when he bumped into me at work.

"I'm so sorry," Mr. Harrison says. "Levi's a little . . . uh . . . moody to say the least. I'd better get going." He picks up the empty cup and throws it away before getting into his car.

"Well, that was strange," I say once they're gone.

Aiden shrugs. "Levi is Anthony's son. He doesn't talk, like, at all. I met him the other day. He's really rude. He definitely doesn't like me."

"Since when does he have a son? Who doesn't talk?"

Mr. Harrison never told us anything about having a family. I wonder if Levi's ever spoken. He seems about my age. I wonder what would make him so . . . different.

"Maybe he's a mute or something, I don't know. Anthony told me the other day that Levi has had a rough few months. He didn't tell me much. I don't think he really even knows. Levi seems to be one big mystery."

"A mystery, huh?"

40

Later that day, I go for a run around the neighborhood. I do this quite frequently. It gives me some time to myself, and I like the way the wind feels against my skin and through my hair.

There's a small, rundown park in the corner of our neighborhood no one uses that much. There are some swings and a slide covered in graffiti. Nothing too interesting. But tonight, when I run past, there's something out of the ordinary.

Levi.

He's lying on top of the monkey bars, one of his arms dangling over the edge. He's too tall to fit over the whole thing, so his feet are drooped over the end. He seems to be asleep, his chest slowly rising and falling while he breathes.

I quietly walk through the grass and sand until I'm below the monkey bars.

"Hello?" I whisper. "Hey, Levi?"

His hat has fallen off his head and into the sand below him. His hair is half flat, half sticking up. He must have kicked off his shoes, because a pair of black Vans are near the swings.

I stand on my toes and gently tap Levi's shoulder. He bolts up and falls into the sand with a loud thump.

I try to hide my laugh, but it's hard. Some giggles escape me. "Sorry," I say, smiling. "I didn't mean to scare you."

He stands up and brushes his hands on his jeans. He's covered in sand from head to toe.

"Here, let me help. I'm really sorry," I tell him, reaching up to sweep sand off his shoulder. He backs away and pulls out his phone. He types something, and then I hear a voice come out of his phone, which surprises me.

"What are you doing?"

I put my hands up in defense. "I was going for a run, and you were on the monkey bars. Asleep."

He shrugs and makes a face, as if he's saying, "And?"

41

"And I just thought I'd come say hi," I tell him.

Something about Levi scares me. Maybe it's his height. Maybe it's the way his eyes seem to pierce through me, when earlier, he wouldn't even look at me.

He types more. "Well, don't. I don't need anyone coming to say hi. Especially not you."

Aiden's right, he is rude. But as much as I want to run away, I stay. Nevertheless, there's a fear in the back of my mind that Levi may hurt me. I know nothing about him or his mental state. He could be psychotic for all I know. I highly doubt it, but there's always a part of me that thinks the worst.

I cross my arms over my chest and roll my eyes. "It's called hospitality. Something you don't seem to know about."

"Hospitality? Is that what you call barging into someone's personal time without invitation? Waking them up?"

"I didn't mean to scare you. Honestly."

"You didn't scare me."

"Then why'd you fall?"

"There's this thing called balance. I lost it."

It's hard to take Levi seriously since he doesn't talk. The robotic voice on his phone has no emotion, so it doesn't say things the way a human would. I know he's trying to seem rude and sarcastic, but it's not coming out that way.

But somehow, he's still intimidating. Maybe it's the way he stands, or the way he runs his tongue across his lip. Something about him is harsh and cold.

"Whatever, Levi." I turn around and leave the park. I'm clearly not wanted here.

Part of me expects Levi to have more to say—or write? He is so confusing. Aiden's right; he is a mystery.

A part of me thinks he will come running over and apologize, or ask to walk me home. He seems unpredictable, and I'm unsure of what he'll do next.

But I don't hear footsteps or fingers typing on his phone. I hear nothing.

And as much as I don't want to admit it, I want to solve the mystery of Levi Harrison.

Chapter Six

LEVI

It's been seven days since I arrived here. One whole week.

One hundred and eighty-nine days without her.

There will be more days to come. More endless weeks stuck here.

I haven't been back to the park. I don't plan on going back anytime soon, or ever for that matter. My goal now is to avoid everyone, especially Delilah. Since the incident at the park, I haven't seen her. But I also haven't left the house in three days.

Technically, I've barely left my room aside from the occasional food and bathroom breaks.

"Levi," my dad says, knocking on my door. "You need to get out of the house. It's been three days."

Wow, way to state the obvious. You're *so* cool, Dad.

If I wanted to leave the house, I would. But I don't, so I won't.

He knocks again, a little louder this time.

Does he think I'm deaf too? Just because I refuse to talk doesn't mean I refuse to hear. There are times I wish I could block everything out, though. We have eyelids to shut our eyes, so why can't we have earlids too? That'd sure help me a lot. I wouldn't have to listen to anyone.

Finally, he barges into my room. I should've locked the door. I should've escaped and jumped out the window. I look at my open window and debate whether or not I should just jump now. There's still time.

"We're going out," he tells me.

I should've gone when I had a chance.

He has his arms folded across his chest as he looks down at me. I stay sitting on my bed, refusing to move. I tap my feet on my carpet, the plushness feeling good beneath my feet.

"Levi, we are going out," he repeats. "Be ready in twenty minutes."

My dad walks out of my room, but I don't get up. I don't want to.

After sitting in the same position for a few minutes, I hear my dad talking to someone. I slowly walk out of my room and down the hall. His bedroom door is shut almost all the way—there's a small space that I can see him perfectly through. He's on the phone with someone, and his head is in his hands.

"Yes, Lilian, I know . . . Lilian . . ." He sighs and runs his hand through his hair.

Why is he talking to Mum?

"How did our son get to be like this?" I swear I just heard his voice crack. Is he crying?

I walk closer, careful not to make any noise. I need to hear what he's talking about.

"Levi used to be so happy. He used to smile. What happened to him?" There's a pause before he talks again. "It's been a rough week for both of us. Levi rarely leaves his room, and when he does, he leaves the house. He barely looks at me. Half the time he glares at me or slams doors in my face. I don't even feel like a father."

Does he really feel that way?

"Yes, Lilian, I'm aware that he's testing me. It's like this is all a big game to him. This is serious . . . Our son has clinical depression!"

I wonder what my mum is saying. There are long pauses after every sentence my dad says.

Does he really think I'm testing him? I'm not testing him, that's for sure. Okay, maybe just that once at the airport, but that was

45

it. I just genuinely hate him and this place. I hate everything and everyone, I can't help it. I can't help that I'm depressed. I can't help that I have mood swings. I physically can't make myself do things I don't want to do, and I mentally can't handle anything anymore. All I want to do is be away from people, because I constantly feel like everything is falling apart. I wish everyone could see that. I wish that they would just leave me alone.

I feel slightly annoyed at my dad for thinking I see this as a game. It's like he thinks I find this funny. Why would I find my situation funny? It's the total opposite. I'm a miserable train wreck of a seventeen-year-old boy who's barely living. All I am at this point is someone that takes up space and breathes to stay alive. I'm nothing more.

"I just want him to tell me something. Anything. Write a note even . . . Why would Delia's death cause all this? I don't get it."

Don't get it? You don't *get it*?

I walk back into my room, not caring if I make any noise. I don't even care if he heard me. His words replay in my mind over and over.

Why would Delia's death cause all this? I don't get it.

You know what I don't get? How someone thinks they can automatically understand every single one of your problems. He hasn't lived in my shoes. He doesn't know what it's like to lose the most important person in your life.

My dad doesn't know how close I was to her. He doesn't know how important she was, and still is, to me. He doesn't know what I've gone through the past six months. He has no idea. And the fact that he doesn't understand why I'm like this because of her death proves that he doesn't care.

He doesn't care, and he never will.

I'm overcome with a sudden feeling of anger toward him. I toss the closest thing to me, which happens to be a chair, to the ground. It causes a loud noise, but quietness doesn't matter right now. I kick my foot against the wall, scuffing it a little. I wish I never came here. I wish none of this had ever happened.

"Levi!" I hear my dad scream. He runs into my room and stops in the doorway. "What's going on in here?"

I continuously punch the wall in front of me. My hands feel numb, not that it matters. My dad runs between the wall and me, but I continue punching blindly. I can feel my fists hitting his stomach, yet he doesn't move.

I can't stand when I do this. It just happens out of nowhere. My mood flips in a matter of seconds, and I hate it. I hate everything about myself. I'm not normal. Normal people don't do this. I hate my whole life and everything involved in it.

My heart starts pounding a mile a minute, and my breathing picks up. My whole body is shaking furiously, and I'm becoming light-headed.

"Levi, calm down. What's wrong?" my dad asks over and over. After punching him for what feels like a long time—but is actually only a few seconds—I collapse to the ground. My legs are too weak and shaky to hold me up. I hug in my knees to my chest and rock back and forth. I take slow, deep breaths to try to calm down.

My dad sits beside me, even though I don't want him here. I push him away, but he stays. He grabs my wrists, and I try to wriggle out of his grip, but he's too strong. I kick my legs to get him to let go, but he doesn't.

"Levi! Listen to me! Relax!" he screams.

My head is pounding, and I can hear my heart beating like a drum. It's like my heart has moved to my brain. I want to scream and yell, but I don't.

"Levi, please!"

And for some reason, I obey. I look up at him, while trying to get out of his grip. He's still holding tightly to me.

"I don't know what just happened to you. I'm not like your mum, I don't know how to handle this stuff," he says nervously. "I know this is hard for both of us. I get that you don't want to be here. I understand. But I'm trying. I'm trying so hard."

A tear falls from his eye and rolls down his cheek. I can't believe that he's crying.

"I know I haven't been the best dad. And I'm sorry. I'm sorry if you hate me, I'm sorry if you don't want to be here. But this is the situation we're in. And if you want it to get better, you have to at least try. We can figure this all out together. Because this is all new to me too. And I just want you to know that you're not alone in this. Please, Levi. Just try. Please."

I breathe heavily, my chest rising and falling. My heart is finally going back to a regular beat. I'm a little more relaxed and not as angry as I was. Though I'm still shaking all over, and my teeth are clenched tightly.

A few minutes ago, my dad thought this was all a game. He seemed like he didn't care. And now, he says this. I don't know what to believe. My head is pounding, and I can barely focus.

For some reason, I reach for my phone and begin a reply to my dad. My fingers shake over the keyboard as I type. I pass the phone over to him, and he reads it.

I'll try.

He looks up and smiles at me. A genuine smile. Not the cheesy "I'm proud you got that goal, son" or the "I'm really not happy with your choice, but it's your life" smile. It's a real smile.

I get up from the ground and feel a little bit dizzy from the sudden motion. I blink a few times to get rid of the pain behind my eyes.

"Are you all right now?" my dad asks.

I nod, and he pats my arm awkwardly.

"Okay, well, if you need anything, I'll be in my room. We can go out another time," he says.

I don't know why I told him I'd try.

I don't know what I've gotten myself into.

All I know is that I'm stuck here for who knows how long, so I might as well try to make it work with my dad.

Chapter Seven

DELILAH

I haven't seen Levi since what happened at the park. Considering I live only a few houses down, I thought I'd see him daily. It's perfectly fine that I haven't run across him, though. He was extremely unpleasant, and I'm not sure I want to deal with his harsh attitude again.

But I haven't stopped thinking about him.

I want to know why he doesn't speak and why he seems so angry at the whole world. Something must have happened to make him this way.

So when I'm at work and see his folder lying open on the front desk, I debate whether or not to take a quick look inside. I glance at the paper on top, but look away after a second. I know I shouldn't do this. I could lose my job. I can't peek into Levi's personal information. But I want to so badly.

I look again, a little longer this time. I quickly read the heading.

Levi Elliot Harrison. 17 years old. Date of birth: July 25.

He's my age? He seemed to be at least nineteen years old. He definitely doesn't look, or act, seventeen years old.

I quickly look again, this time at the diagnosis section.

Severe depression. Violent mood swings. Anx—

"Levi, you can come in now," someone says, which causes me to jerk my eyes up quickly.

Is Levi here?

I see him walk across the waiting room, his hands shoved deep into his pockets and his head down. He's dressed in all black like the last time I saw him, except this time he's not covered in sand.

How did I not notice he was here?

My heart rate speeds up as I realize that Levi may have seen me reading his information. I could get into so much trouble. I didn't read much, though. It's not a big deal; I'll be fine.

But I still want to learn more. I didn't get to finish reading his diagnosis. What if there are reasons for his mental health in his files? There has to be. He can't be a giant secret to everyone.

"Delilah?" I hear Candace ask.

Oh no. I'm caught. If she knows I was reading Levi's files, I'm going to be fired. What if I end up going to jail? *Did* I violate the law? All I did was look at his birthday and some of his diagnosis. I'm not a criminal.

"Can you come here please?" she says with the same cheery smile she always has.

Here it comes.

My stomach gets queasy as I walk over to Candace, and I rub my sweaty palms on my jeans. I never should have looked in that file.

"Y-Yes? What do you need?" I say, trying not to sound as nervous as I feel.

"Levi's folder," she says.

This is it. She knows. She saw.

I am going to die.

Tell my parents I love them.

"I seem to have misplaced it," she says. "Would you happen to know where it is?"

I feel my heart rate slow down, and I let out a breath I didn't know I was holding.

"It's on—" I start to say. But this is my chance to find out about Levi firsthand. "No, I haven't seen it. Do you want me to look in your office?"

"That'd be great! Thank you! Come on in!"

I smile at Levi when I walk past him, but he doesn't even look my way. He stares up at a painting on the wall, his gaze frozen on it.

He's the same as he was the first time I saw him. I guess I should have expected that. I'd just thought maybe he'd be different now that we've talked.

I go over to the desk in the corner and start slowly rummaging through the drawers. I listen to what Candace is saying and look up every minute or two to see Levi's responses. I don't want to make it too obvious that I'm eavesdropping. I really shouldn't be here.

"So, Levi, how have you been?" Candace asks him.

He shrugs.

"Your father told me about last night. Has that happened before?"

He nods.

What happened last night, and was it something bad? There are so many possibilities.

"Want to tell me how you feel when it occurs?" she asks. Her tone is like the typical therapist. It's overly perky.

He shakes his head no.

"Have you ever told anyone when it happens?"

He shakes his head no again.

"Well, I can't help you unless you tell me."

He cracks his knuckles nervously and chews on his bottom lip.

"You've got to try if you want to get better, Levi."

Levi glances over at me, and I quickly look into the desk drawer. I hope he didn't catch me watching him.

I look back up to see him writing on the whiteboard. Candace smiles and seems surprised that Levi is actually writing.

He lifts it up to show what he's written.

When it happens, I hate everything and everyone, and I just want to ruin everything.

"Why do you want to ruin everything?" Candace asks.

He thinks for a second and rubs the back of his neck. He hesitantly writes something on the board.

Because everything has ruined me.

Candace leans back in her chair, probably thinking about Levi's answer. I know I'm thinking about it.

My hatred and curiosity for Levi has suddenly changed. I now feel extremely sorry for him. He feels ruined, and here I am trying to figure out why. What a horrible thing to do. It's Levi's personal business, and I shouldn't interfere with it. I wish I'd never looked into his folder or come into this room. I'm about to get up and leave when Candace starts talking.

"Well, Levi," she says. "What you experienced was an anger attack. Do you know what that is?"

He shakes his head.

Since working here, I've found out a few things about mental health. And I know exactly what Levi is experiencing. There have been many patients who have anger attacks, but they're usually older. I feel bad that Levi has to go through all this, and he's my age. I can't even imagine what it's like.

"It probably felt like a panic attack, and I know you have those too. It happens when you get overly upset about something. It's like the anger just explodes out of you. It has nowhere to go but out. And you probably feel like you have no control over yourself when it happens, which is normal. I'm going to put you on another pill once a day to see if that helps. You can try that for two weeks, and you should feel a difference."

Another pill? How many does he take?

I wish I wasn't finding out these things. I feel so selfish for wanting to snoop into Levi's personal business. It's his life, not mine. I should just let him be.

I walk out of the room and return with Candace's folder, telling her I forgot I had seen it on the front desk. Levi watches me intently as I exit the room, and I can feel his eyes piercing through me.

Once I leave, I sit down in one of the plush waiting room chairs. I relax for a few minutes and think about what just happened.

Levi experiences panic and anger attacks. I thought he just had anger problems, but he has so much more. Something caused him to be how he is. And all I can think about is what he wrote on the whiteboard.

Everything has ruined him, so he's trying to ruin everything.

It suddenly makes sense why he's so cruel. I bet he feels like everyone is out to get him, or maybe he thinks everyone will hurt him.

And just thinking about what Levi may be going through hurts my heart. He is suffering.

Levi definitely is not a simple person. He has many things going on in his mind, and I sense he's fighting a war with himself.

I hope he wins.

Chapter Eight

LEVI

I'm being dragged to a football game today, and as much as I don't want to go, I have to. After what happened the other night, my dad doesn't trust me to be home alone. He doesn't want me to hurt myself or anyone else. So basically I have no choice in anything from now on. Not that I'd choose much anyway.

"You can sit with the team or sit in the bleachers, whatever you'd like," my dad tells me as we walk to the field. I'd like to go home, that's what I'd like.

I can see the annoying twelve-year-olds already. They're running around the field, probably telling mom jokes to each other or picking boogers. I don't really remember what I did as a twelve-year-old, mostly because it was my awkward phase. I don't like to look back on my long hair that flowed in the wind, thank you very much.

I walk toward the bleachers since I don't want to sit with a bunch of the booger pickers. I head close to the top, away from the few people that are watching the game. I watch the boys practice, and one of them falls flat on his face while running to give his friend a high five. That pretty much sums up my childhood football career, I did it all the time.

"Hey, Levi!" I hear someone say.

Please, no.

I turn around and see Aiden walking up the bleachers, followed by Delilah.

"Mind if we sit here?" Aiden asks, already sitting down next to me.

Yes, I do mind.

"See number seven? That's my brother!" Aiden tells me excitedly. "Today's their last game of the season! I hope they win!"

Aiden continues to talk, but I don't really listen. I stare at the spilled popcorn on the bleachers and zone out. I wish I was anywhere but here.

I look up from the field to see Delia waving through the fence. I go over to her and smile.

"Last game of the season," she says, smiling widely. "You better win."

"I'm so nervous," I tell her.

"Why? You're, like, the best player!"

I feel my cheeks blush. "I'm just not feeling too good about tonight. Have you seen the other team?"

"Yeah, you can beat them, though. Don't be so nervous. I can be your good luck charm. If you get nervous, I'll be here to cheer you on. Even if you lose, I'll still cheer you on."

I laugh. "Just please don't yell my name when I'm on the field. I lose focus."

"I can't make any promises."

I roll my eyes. "You're lucky you're cute."

She sticks out her tongue and smiles widely. "That's one of the reasons I was put on this earth. On the seventh day God said, "There shall be a Delia to distribute her looks and delightful smile throughout the world."

"Why can't it just be for Levi Harrison?" I whine, sticking out my bottom lip.

"You, Levi, are my universe. But you can't steal me from the world. They need someone as fantastic as me too."

"Levi? You okay?" I hear Aiden ask, breaking my thoughts.

I blink a few times, since my vision has blurred. My sight refocuses, and I'm still fixated on the spilled popcorn. I look up at Aiden, who is staring at me. So is Delilah.

"You zoned out for a few minutes. You looked so focused," Aiden says.

I scrunch my eyebrows and rub my eyes, trying to get rid of the memory.

I hate when I get random flashbacks. They always come at the worst times, and they can happen anywhere. Just when I'm not expecting it, one comes. It messes with my brain and causes my emotions to take over. Every time they happen, I feel like I sink deeper and deeper into sadness—and someday, I might not be able to get back up.

I look around the park to distract myself and forget about the flashback. I count how many people are here so far. There are seventeen. I see a concession stand at the opposite end of the park and get off the bleachers.

"Where are you going?" Aiden asks.

Can't he just let me be? I don't get why I'm questioned for every single thing I do. I roll my eyes and point to the concession stand.

"Oh, I'll come!" Delilah says. "I was gonna go anyway."

Great. Just who I wanted to be with. I don't like being around her. There's something about her that makes me nervous and angry and sad all at once. I think it's because she reminds me of Delia.

"Get me a hot dog!" Aiden yells as we leave.

We walk over to the stand in silence, which isn't surprising. I live in silence.

Once we get there, I notice how Delilah frequently changes the position she stands in while we wait. First she has her arms by her sides, then crossed in front of her, then her hands are on her hips. It's like she can't find a comfortable standing position. I wonder if she knows that she's doing it. Maybe she's nervous about something.

"What do you want?" the lady at the counter asks me, sounding bored and tired.

I point to a pretzel.

"Excuse me, what is it?" the lady at the counter says.

I pull out my phone to type the answer, but Delilah starts to order.

"We'll get a pretzel and two hot dogs."

I'm taken aback by how she knew what I wanted. Most people get confused when I point to things, because they're unable to tell what I point to. But she understood.

She looks up and smiles awkwardly at me as we wait.

"Is this the first game you've been to here?" she asks.

I nod.

I don't know why she's being nice to me, since I've been nothing but rude to her. And I probably will continue to be rude. That's who I am. Being rude is easier than breaking down.

"Here you go. That'll be $4.50," the lady says.

I reach into my wallet to pull out money for my pretzel, as this time I have American money.

"It's fine, I got it," Delilah tells me. Before I can pay, she gives the lady a five-dollar bill.

When people are nice to me, I start to question if it's pity. She probably feels bad for me. She probably knows a little bit about me since she works at my therapist's office, which gives her even more of a reason to feel sorry for me. I don't want people's sympathy.

We get our food and head back to the bleachers. Delilah points out different people at the game and tells me about them. So and so has an obsession with pickles, this guy has been married four times, that girl is from Italy. It's like she knows everyone. As she talks, I get the feeling this is a close-knit town. I'm an outsider, and I think I always will be. Just like everywhere else I go.

We watch the game, which is as boring as I remember it. It's just a bunch of boys trying to get a goal and running around the field. I don't understand how people enjoy it. I don't understand how I once enjoyed it.

The game goes on for almost two hours. My dad's team lost, which means Aiden's brother lost.

"Aiden!" his brother, Hunter, says as he runs over to him. "We didn't win." He frowns and looks down at his feet.

"It's okay, you always have next year! I think you did amazing!" Aiden tells him, giving him a hug.

Hunter shrugs. "I guess so."

"Tomorrow, you and I will go out for ice cream and do whatever you want. How's that sound?" Aiden says.

Hunter's face lights up. "Really? That'd be awesome!"

"It's a deal then. I'll see you tonight when I get home, and we can plan our day."

"Where are you going?" Hunter asks, pouting again.

"I told you . . . I'm, uh, hanging out with Delilah and some friends."

Delilah raises an eyebrow at Aiden. I wonder what's happening.

Hunter shrugs. "Okay, I'll see you later then. We're going out for pizza!"

"Have fun!" Aiden yells as Hunter runs to his mom.

My dad comes over looking extremely tired. He rubs the side of his face and yawns.

"I am worn out," he mumbles.

"It was a close game," Aiden tells him.

My dad nods. "I've gotta go take the team out for pizza," he tells me. I sigh. I do not want to go out for pizza with a bunch of annoying boys. I thought pizza was only for winners, anyway.

"Well, he can hang out with us," Delilah says. "We're gonna be with a few friends."

Aiden shoots her a wide-eyed glare, and she just smiles.

"That'd be great! It'd give you a chance to meet some kids, right, Levi? Go ahead, it'll be fun!" my dad says.

I glare at my dad. What's worse? Twelve-year-old boys or people my age? I debate for a few seconds before my dad speaks up again.

"Have fun, Levi," he says, walking away.

I guess I had no choice in that decision, as usual.

Aiden whispers something to Delilah, and she shrugs.

"We're going to a little party. It won't be anything too big," she tells me. "Let's go."

I follow them to the car, and I'm overcome with anxiety. I'm always hesitant getting into cars with people, especially people I don't know that well. I should have thought of that sooner before I "agreed" to go with them. I look around to see if my dad has already left, and the spot he parked in is now empty. I have to go with Delilah and Aiden—I have no choice.

"C'mon," Aiden says, motioning me to get in the car.

I type quickly into my phone, "How long have you had your license?"

"Almost a year," Delilah says. She glances over at Aiden quickly.

I nod and take a deep breath. "Have you ever gotten into an accident?"

"No."

"She's a really good driver," Aiden says. "Don't worry."

Telling me not to worry will not make my anxiety level decrease. Regardless, I take a deep breath and sit in the back seat.

A little party.

There are at least ninety people here, and it's not even that late. We shove through a bunch of people to get into whoever's house this is. The house is huge. People are all over the yard, and there are even more inside. Loud music is blaring, and the stench of alcohol and sweat surrounds me.

I notice some people are staring at me, mostly girls. Maybe it's because I'm new here. No one has ever seen me before. I'm used to being looked at like I'm different, though. I am different.

A girl dashes out of the house, mascara running down her face. She's sobbing uncontrollably as she leaves. Her boobs seem to defy gravity as they bounce with each step. I try not to stare.

"Aiden! Delilah!" someone screams from behind me. "You made it!" I turn around to see a blonde girl with a beer in her hand. She's wearing a tight black dress that seems like it'll burst at any second. She pushes through some guys and walks over to us, stumbling in her heels.

Aiden rolls his eyes and waves.

"Who's this?" she asks, looking over at me. "You're ca-ute." She points to me and taps my chest weakly. She smiles and takes a sip of her drink, half of it missing her mouth.

"Taylor, this is Levi. Levi, this is Taylor," Aiden mumbles. "Nice seeing you. Good-bye."

Aiden grabs my wrist and pulls me away.

"She's extremely drunk," Aiden mumbles.

No, really, I couldn't tell.

"She moved here three years ago. She used to hang out with us, until she became, ya know . . . That. Whenever she's drunk, which is a lot, she believes we're still friends. She's a clingy drunk. I'd stay away."

I nod.

We walk through the house to the most crowded room. Delilah and Aiden say hi to a lot of people—they definitely know almost everyone. I don't know if they're popular around here, or if everyone just knows one another.

I look around, taking in my surroundings. People are dancing on the table and making out all over the place. Two guys continuously slap each other in the face, screaming the whole time.

I hate parties.

I nervously crack my knuckles and run my hand through my hair. My anxiety is increasing every minute. We've only been here for about twenty minutes, and I already can't take it. I can't handle all these people and the atmosphere. The loud music has already given me a headache, and I can feel the beat in the pit of my stomach. It makes me want to throw up.

"Do you want a drink?" Aiden asks me.

I shake my head no.

I refuse to drink because I'm afraid that if I do, I'll get drunk and speak. And I cannot talk. *Ever.* Who knows what I'd say if I were drunk. I could tell someone something personal, really personal. That is one of my biggest fears.

After a few minutes of talking, Aiden and Delilah go off to do whatever. I don't really pay attention to where they went. I'm too busy trying to breathe. I stand in the corner of the kitchen, away from everyone. I try to calm myself, but I can feel an anxiety attack coming. I lean against the counter, resting my head on my hand.

"You okay?" some girl asks me, raising her eyebrows.

I wave her off, and she shrugs before walking away.

I am not okay. I will never be okay.

Taylor walks over to me and leans against me.

"So, Levi, right?" she asks. She giggles. "You're so cute. I like that," she says, pointing to my lip ring. Her finger touches my lip, because she's so close, and I can smell all the alcohol she drank. "Wanna go do something?" She wiggles her eyebrows and laughs again.

I look away and shake my head.

"Oh, so you're one of those guys. Playing hard to get, huh?"

The kitchen becomes crowded as people lie down on the counter and drink alcohol off each other. Everyone is screaming and chanting and laughing. I wonder how people can act like this. They're so immature and disgusting.

I've never liked parties.

I push away from Taylor and walk away from her.

"Levi, come back!" she whines.

I start to become lightheaded, so I stumble down the hall and try to find an empty room. I finally locate one upstairs, after several awkward encounters with other people. I go inside and lock the door so no one can come in.

Breathe, Levi.

I check the time on my phone. 10:34. I've been here for almost an hour.

My heart is racing, and my hands are shaking. I sit on the edge of the bed and hang my head in my hands, trying to relax. My breathing is abnormal, and I'm sweating.

Now is not the time.

I can feel the tingles throughout my whole body start to increase. Soon I'll be shaking furiously.

No, stop, please.

I can hear my heart pounding. It's louder than the music that continues to blare. Everything seems to get louder and quieter all at once.

My vision is blurry, fading in and out. I look at my hands, which are shaking uncontrollably. I feel like I'm in a daze.

This has happened before—a lot, actually—when I'm around too many people. This is why I avoid being in crowded public places. This is why I like to be alone. A few friends is different from a party of one hundred people.

My breathing increases as I try to relax, but nothing is working. The music gets quieter, and then everything is silent. All I can hear is my heart racing, and the ringing in my ears. All I can feel is my shaking body. I feel like I'm stuck in an earthquake. Except the earthquake is myself, and there's no escape.

Why does this happen to me? Why do I deserve all this?

My thoughts become jumbled as I try to do what my therapist told me.

Count to ten.

I slowly count to ten.

It doesn't work.

Breathe in through your nose and out through your mouth.

I do that a few times.

It doesn't work.

I squeeze my fists repeatedly, another thing my therapist told me. It makes me focus on something other than my panic attack.

I just have to let the anxiety run through my body. I can't do anything to stop it. It could last for a while, or it could be over in a few minutes.

The violent shaking continues to increase. I need to stop this.

Xanax.

I fumble in my pockets for my wallet, looking for my pill.

C'mon. I have to have some in here. I always carry it with me.

I finally find it and quickly run to the bathroom that's connected to the room. Thankfully, no one is in here. I swallow the pill with some water and sit down on the cold tile floor to let it sink in.

The symptoms slowly fade away.

It's 11:01.

There's a text from my dad.

Hope you're having fun. Be home by 12.

Oh, yeah. I'm having tons of fun. Just hanging out with my anxiety. We're having a swell time.

I lean my head back against the wall and squeeze my eyes shut. Finally, my body is still. I'm all right.

A light turns on, and I snap my head toward the bathroom door.

"Levi, are you okay?"

Why can't I just be alone?

Chapter Nine

LEVI

was worried when I couldn't find you."

Delilah comes and sits beside me on the cold tile floor. She looks at me with wide eyes. She seems scared and very concerned.

I move over a little so she's not so close.

"What happened? Did someone do something to you?" she whispers. She's talking quietly, but there's no one around that would be able to hear us.

I shake my head no, not looking up at her.

Instead, I watch her through my peripheral vision, and can tell she notices my abnormal breathing and my shaky hands as I reach up to fix my hair.

She leans her head against the wall and turns her body so she's facing me. "Why are you shaking? Levi, what— Wait, you're having a panic attack, aren't you?"

I slowly nod.

She speaks quietly, barely audible. "I'm really sorry. I honestly thought it was just a few people. Aiden said it was just some of his friends hanging out. He didn't say it was *this*. If I had known, I wouldn't have come either. It's sorta overwhelming. I hate stuff like this."

Delilah seems like she's being truthful, and I believe her for some reason. There's just something about her words that makes me believe she's not lying.

"Do you need anything to stop it? Are you going to be all right?" she asks, concerned. "I can go get you some water or something."

I give her a thumbs up to indicate I'll be all right.

We sit in silence for a minute or two. The only sound is the muffled noise from outside the bathroom. I can still hear the music and people screaming. It makes my head pound just thinking about it.

"Do you want to leave?" she asks, peering over at me.

I look at her for the first time and see the sincerity in her eyes. It's not pity like I thought it was earlier. It's empathy.

I nod slowly.

She stands up and reaches down to lend me a hand. She smiles a little and nods slightly, as if she's saying it's okay.

I hesitatingly accept it.

"Just follow me. If you get nervous, let me know. I just need to find Aiden," she tells me as we leave the bathroom. She's still talking quietly, and I like it for some reason. It makes me feel like I can trust her, like she'll keep this all a secret. She's not treating me like a child or getting upset with me like everyone else. She's just acting natural about it. "Are you okay now?"

I nod.

She weaves in and out of the crowd of people as we move through the house. I focus on Delilah, careful not to lose her. I try to ignore the many people surrounding me. I don't need more anxiety.

We make it to the kitchen and see Aiden standing with a group of people. He has his arm around the waist of a girl while they talk. Aiden laughs at something the girl says, and she moves slightly closer.

He notices us and waves.

"Well, hey guys!" he says excitedly. "How's everything going? Having fun?"

Delilah takes a deep breath. "Levi and I are leaving!" she shouts over the noise.

"The party's just starting though!" Aiden says, wiggling his eyebrows.

Delilah rolls her eyes. "Do you want to stay? Or leave with us?" she asks him.

He waves her off. "I'm staying!" He glances over to the girl beside him and smiles.

"All right. Have fun," she says, rolling her eyes but smiling.

"Bye, guys! See you later," Aiden says, before turning back to the girl, seeming to forget about everyone else instantly.

I follow Delilah outside. Every few seconds, she makes sure I'm still behind her until we've made it to the car. She gets into the car and looks over at me confused when I don't get in.

I stand outside the car and light a cigarette.

"You're kidding, right? You are seriously not a smoker," Delilah says after she rolls down the window.

I shrug. I'm not really a *smoker*. I'm just so nervous right now, I need something to take my mind off the anxiety. It's just a little stress reliever. It's not like I'm addicted.

"I shouldn't be as surprised as I am," she says, rolling her window back up.

I'm relieved to be out of the party, and my anxiety has finally decreased. I can breathe normally again, and my body has stopped shaking. I can relax a little now.

I get in the car once I'm done smoking, and Delilah starts the engine. I'm more relaxed getting into the car this time, mostly because I don't want to go to sleep and have today be over with.

"I was thinking we could go get something to eat, then go home. Is that okay?" Delilah asks as she drives. "Only if you want to, though. We don't have to."

I think for a few seconds. I am hungry, but I don't really want to go. I'm exhausted too. But Delilah helped me out. Though she's still a girl who makes me uncomfortable.

However, I'm quite hungry.

I nod, and she smiles.

"Okay, there's a place around here that should be open," she says. "I really am sorry about tonight."

I'm not quite sure why I agreed to go out. If she had asked a few minutes earlier, I would've said no. This is very unlike me.

We drive for a few more minutes before she pulls into a small diner. A red neon sign reads "Breakfast 24/7." I text my dad to let him know I'll be home soon.

Wait, since when do I care about curfew? Or my dad?

We get out of the car and head into the diner.

Delilah and I sit at a table, and the waitress hands us menus. I get pancakes, and Delilah gets waffles. We both get chocolate milk.

We sit in silence the first few minutes. I feel like no one ever knows how to start a conversation with me, which is understandable. I'm *me*. Plus, it's kind of hard to have a conversation with someone who doesn't talk.

Delilah finally starts to speak. "So, uh, what grade are you in?"

I type something in my phone and press speak. "I dropped out."

She scrunches her eyebrows and stirs the straw in her milk. "Oh. I'm a junior."

"What's a junior?"

"Oh, right, Australia doesn't call it that. Um, what you call Year 11, I think."

I nod. "I would've been in Year 11 this year."

"Oh. When did you drop out?"

"This year. I was homeschooled for a little, but it came to the point where I wasn't getting out of bed. And I assume you know why."

Her cheeks turn slightly red. "What?"

"I saw you looking at my folder."

Her eyes widen, and she looks down. "I'm really sorry. I didn't, I was just . . . I'm sorry."

"I shouldn't even be acknowledging your existence for being so snoopy."

If I actually talked, she would be able to tell that I'm being sarcastic. I don't really care that she read my folder. The only thing in there is the information sheet that has the diagnosis. My diagnosis is pretty self-explanatory anyway.

"I was just curious. I'm sorry," she says quietly.

I start to type that I'm just kidding, but she speaks again.

"It's just that . . . Well, when patients like you come in, I like to know why they're like that. My dad left when I was five years old, and he suffered from anger problems. No, that's the wrong way to put it. He didn't suffer, he was more, like, overtaken by it. It controlled what he could and couldn't do. Some things would make him so upset, and he'd have random outbursts. And I just want to know why he left, if that makes sense. And sometimes I think if I knew how other people with similar issues thought and acted, it'll bring me closer to solving why he couldn't live with us anymore. Sometimes I feel like I caused his anger, and he left because of me. I feel like I was maybe a burden or something . . . Like, what if he hated me? And that's why he left . . . I don't know, it's stupid, I know. But . . ."

"It's not stupid."

She looks up from the table, where her gaze was frozen. "It's not?"

I shake my head no.

"It makes perfect sense."

"I shouldn't have even told you that. I'm sorry. You probably don't even care."

"Please stop being sorry."

"Sorry—Oops." She smiles a little and bites her bottom lip.

The food comes out, and we eat in silence. I think about what she told me about her dad. It was something deep and personal. And I feel like she deserves to know a little bit about me. Maybe it will give her hope about her dad.

Sometimes I forget that other people have problems too. I live in my own world and think that I'm the only one who suffers.

Everyone has their own issues, no matter how big or small. We're all people that live different lives with different troubles. It's comforting to think that Delilah can share one of her problems with me, someone she barely knows. Maybe she only told me because I have no one to tell. Or maybe she's slightly drunk too.

Or maybe she just trusts me.

I didn't think anyone could ever trust me. I don't even trust me.

I put my fork down, and she looks up. I type quickly on my phone, and she appears confused.

"I don't know if this will help," the robotic voice says, "but I've been like this for six months. My girlfriend died really unexpectedly. It messed me up. It turned my life upside down. I stopped doing everything. My whole life spiraled downward and just kept getting worse. And maybe your dad felt that way too, I don't really know. There's no way of knowing. It could've been anything, really. I just thought I should tell you that."

Delilah doesn't say anything for a few seconds, and she just looks at me.

"I'm sorry about your girlfriend," she says quietly.

"Please do not be sorry."

She rests her head on her hand. "You know, you're turning out to be different than what I thought," she whispers.

"It's that stupid new pill. Making me all sentimental."

But it's not stupid. I kind of like the way it's making me feel.

I'm starting not to feel so numb anymore.

I can actually feel a little again.

Chapter Ten

Delilah

I head to Aiden's the next morning to see how he's doing, even though he's probably still asleep. I wonder how long he stayed at the party.

I walk into his house and see Hunter watching television. He turns around and waves.

"Hi, Delilah!" he says happily.

"Hey! Is Aiden awake?" I ask him.

He nods. "Yeah, but he's still in bed. Mom said I'm not allowed to bother him."

I head down to Aiden's room and find him lying on his bed, his face shoved into the pillow.

"Aiden?" I whisper.

He mumbles something and slowly rolls over. He squints at me and wiggles his fingers in an attempt to wave.

"How long did you stay at the party?" I ask him

"I dunno. A long time. My mom almost grounded me. I lied and said I was at your house, so if she asks, that's where I was."

I roll my eyes and laugh.

I tell him what happened with Levi, leaving out how he had a panic attack and what he told me about his girlfriend. Those are personal things that no one else should know. Even though Aiden is my best friend, it's not right for me to tell him.

"So he actually, like, was nice?" Aiden asks, sitting up a little.

I nod, smiling. "Yeah, it was different from all the other times I've been around him."

Levi has definitely changed. I thought he would never want to be near me, let alone have breakfast at midnight with me. He told me a secret of his, even though it wasn't the whole story. He opened up, which was surprising. Maybe he trusts me.

"We should hang out with him sometime," Aiden says. "Maybe he wants some cool friends like us."

A few days after, I decide to go to Levi's. I haven't seen him since the party. If he went to school, I would've run into him there. I wonder what he does all day.

Aiden and I are going to see a movie tonight, so I thought I'd invite Levi. After what he told me about his girlfriend, I don't want him to feel alone. Plus, Aiden thinks it's a good idea for him to hang out with us. It might make him more comfortable here.

Mr. Harrison is in the front yard when I get there, mowing the lawn. He waves when he sees me.

"Hey, Delilah, what's up?" he asks.

"I came to see Levi. Is he inside?" I ask.

He smiles. "Yeah, he's in his room, the one at the end of the hall. You know, I'm glad you let him hang out with you guys the other night. He's sort of, I don't know, separated. It's hard to get him to do things. I'm happy you and Aiden are here."

I smile and nod. "Yeah, it was nice hanging out with him."

I walk inside before he can question me about that night. I don't want to be the one to tell him that his son had a panic attack all alone at a huge party. I wonder if Levi even told him about it.

Probably not.

I walk down the hall to Levi's room and knock on the door. It opens after a few seconds, and he stares at me for a while before walking away from the door.

"Hey," I say quietly. I don't really know what to do. I feel really awkward right now. Finally, I clear my throat and speak up. "So, uh, Aiden and I are going to the movies tonight, and we were wondering if you wanted to come."

He types something in his phone. "Why would I want to come?"

I scrunch my eyebrows. "I don't know. We thought maybe you'd want to. If you don't like movies, we can do something else."

"No. Why would I want to hang out with you guys?"

I'm taken aback by what he wrote. I didn't expect this kind of response.

"I thought you'd want to because . . . the other night . . ."

"The other night meant nothing. I was drunk. Whatever I told you was false. I don't care."

Why is Levi being like this? The other night he was so shy and kind. But now he's being a cocky jerk. He seems like he's constantly changing.

I don't think he was drunk at the party. I don't even think he had anything. I rack my brain to try and remember if I saw him drinking. He never did, as far as I know.

He's lying to me.

"Levi, you weren't drunk," I tell him, crossing my arms over my chest.

"Yes, I was. You were barely even with me. I think I would know if I was drunk."

I roll my eyes. "Why are you being like this?"

"What do you mean? This is me. You don't even know me."

He stands up from his bed, towering over me. He looks down, his blue eyes piercing through me. I'm suddenly nervous again and at a loss for words for a few seconds.

"I thought I could get to know you. I'm sorry for trying, okay, Levi? Sorry for trying to help you. If you want to be like this, be my guest. You can be a jerk for the rest of your life."

"Good. Because I don't care what you do with your life, so you shouldn't care about mine."

Each thing he says is like a knife being thrown at me. Maybe because he was so kind the other night, I thought he actually wanted to hang out with me.

I guess I mean nothing to him.

I look around his room and see a weekly pill container. I notice Sunday to Thursday have pills in them, even though it's Friday.

He hasn't been taking his pills since the party, which was Saturday.

"You stopped taking your meds," I mumble without meaning to.

His eyes dart over to the container. "No, I just refilled them." He rubs his nose quickly and looks away from me.

He's lying again.

I look at him, and he bites down on his lip.

"Why?" I ask.

"Why do you care? It's none of your business."

"You're right, it is none of my business. But you know what? This is your health on the line. You should care for yourself."

"Since when do you think you know everything about me?"

Levi is just putting words in my mouth. He's being so rude about everything. I was just trying to be friendly.

"I never said I knew everything! I'm just trying to be here for you! Because that's what I would want if I just moved to the total opposite side of the world!" I don't want to yell, but I am. I can't help it.

"I don't need you! I don't need anyone! Just leave me alone!"

"Fine, Levi, I will. I'll leave you alone. Sorry for trying to help," I say, leaving his room and shutting the door.

I leave without saying good-bye to Mr. Harrison.

What happened with Levi keeps replaying through my mind. Every word, every movement. I wish Levi actually spoke so I wouldn't have to interpret the robotic voice. It makes fighting more difficult because there's no emotion in its voice.

For some reason, the robotic voice makes me even madder.

I don't know why Levi suddenly went back to how he was before. It definitely has to do with his pills. I know he was taking them before, because he said they were making him sentimental.

Why would someone stop taking pills? If they help, why stop?

I know I will never understand how Levi's mind works, nor do I truly want to. It's his personal business. He's putting himself in jeopardy by not taking his medication.

I'm worried about him.

Maybe he just forgot. That's a possibility, right? Maybe his mind was somewhere else, and he didn't remember to take them for a few days.

I hope that's why. I hope he's not intentionally stopping.

But something in the pit of my stomach tells me it's intentional.

Levi doesn't want to be happy.

Chapter Eleven

LEVI

I anxiously sit in front of my laptop, staring at Caleb's icon on Skype.

C'mon, Levi. Just press call.

We've planned to video chat today, with my mum too. She doesn't understand how the whole Skype thing works, so Caleb is helping her. I've kept my finger wavering above the button to call for a few minutes now. I don't know why I'm so nervous to see them. It's my mum and Caleb, the two most familiar people in my life. But for some reason, there are butterflies in my stomach.

I'm anxious to see them again; it feels like it's been forever. I feel like I'm in a whole other world, not just a different continent. Nothing is the same here.

Caleb's smiling icon pops up, saying he's calling me. They probably think I've forgotten or that I don't want to talk to them, but I do. I always mess things up, don't I?

I press accept and wait for the call to connect. I can hear them, just not see them.

"Caleb, it says the webcam isn't working. What's that? Where's the webcam?" I hear my mum say.

"Lilian, Lilian. Stop pressing random buttons! I got this!" Caleb says, laughing hysterically. He sounds happy. He's making the hiccup noises he makes when he laughs too hard. I missed that.

It's been twenty-one days without them. It's nice to hear their voices, but I want to see them now. But just hearing them is making me happier already. I didn't think it was possible to miss Caleb this much; I thought we would both stop being friends once I moved out here. But he hasn't given up on me.

"Look, oh my goodness, I can see Levi!" I hear my mum say. "Caleb, hurry! I want him to see us too! Oh my gosh, I miss you so much, sweetie!" My mum babbles on and on about how much she misses me. It makes me miss her even more. I didn't realize how homesick I really was.

"Levi, can you hear us?" Caleb asks. I nod.

"He nodded!" my mum says excitedly.

"Wait . . . Got it!" Caleb says. Shortly after, they pop up on my screen, smiling widely. They both cheer excitedly. I clap my hands to show that I'm excited too.

"Hi, honey!" my mum says happily. I wave, and she smiles even more. A few tears slip from her eyes. She wipes the tears away quickly, and she's still smiling.

I blink a few times to stop myself from crying too. I type into the message part.

mum if u cry i'll cry:-(

"Sorry, Levi, sorry!" she says, frantically waving her hands.

We talk for a while, with her asking questions, like how my dad is and how I'm feeling. It's nice to talk to them again. They're the only ones who really know how I feel.

Caleb tells me all about what's happening back home. I guess people keep asking about me, which is weird. They didn't seem to care when I was there, so why do they care now?

"I've been on the search for a new FIFA partner, but no one wants to play with me," Caleb says, pouting. Typical Caleb.

ur such a loser!

Caleb laughs. "I am not! FIFA is fun!" he says, defending himself.

Now I wish I was playing that stupid football video game with Caleb. When I left, I couldn't wait to leave. I wanted to be away from everyone. But now that I've been away, I want to go back home. I'd rather be there than here, that's for sure. I have no one here. I thought I was lonely back home, but I really wasn't. I had a caring mother and a great friend, and I treated them terribly.

I realize now how much I had. I just wish I could redo some things.

"Can we have a tour of your room?" Caleb asks.

it's kinda boring but yah sureee

I get up from my bed, carefully balancing my laptop while I walk around my room. They make comments about how I need more decorations and things in my room. I don't really care, though. What's the point of decorating?

"You need to clean!" my mum says, laughing. I look around at all the clothes on my floor, slightly embarrassed. I didn't think they'd want a tour of my room, so I didn't see the reason for cleaning.

I start to head back to my bed when my mum says something.

"Wait, Levi, go back a little please."

I take a few steps back, unsure of what she wants to see.

There's a long silence, and I hear her sigh. I know I've done something wrong. Things were going so well too. What have I done now?

"Levi Elliot Harrison," she says quietly.

Uh oh. The full name is never a good sign.

I look at Caleb, who looks as confused as I am. I chew on my bottom lip and head back to my bed, waiting for my mom to speak up.

"You stopped taking your pills."

There it is. Of course she noticed. Out of all the things to see, she just had to see that.

Her voice gets quieter, and I can tell she's trying not to cry. "Why did you stop?"

This isn't really something I want to get into with her. It's stupid why I stopped. She won't understand. This isn't the first time this has happened, either. I think she always blames herself when I stop taking them, like somehow she caused it. I feel bad for making her feel that way, but I can't help it. I don't like taking them. They always cause me more problems.

I quickly think of an excuse.

I forgot to take them, I was feeling better so I just forgot. I'm sorry. I promise to remember.:-)

I know she doesn't believe me because she doesn't say anything for a few seconds.

"Have you taken them today?" she asks. I shake my head no. "Please, take them right now. So I don't have to worry."

Now I have to take them. She's on a total different continent, and she'll be worrying about me. I can't do that to her.

I get up and quickly take the pills. She smiles a little afterward, clearly still upset. The atmosphere has changed drastically.

I'm such a screwup.

I nervously scratch my nose and chew on my bottom lip.

"So, uh, have you made any new friends?" Caleb asks, trying to change the subject.

As if on cue, Aiden walks in.

Not that he's a friend, but he's someone.

"Who was that?" my mum asks.

Aiden plops on the bed beside me, bouncing the mattress a little. I glare at him, and he smiles.

"Hello there! I'm Aiden! You must be the lovely Mrs. Harrison!" he says cheerily.

What in the world?

My mum smiles. "Call me Lilian! Are you Levi's friend?"

I wait anxiously for him to say no. My mum will be crushed. I hold my breath for a few seconds, ready for more tension to be added.

Aiden looks over at me and back to the laptop. "Yeah! We're neighbors. I help Anthony with soccer stuff too! Levi's great!" He puts his arm around my shoulders and smiles.

Well, I guess this is better than my mum thinking I have no friends. But I don't appreciate his extreme closeness. I wriggle out of his arm and roll my eyes.

"That's fantastic! Oh, I'm so happy to hear that!" my mum says.

Aiden talks to them for a few minutes, and he's extremely nice. I never noticed how talkative he really could be. He always laughs at the right times, and he's making my mum laugh too. It's nice to see her happy. I'm so used to seeing her upset and sad, it's rare to see her this happy.

Maybe Aiden isn't as bad as I thought.

After a few minutes, Aiden leaves to go do something. I'm pretty sure he just wanted food, though.

"Aiden seems great! I'm so glad you met him!" my mum says once he's gone.

uhhh yeah, he just kinda showed up one day

After a few more minutes of talking, my mum and Caleb decide to leave. We talked for over an hour, and it's getting late over there. I hate the fact that the time zones are so different. I feel even more separated from home.

We say our good-byes, or they say theirs and I type mine, with a few more tears from my mum. She makes me promise to take my pills.

I hate making promises, because I always break them.

I click the end button and watch them fade away from the screen. I stare at the laptop for a few minutes after they're gone, wishing they were still there.

I miss them already.

I can hear someone moving around the house, either my dad or Aiden. I head out of my room and find Aiden in the kitchen eating a banana.

"Hey, that kid Caleb is pretty cool. Your mom is nice too!" he says with his mouth full.

I shrug and sit in one of the chairs. I pull out my phone and type something. "Why were you so nice? You could've easily said we're not friends. It's not like we've actually hung out or that I like you."

Aiden shrugs. "I dunno. It's easier to be nice than to be mean. Plus, I didn't want your mom worrying about her little boy," he says, teasingly.

I roll my eyes at his remark.

"Whoa, whoa. I just did something kind for you, and that's how you repay me?" he says, laughing.

I shrug and turn away from him.

"This whole tough guy act isn't going to last long, I hope you know that," Aiden says, gesturing toward me. "You can try to be all cool and mean, or whatever you're trying to do, but it isn't going to work with me."

I look back at him and raise my eyebrows.

"You know exactly what I'm talking about. Don't try to act all innocent and naive."

And I do know. I know I come off as inconsiderate, but I can't help it sometimes. At first I did it to keep people away, and now it's a part of who I am. I keep everyone away.

I'm not sure I can do that with Aiden. He won't stay away for some reason.

"You're literally stuck with me," Aiden says, laughing. "This is, like, my second home, whether you like it or not." He takes another bite of his banana and chews it loudly. "I'm not going anywhere."

Chapter Twelve

LEVI

Since video chatting, I've been missing something a lot.
FIFA.

I don't even know why I miss it. I never really enjoyed playing it. I think it's because it's something Caleb and I did together, and I miss Caleb. I guess playing it might make me feel closer to home. Is that stupid?

I've been pacing the hallway for the past few minutes, debating whether or not to leave the house. I figured that Aiden might have FIFA, or some other game that will keep me busy. I don't want to play with Aiden, but he's my only chance. The FIFA withdrawals are giving me anxiety, and I'm not really sure why. I think I'm just extremely bored and looking for something to do.

Is this what homesickness is? Or am I going insane?

I'm already insane, actually.

When I want to do something, it usually causes me to have to do it. I get jittery and anxious if I don't, and get completely wrapped up in thinking about it, so I'm sort of forced to do whatever it is. Today, it's FIFA. Something like this hasn't happened for a while. It's usually something that connects to Delia, but today it's Caleb.

I can live without FIFA.

But I want to play it.

I don't need to play it.

Yes, I need to play FIFA.

I'm a mess.

I finally run down the stairs and open the door. My hand stays on the knob a little bit before I walk outside. I take the first few steps down my driveway and stop.

This is weird. This is really weird. Is it weird?

I shake my head and continue walking to Aiden's. Good thing my dad isn't home, or he would've questioned me. He's been trusting me a little more; he leaves to do quick errands, but he's never gone too long. I understand why he's afraid to leave me alone. I'm unpredictable.

When I get to Aiden's, he isn't outside like I hoped he would be. I hesitantly ring the doorbell and wait for him to answer. After a few seconds, an unfamiliar face opens the door. I'm guessing it's his mum.

"Hi, can I help you?" she asks.

I open and shut my mouth, unsure of what to do. It's not like I'll speak to her, and she is expecting an answer. I bite on my lip ring and pull out my phone to type something. I pass it to her, as I don't want the robotic voice to speak. That voice surprises some people, and I'm trying to make this less awkward than it has to be.

Is Aiden here?

"Aiden is at school. He should be home soon. Do you mind me asking who you are?" she says, raising an eyebrow suspiciously. She probably expects me to be at school too.

I forgot all about school. I should've realized that's where Aiden would be.

Thankfully, Aiden pulls up in his car. He grabs his bag and gets out, drumming his fingers against the door. He notices me standing at his front door, and he looks surprised.

"Hey, Levi! What are you doing here?" he asks, walking over to us. "Mom, this is Levi. He's Anthony's son."

"Oh, nice to meet you! Aiden told me about you moving in," she says. I feel my cheeks heat up, slightly embarrassed. I wonder what Aiden said about me.

"So, uh, what are ya here for?" Aiden asks.

His mum heads back inside, leaving us alone in the yard.

I type in my phone, "I was wondering if you have the game FIFA."

"Yeah, I'm pretty sure we have it! I'm, like, blind, so Hunter usually plays. Do you wanna borrow it? Here, come inside."

"Actually, I was wondering if we could play it."

Aiden stops walking and turns around, a big smile growing on his face.

Great, he's going to laugh at me. This is so embarrassing.

I type in more. "I don't have anything to play it with at my house, and I thought you'd have it. I'm sorry if that's weird."

I'm suddenly regretting coming over. This is really awkward. I basically just invited myself into Aiden's home to play FIFA. If that isn't strange, I don't know what is.

"No, no, that's not weird at all! Of course we can play! I kinda suck at it, but that's all right," Aiden says, leading me into his room. He rummages through a drawer, pulling out his glasses. "I'll need these to see," he says, laughing. "C'mon, let me show you around."

He takes me on a brief tour of his house, which is almost exactly the same as my dad's. I wonder if all the houses in the neighborhood are like this.

I'm surprised that Aiden is willing to let me come into his house and hang out with him. This is considered hanging out, right? I feel like I haven't done something like this in forever. Aiden is so kind when all I've been to him is rude.

We head to the living room to play, and Aiden sets it up. He hands me a controller and sits down on the couch beside me.

"Just warning you, I really am terrible," he says as the game starts.

I didn't think it was possible to be as bad as Aiden is. Half the time he runs in the wrong direction or doesn't move at all. He keeps screaming too—it's quite funny to watch.

"All this green is so frustrating!" he screams after a few minutes.

Playing FIFA makes me feel better. I feel a little closer to home while playing the game, because it's so familiar to me. Aiden isn't anything like Caleb, but that's okay. He's not a bad guy—he's pretty nice. I'm just not sure if he's being nice because he pities me or if that's just how he is.

"No, I'm the better FIFA player!" Caleb says.

"No, I am, and you know it!" I say.

"I've won the past three games!"

"I was distracted," I say, blushing.

"By what?"

"That girl," I say, pointing out the window to a girl outside.

"Who? Delia?"

"That's her name?" She had just moved here and sat across from me in English. She was so interesting, always writing in this blue notebook, though I don't know what. She had these cool glasses and wore pretty dresses.

"You like her, don't you?" Caleb asks, wiggling his eyebrows.

I feel my cheeks blush. "Psh, what? No! She's just . . . different, that's all."

He rolls his eyes.

"Let's get back to FIFA," I say, turning the game back on.

"Levi, why aren't you running anymore?" I hear Aiden say. He waves a hand in front of my face, and I push it away. "You always get distracted," he says, laughing.

Distracted is a way to describe it, I guess. I see my player standing in the middle of the field, and Aiden has paused the game.

"Is everything okay?" he asks.

I nod quickly and wave my hand so he'll start the game again. He shrugs, and we continue to play. About halfway through, the door opens, and I hear a familiar voice.

"Hey, Aiden! I found this really cool—What is he doing here?" Delilah is standing in front of us, crossing her arms over her chest. She looks confused when she notices me.

Aiden pauses the game again.

"Levi and I are playing FIFA! Wanna join?" he asks, patting the spot on the couch beside him.

"No, that's okay. I'll let you go back to your game. Sorry for interrupting." She starts to head out, but I stand up and quickly type something.

"No, it's okay. I'll leave. Thanks for having me, Aiden."

"No, Levi, it's fine," Delilah says.

"It's okay."

"Levi."

"Delilah."

Both of us are stubborn; I've quickly learned that about Delilah.

"You were here first. I don't want to interrupt," she says, opening the door.

"Why can't we both stay?"

Wait, what. What did I just type? Clearly my fingers aren't cooperating with my brain.

"Wait, what?" Delilah asks, saying exactly what I'm thinking.

I bite my bottom lip nervously and rock on my heels.

"Why would you want me to stay? You clearly hate me," Delilah says.

I don't type anything because I'm not sure what to say to that.

"Thought so. Bye, Levi. Bye, Aiden, I'll call you later." Delilah slams the door shut. She's gone as quickly as she came.

I head back to Aiden, who was observing the whole thing.

"Well, that was awkward," he says.

I nod and sit back down on the couch.

"You wanna keep playing?"

I shake my head no, and Aiden sits beside me.

"Don't be upset because of her. Delilah is just really sensitive and takes everything personally. You may not hate her, but she feels that way. She'll get over it, don't worry. I thought you hated me, but hey, look at us now!"

I feel bad that I was so mean to Delilah, and Aiden too. I feel like everything is changing inside me since I've started taking the pills again. This is partially why I stopped taking them last week. I'm afraid of how they make me feel.

I'm afraid that I can actually feel again.

I'm afraid of being happy.

Chapter Thirteen

DELILAH

I'm woken up to a sudden jumping on my bed. I open my eyes slowly to see Aiden looking down at me, his face a few inches from mine.

"Aiden, what are you doing here? What time is it?" I mumble, turning my head.

"Levi is missing," he says quietly.

He gets off of me and stares. I check the time, and it's 10:52 in the morning.

"What do you mean, he's missing?"

He shrugs. "Anthony called me a few minutes ago. He said Levi wasn't in his room, and his window was open."

I sit silently for a little. Aiden has been hanging out with Levi more since I saw them playing video games, so I guess they're friends. I'm not sure because Aiden doesn't really tell me about Levi, mostly because he thinks I don't want to have anything to do with him.

"I'm worried, Del," Aiden whispers.

"It'll be okay. He couldn't have gone too far."

"You don't know Levi. None of us do, really. He could be anywhere."

I chew on the inside of my cheek and rest my head on my hand.

"I was with him last night. He seemed fine," Aiden says.

"Isn't that the second night in a row?" I wonder what Levi and Aiden do. Levi doesn't seem to want to do much.

"Yeah. Anthony trusts me with Levi. What if I did something? Do you think I said something that upset him?"

"Aiden, I'm sure you didn't do anything."

He shrugs. "Will you help me look for him?"

I nod slowly. Levi may not be my friend, but Aiden is my best friend. I know he'd help me with anything.

I may also be worried for Levi too. Don't tell Aiden.

I quickly get dressed, and we head out to look for Levi. We pack some waters, food, and flashlights. We could be looking for Levi all day.

Aiden and I decide to split up. Anthony and Aiden are driving through town, so I've decided to look through the neighborhood. Maybe he just left for a walk or something.

I highly doubt that, though.

After half an hour, no one has found Levi. I've asked neighbors, I've gone through yards, I've even checked sheds. He's nowhere.

I try to think of all the places I've seen Levi. There are not many—the therapist's, his house, Aiden's house, and the park.

The park! I can't believe I didn't check there sooner. I run down to the park and search for Levi. It can't be that hard to find a six-foot-tall boy dressed all in black.

He's not in the obvious places, like the swings or the slide. I check the basketball field, but he's not there either. I head toward the fenced-off area, and I see Levi hidden in a bunch of trees. He's hugging his legs into his chest and is looking down. I crawl through the huge opening in the fence that's been there forever. I quietly walk over, not wanting to scare him like last time. As I get closer, I can hear him crying.

"Levi?" I whisper.

He looks up at me through the trees, his eyes red and swollen. His cheeks are rosy and blotchy and tears stain his face. His shirt is all wrinkled and dirt covers his jeans.

When he sees me, he quickly gets up and starts to run. He runs fast, rapidly getting farther away from me and deeper into the trees.

I run after him, worried for his safety. He's clearly upset about something, and he could decide to hurt himself.

The trees get more numerous as I run farther away from the fence. I've lost Levi; he could've gone anywhere. I look in every direction and finally see him lying on the ground. His pants are ripped, and there's some blood on his leg. He must have fallen in the short time since I lost him.

"Levi!" I shout, running in his direction.

He tries to scoot away from me, and he's crying even harder now. Something is seriously wrong.

I peer down at the small cut on his leg and look at his eyes, which are filled with tears.

"Just let me help, all right?" I say.

He slowly sits up and allows me to sit beside him. He doesn't look at me—he stays turned away. I can still hear him crying.

I grab the water out of my bag and pour it over his cut. I gently wipe it with a tissue I found in my bag, and he winces.

"Sorry," I mumble.

We sit in silence for a few minutes. I'm unsure of what to say or do. I'm not good at things like this, especially with Levi. He's so different and hard to understand. I don't know why he's so upset right now. I decide to start with simple questions, the way I've seen therapists do.

"Why are you out here?" I ask quietly.

He stays turned away from me.

We sit silently some more. Questions aren't going to work because I know he won't answer, so I just start saying what's on my mind.

"I know you don't like me, and I haven't always been so great to you. But you're clearly hurting, and I don't want to see you upset. It's not good to keep it all inside, trust me. You don't have to tell me everything, or anything if you don't want to. I just . . . I think it'd help if you told someone. Maybe Aiden—you trust him, right? Just so you're able to get it all out, you know?" I take a deep breath. "You probably don't want me here, but I am, and I'm not leaving you here alone."

He doesn't respond for a few seconds. Then he slowly turns around and faces me. His eyes dart around, avoiding mine, and he nervously bites his bottom lip. At least he has stopped crying. He takes out a piece of paper from his pocket, along with a pen. He quickly writes something and passes it to me. I wonder why he's carrying paper and a pen.

It's been 210 days since she died. And it hurts. A lot. Days go by, and she's not here. I hate being here without her. I hate everything. I just miss her so much. It's so hard to get through every day.

I look up at Levi after I read it, and he finally looks me in the eyes. He suddenly bursts into tears, and starts to sob. I put my hand on his back to comfort him, and he flinches at first.

"It's okay to be sad, Levi," I whisper. "You don't have to go through this alone."

He takes in a quick breath and collapses onto me, his head resting on my shoulder. It takes me by surprise, and I slowly wrap my arms around him. He cries into my shoulder for a while, his tears soaking my shirt. I don't say anything, I let him cry.

I didn't expect this from Levi. He seemed unbreakable to me. But in reality, he's hurting every single day. Today it was all too much for him, and he broke down. It seems that every time I'm with Levi, I see a different side of him. He's a giant mystery waiting to be uncovered.

I wonder how long it's been since he's actually cried. I think he tries to hold it all in and not think about his sadness. He tries so hard to be strong and tough, but he's just like everyone else. In fact, he feels emotions even more than others.

Suddenly, my phone rings. Levi picks his head up and wipes his eyes. I take my phone out of my pocket, and see it's Aiden.

"Anything?" Aiden says the second I pick up.

I look over at Levi, who is sniffing. I reach for a tissue and hand it to him. "Yeah. I found him."

Levi looks over at me. He looks so young and fragile, like he could crumble with the slightest touch.

"You did?!" Aiden asks. "Where is he?"

"He's at the park. Just give him some space, okay? He's all right. I'll bring him home, and we'll meet you guys there."

"Okay. I've gotta let Anthony know! Bye, Delilah!"

Aiden hangs up, and I look over at Levi.

"That was Aiden. Do you want to head home now?"

Levi shakes his head. He's looking at the cut on his leg, trying to wipe off the dirt.

"Does it hurt?" I ask him.

He shakes his head.

"Does anything hurt?" I'm not sure if he hurt himself anywhere else when he fell.

He nods and points to his chest.

"Your chest hurts?"

He shakes his head. He hesitatingly reaches for my hand and brings it up to his chest. I can feel his heart beating.

I realize what he's telling me, and I nearly start crying too.

Levi's heart hurts.

Chapter Fourteen

Levi

Delilah and I walk back to my house in silence. I feel awkward after what happened in the park. She just saw me cry like a little baby, and the worst part is that I cried into her shoulder. *Her shoulder.* Guys aren't supposed to be the one crying on the girl; it's supposed to be the other way around. I'm such a loser.

When Delilah found me, I just wanted to be invisible. I wanted Delilah to turn around and leave, like maybe she didn't see me. But of course she found me among the trees, sobbing.

Why did she have to be the one to see me cry?

I don't know if I'm so emotional because of the pills, or because of what's happening to me. I've been taking them every day, and I've just been feeling so much. It's like everything inside me is changing. Or I'm just hormonal. I feel like if guys had periods, this is what it would feel like.

I take my pack of cigarettes out of my pocket and light one almost immediately. I bring it up to my lips and inhale slowly. Delilah glances over at me and sighs, looking disappointed but understanding at the same time. I toss the cigarette to the ground after awhile and squish it onto the pavement. Delilah looks down at it and continues walking.

I honestly thought Delilah would make things worse when she sat down beside me. I thought she was going to yell at me or say something horrible, but she didn't. She actually helped me. She comforted me a lot. It was nice to know that she was there for me. I still feel uncomfortable around her, just because she reminds me so much of Delia. She looks exactly like her, and I'm starting to see similarities in their personalities. It scares me.

"What are you thinking about?" Delilah whispers. She must've noticed my pace slowed down as we walked.

I nervously rub my nose and shrug.

"I won't tell Aiden about what happened back there if you don't want him to know."

I nod my head. It's good to know that she won't share that with him. I don't want everyone to treat me like a child.

I turn my phone on, and multiple texts and missed calls from my dad immediately pop up. I type something on my phone and press speak. "Can you tell me something funny?"

Delilah looks over at me. "What?"

"Tell me a funny story." I want something to keep my mind from thinking about Delia and getting upset again. I think Delilah realizes that, so she starts to talk.

"Umm . . . Okay, I got one," she says, a small smile growing on her face. "In second grade, we had a dinosaur play. And of course I had a solo. You'll never guess what I was."

I look over at her with raised eyebrows. She looks so cute.

She giggles a little and starts talking again. "I was the baby dinosaur. I had to come out of this giant paper egg—it was huge. I sang this song in a high-pitched voice, and then I was *born*. Like, I had to literally jump out of the egg. So I jumped up to be born, and as I sprang up, I stepped on my costume. Well, it ripped in half and fell down to my ankles! Thankfully, I had clothes on underneath. People teased me all the time about it. It was so embarrassing! I even had a huge binky around my neck and a giant bonnet." Her cheeks are slightly red, and she covers her face with her hands. "It was horrible! I didn't know what to do. I looked behind the curtains at my teacher, who told me to continue. I heard all the kids behind me gasp!" she says, her voice muffled.

I can only imagine this happening. I wish I had been there to see it. I smile as I imagine it.

"Hey, you have a dimple," Delilah says, poking my cheek.

I roll my eyes and swat her hand away, trying not to smile any wider.

"I've never seen you smile before," she whispers.

I shrug and continue walking.

Delilah's right, though; she's never seen me smile. Barely anyone has these past few months.

Aiden and my dad pull up to the house at almost the exact same time we get there. My dad runs out of his car and pulls me into a tight hug.

"Don't ever scare me like that again," he says. "Do you know how worried I was?"

I notice that his hands are shaking slightly. I didn't think he'd care if I was gone for a few hours.

"Thank you for finding him, Delilah. And thanks for your help, Aiden. I don't know what I would've done without you guys," my dad says.

"No problem!" Aiden says. "I'm happy Levi's all right."

"Yeah, same here," Delilah says. "You guys want some alone time?"

"That'd be great," my dad says.

"Okay. I'll see you later, Levi," Delilah says, waving as she walks away with Aiden.

I could've sworn I saw some sadness in her smile as she left. Maybe I'm wrong, as I don't know why she'd be sad.

My dad tells me we have to talk, which I was expecting. We go inside and sit down at the table, and he has a stern look on his face. He asks me what I knew he would ask.

"Why did you leave?" he says.

I write down everything that happened. I let him know what was going on in my mind. I tell him I needed to be alone in order to figure some things out. I had been thinking a lot about Australia and Delia, and especially moving to Maine. I felt trapped and just needed some time to sort my thoughts. I was feeling flustered and anxious about everything, so I decided to leave. Figured that maybe I would feel better if I was gone for a little. It feels good to let it all out for once. I leave out the part about it being two hundred and ten days since Delia died.

Although he didn't say too much, he seemed to understand, and I think he felt good when I finally told him something about how I have been feeling. When I'm done, he gives me some new rules to follow. I have an earlier curfew, and I have to keep my door open at all times. I'm kind of annoyed, but I guess I was expecting it. He doesn't really know me yet, and he's worried. He can't trust me, which I understand because no one trusts me.

Once his speech is over, I head to my room. A few days ago, at a therapy session, Candace advised me to write things in a notebook. She said to write down my feelings, like what I'm worried about or struggling with. She also said to write down if anything good happens, which so far it hasn't. She says it's a way to clear my mind. I don't know if it works, but I'm trying. So far I've only written in the notebook twice.

Everything that has happened in the past few months has been building up inside me. It's like all the bad things are stacking themselves up inside me, slowly getting taller and taller. I'm afraid one day there won't be any room left for the good things. It seems like writing things down makes the bad stuff shrink a little, like they're leaving my mind.

Candace says there's a switch inside me that I can turn on and off. I don't really understand the metaphor. She says right now the switch is on, and that's why I'm miserable. I'm capable of turning off the switch, apparently, and once I do I'll be happier. But how am I supposed to turn off a switch when I don't even know what it's for?

I like my own metaphors much better. How is someone supposed to tell you how you feel? Only you know that.

I guess that's why I'm writing in this notebook right now. I'm writing *my* thoughts and feelings, no one else's.

A few hours later, I hear a knock on my door. I open it up to see Delilah standing there.

"Uh, hi. I, uh, came to see how you're feeling," she says. It comes out more like a question than a statement.

I shrug and sit down on my bed. I quickly hide my notebook under the pillow so she doesn't see it. She awkwardly walks into my room, looking at my pill containers again. It doesn't bother me, I know she's just curious. Everyone is.

She walks over to them and reaches into her pocket. She pulls out a bag of Skittles and takes out a few.

I look at her with a confused expression. She smiles and puts one Skittle into each section of the container.

"Maybe they'll make it easier to take the pills," she says. "It makes them seem less terrible."

I find myself smiling again.

I type something into my phone. "Skittles are my favorite candy."

She smiles and sits down beside me. "They're my favorite too."

She reaches into the bag again and hands me some Skittles. I eat all the red ones first, like I always do.

"Is red your favorite?" she asks.

I nod. I look down at my hand, which now has rainbow spots all over it.

"Me too. I guess we have more in common than we thought, huh?"

I shrug and toss another Skittle into my mouth.

I hate to admit it, but Delilah isn't so bad after all. She may have been one of the reasons why I stopped taking the pills, but she's a reason to keep taking them now.

When she says she has to leave, I actually want her to stay.

Chapter Fifteen

LEVI

My dad walks into my room around ten o'clock the next morning to check in on me.

"How are you feeling?" he asks quietly while he stands in the doorway.

I sit up in bed and shrug.

"Do you feel up to going out for some breakfast? I thought it would be nice to get out of the house, maybe," he says, walking into my room.

I run my hands through my hair and nod. Going out for breakfast would be nice . . .

I hesitantly nod. My dad smiles widely.

"Great! Whenever you're ready, we can go."

I know my dad is trying to be a real father and make up for all the time he lost. I think he feels bad about my situation, like most people do. Maybe he thinks some of this is his fault, and that's why he's always trying so hard. It's no one's fault but my own. I hope he knows that.

I slowly pick myself up out of bed and get dressed. When I'm ready, I walk into the kitchen to find my dad sitting at the table with his car keys in his hand.

"All set?" he asks.

I nod.

He walks outside to the car, and I follow behind. I have no idea where we're going or what restaurants are around here, besides the one Delilah took me to. I wonder if I'll ever really get to know my way around here. I doubt it. I won't be here long enough. I'm almost certain that the longest I'll be here is two months. I probably won't get better or my dad won't be able to handle me. Either way, I know I'll be back in Australia soon, facing the same problems I had when I left.

My dad talks a little during the car ride, but mostly it's silent besides the humming of the tires on the pavement and the radio softly playing music.

"We kind of need to discuss what happened yesterday some more," my dad says abruptly.

I sigh and type into my phone, "What about it?"

"If you're ever feeling bad, I don't want you to just leave like that. You can talk to me, or we can go to Candace if she's free. Your mum is also just a phone call away, or in your case probably a text."

I nod. Then I realize he's driving and has his eyes on the road, so I type some more. "Okay. I won't do it again."

"You can say you won't do it again, but how can I be sure?"

I form my lips into a straight line and take a deep breath. "You can trust me." I don't even know if I can trust me. I want to, but there's always some doubt.

"I want to trust you, I do. It's just . . ."

I know it's hard to believe me. I keep on making mistakes that make me less and less reliable. I can't help it. Things just keep happening, and I can't stop them.

"I promise. If I run away again, you can send me to a facility here or something." I know I shouldn't be making this promise. I shouldn't have even said it. I regret pressing speak the second I hear it. Now I can't run away again. I refuse to go to another psychiatric hospital.

My dad smiles a little. "I believe you."

Great. Now I know he's going to remember this forever.

"I wouldn't send you to a facility, don't worry," he says. "But just the fact that you said that makes me believe you, considering your mum told me how much you disliked the one in Sydney."

I feel somewhat relieved when he says that.

I look out the window at people, watching mothers push their babies in strollers and kids walking their dogs. I notice two familiar people walking out of a store.

"Hey, there's Aiden and Delilah!" my dad says happily, noticing them at the same time I do. "Wanna invite them for breakfast?" he asks. Before I have any chance to respond, he pulls over and rolls down his window. "Delilah! Aiden!"

"Hi!" Aiden says. Delilah waves.

"We're going to get some breakfast, want to join us?" my dad asks.

I roll my eyes and place my head in my hands.

Delilah looks at Aiden, and they converse for a few seconds.

"Yeah, we'd love to," Aiden says.

"We're going right there," my dad says, pointing to a building that's a little farther down the road.

"Okay, we'll meet you there," Aiden says. They get into their cars, and we all head to the restaurant.

I don't really want to have to sit through a breakfast with everyone. I'm slightly embarrassed over what happened yesterday and don't feel like facing them both today. They probably think I'm insane. They probably don't even want to go to breakfast with us—they're just being nice.

We pull up to the restaurant, with Delilah and Aiden close behind us. We are seated at a table in the corner, away from everyone else, which is good. It's a little more private in case they bring up yesterday's events. No one will be able to overhear. It's bad enough that three people have seen me in such a rough state; I don't need other people hearing about it.

"This place has really good scrambled eggs if you like those," Delilah tells me. She's sitting across from me. I'm next to my dad, and she's next to Aiden.

I nod.

I end up ordering the scrambled eggs.

"So, are you feeling better now?" Aiden asks. There it is. The question I've been waiting for.

I nod.

"Okay, good. We were worried!" Aiden says. Delilah smiles at me.

I shrug and smile a little. They shouldn't have been worried about me. I don't like when others worry about me or my problems. They're *mine*, so I should be the only person worrying.

Our food comes out shortly after we order. Delilah was right, the eggs are good.

Just yesterday, I had been running away from Delilah, and here I am now, sitting across from her. I notice that she only takes small bites of her food and stirs her coffee before every sip. She notices me smirking when she stirs her coffee for probably the tenth time.

"What?" she asks, raising her eyebrows suspiciously.

I shake my head quickly and wave my hand to dismiss her.

"Okay . . ." She laughs a little, stirs her coffee some more, and takes a sip.

Aiden and Delilah aren't that bad. I first saw them as annoying, and I think I was kind of hoping I wouldn't like them. But there really isn't any reason to dislike them—and I've tried to find ways. They cared enough to help find me yesterday, and now we're eating breakfast together. When my dad invited them out with us, I was kind of mad. Now, I honestly don't mind it too much. I can't think of too many people who would willingly spend time with someone like me.

I wonder if it will last, or if they'll just give up on me like everyone else.

Chapter Sixteen

LEVI

L evi, stop eating the candy! We have to save it for trick-or-treaters!" my dad says, laughing and slapping my hand out of the bowl. I toss a piece of candy into my mouth and shrug.

Halloween never really interested me. I always just stole a bag of candy from my mum and hid it in my room. It was easier than going through the hassle of finding a costume that I'd only wear once.

"Do you want to give out candy or have me do it?" my dad asks.

I point to him. I don't want to be standing here all night giving out candy. I'll probably watch some scary movies or sleep.

Caleb stands beside me, flexing in the mirror.

"What are you doing?" I ask him, trying not to laugh.

"I'm punk rock, I'm acting tough," he yells.

I burst into laughter, and Caleb glares at me. "Putting on a fake tattoo sleeve and wearing eyeliner doesn't make you punk rock."

"Excuse me, it's called guyliner."

"Who are you even dressed as?" I ask him, still laughing.

"I've told you! Billie Joe Armstrong from Green Day!"

"Then you can walk a lonely road trick-or-treating down your boulevard of broken dreams, because no one will know who you are."

"Shut up. You're dressed as a penguin!"

"My penguin is cute," I pout. I cross my arms over my chest as best as I can since I'm in a full penguin suit. "And Delia is going as one too."

"How adorable," Caleb says sarcastically.

"You're just jealous," I say, walking out of the room. I end up stepping on the fabric that's covering my foot and falling down.

"Looks like wittle Levi has to learn to waddle," Caleb says in a baby voice. He starts cracking up and holds on to his stomach as he laughs.

"I hate you," I mumble, my voice muffled since I'm face-first in the carpet. Even I start to laugh at myself.

Delia walks in and sees me on the floor. "Did he fall again?" Even without seeing her, I can tell she's smiling.

Caleb nods, still laughing.

"You'd think a sixteen-year-old would be able to walk with ease," she says, giggling.

"I can't help it. I tripped on the fabric."

"You're such a dork," Delia says.

"But I'm your dork," I say, smiling cheesily.

That was last year, when I was forced to go trick-or-treating. It ended up being a lot of fun, even though I was mistaken for a twelve-year-old boy in my costume.

Someone knocks on the door, so I grab a handful of candy since my dad is upstairs. It's still really early for kids to start coming, but maybe Americans start earlier.

I open the door to reveal a smiling Aiden and Delilah. I wasn't expecting them to be here.

"Happy Halloween!" Aiden shouts, walking inside. He shoves a bag into my hands. "That's your costume. We guessed on the size, but it should fit."

What? They got me a costume?

I stare at the bag, not moving. I'm kind of shocked. I wasn't planning on going out tonight. I especially wasn't planning for them to show up with a costume for me.

"C'mon! Look at it!" Aiden says.

I look into the bag and pull out the costume. It's a giant bag of Skittles. I hold it up in the air, holding back a smile. I bite on my lip ring and hold the costume tightly.

"Do you like it?" Delilah asks.

I nod very fast.

"We were so nervous you would hate it! Let's go get ready then!" Delilah says, a grin growing on her face.

She runs into the bathroom, Aiden goes downstairs, and I go into my room. I put the costume on over the clothes I already have on. It fits perfectly. Caleb would find this hilarious. I decide to take a picture and send it to him. He responds almost immediately, which I didn't expect. It's not Halloween in Australia—it's already early tomorrow morning.

Caleb: *Hahahaha! Wish I was there to see it.*

I smile and put my phone in my pocket, which is quite hard since I have the Skittles costume on.

I've hung out with Delilah and Aiden a few times since we all went out for breakfast. I'm not sure if we're friends; maybe acquaintances. They live close by, and they always seem to be showing up at my house randomly. And they're starting to grow on me.

I walk out of my room and Aiden is standing in the living room. He's dressed as a giant banana.

"We're going with the food theme," he says, referring to our costumes.

Delilah walks out dressed as a hot dog. She looks upset, and Aiden starts laughing.

"Aiden, you told me you got me an ice cream cone, not a hot dog," Delilah pouts.

"What's the fun in ice cream? This way I can call you hot, dawg," Aiden tells her, laughing even more.

Delilah rolls her eyes, but I can tell she's trying not to laugh too. "You're so weird!" She slaps his arm.

I wonder if they're dating or just friends.

My dad walks into the room and smiles. "I thought you had no plans tonight, Levi."

"We surprised him!" Aiden says, still rubbing the spot where Delilah hit him.

"Let me go get my camera! You all look great!" My dad runs off into his room, quickly returning with his camera. "Go stand over there, the lighting is good!" He pushes us all to one side of the room. "Levi, smile just a little, please."

I smile—not a teeth smile, but I smile. I notice Delilah quickly look up at me and back at the camera before the photo is taken. She puts her arm around me and her other arm around Aiden, since she's in the middle. I look down at her, and she beams. I hesitantly wrap my arm around her too.

"Perfect!" my dad says, taking the picture.

"Okay, let's go then!" Aiden says, grabbing three pillowcases and giving one to each of us.

We walk outside, the sun still slightly setting. We get some weird looks from younger kids that we pass.

"Are you a banana?" a boy dressed as a pirate asks Aiden.

"Yes."

"That's stupid."

"Actually, bananas are quite delicious. They are also high in potassium and magnesium. They'll help stop your poop too, young boy," Aiden says in all seriousness.

"You're weird," he says, walking away.

Delilah starts laughing and so does Aiden. I can't believe he just said that.

"Did you see the look he gave you?" Delilah says in between laughs.

"Just spreading my knowledge," Aiden says.

We go to the house next door to mine, and Aiden rings the bell. I've never seen the people who live here. An old woman opens the door and squints her eyes.

"Aren't you a little too old to be trick-or-treating?" she asks. She shuts her door a little, so it's only open wide enough for her to see us.

"Ma'am, there is no age limitation on Halloween," Aiden says. Delilah is trying really hard not to laugh.

"Are you hooligans that are going to rob me?" the old lady asks.

"No, no! All we want is some candy!" Aiden says.

She squints some more, but finally sticks her hand out with three pieces of candy.

"Have a nice night!" Aiden says as he walks down the stairs.

"That was strange," Delilah says.

"I never even knew who lived there," Aiden says. "Now I see why."

After two hours of trick-or-treating, we've gone to every house in the neighborhood. It was really fun, surprisingly. The neighbors thought it was funny that we dressed up, and they loved our costumes. Some people gave us odd looks, but that's okay. There were also some of those annoying people that force you to say trick-or-treat. Thankfully, Aiden explained my situation so I got the candy without saying anything.

We're heading back to my house now, and we're walking extremely slow. I forgot how much Halloween exhausts me. Aiden rummages through his pillowcase, looking for some Twix.

It's weird how things have turned out with them and me. Things are still slightly awkward with Delilah, but it's getting better. I'm getting closer with Aiden—I may even consider him a friend. I'm not sure yet.

I hold up a piece of unfamiliar candy to Delilah. Most of this American candy isn't in Australia, and if it is, it's usually only in a few special candy stores.

"That's Reese's. There's peanut butter in the middle. They're really good," she tells me.

I open up the package, and there are two cup-like chocolates. I take one for myself and give one to Delilah. She smiles as she slowly takes it out of my hand.

I take a small bite at first. It's surprisingly very good.

"Do you like it?" Delilah asks, chewing on her Reese's.

I nod, taking another bite.

I can't help but think that Delia would have loved to be here. She always liked holidays, every single one. She would have loved trying all the American candy and dressing up as food.

I try to push the thoughts out of my mind and focus on Aiden and Delilah, not Delia.

"Hey, guys," Aiden says. "There's this haunted house starting at ten o'clock tonight. It's eight thirty right now. Do you wanna go?"

Delilah says yes, and they both look at me, waiting for my answer.

The last time I went to a haunted house, I was ten years old, and I ran out screaming. I haven't gone to one since. It was extremely traumatizing and embarrassing.

For some reason, I nod.

We're standing outside the haunted house, waiting in line. We're no longer in our costumes, we're dressed normally.

It's pitch black outside, the only light is the green luminescence of the haunted house. I can hear groans and screams coming from inside. I have to admit I'm nervous.

"If someone jumps out, you guys better protect me," Delilah says.

"I can't make any promises," Aiden says.

"Levi seems like he'll be able to. You won't get scared, right?" Delilah asks me.

I shake my head no, even though I know I will get scared.

Before I know it, it's our turn to go in. I hear Delilah take in a deep breath before we step inside.

At least this time I know I won't scream.

We walk through the path . . . nothing too scary yet. There are just some weird noises and pictures on the walls. All of a sudden, a giant, bloody zombie jumps out. Aiden screams like a girl and

106

jumps at least a foot back and crouches to the ground. Delilah stops breathing for a second, and I do too. She starts laughing at Aiden afterward.

"You're such a wimp!" she says.

"I can't help it! He attacked me!"

"He jumped out! He didn't even touch you!"

We continue walking extremely slow, all of us nervous about what will happen. My heart is racing, but not in a bad way. It's just the adrenaline, not real fear for once. At least I don't think so.

A man with a chain saw runs out into our path, standing in front of us and starting to wave the chainsaw wildly.

"No, no, no, no, STOP!" Aiden screams, moving backward. He crashes into me and screams even louder before he realizes it's just me.

"Oh jeez," Delilah mumbles. We've all ended up huddled together, not moving. Aiden is hiding behind me, and Delilah is behind him.

I'm so nervous; I didn't expect it to be this lifelike.

Suddenly, a bloody woman jumps out, screaming. She quickly runs back and disappears.

Delilah screams and grabs my hand tightly, putting her head to my chest. I can feel her heart beating quickly and hear her fast breaths.

Aiden is continuously screaming and gasping. He keeps pushing Delilah and me to the front. Although I am actually scared, it is kind of funny to watch this unfold. Aiden is terrified.

The chainsaw starts up, and I hug Delilah tightly out of fear. She may think I am protecting her, but I am hugging her because I am so terrified.

"Why did we come here?" Delilah mumbles, still not letting go of my hand or moving away from me.

There are strobe lights going off, and people screaming everywhere. As we creep along, we hear a ferocious dog barking in the dark. A woman with giant fangs and long hair jumps out at us unexpectedly.

Aiden screams and then announces, "I just peed myself!"

I can hear Delilah laughing a little.

"Guys, I really peed. This is bad. This is really bad."

The guy with the chainsaw starts chasing us, and Aiden finally flips out.

"CAN YOU STOP THE FREAKING CHAINSAW AND GET OUT OF HERE? JUST STOP!! I JUST PEED MYSELF. JUST SHOW ME THE EXIT," Aiden screams.

The chainsaw stops, and the guy leaves slowly. As we seem to be approaching the exit, Delilah awkwardly moves away from me and stops holding my hand. I wipe my sweaty palm on my pant leg, breathing a sigh of relief that it is almost over. It appears we made it through the worst part.

"Levi's going in front from now on," Aiden mumbles, holding his hand in front of the wet spot on his pants. I can't believe he actually peed himself.

We make it out within the next few minutes, the rest not being too scary. Aiden still screamed occasionally whenever a hand popped out or someone walked by. Delilah kept making tiny shrieks and squeaking noises.

"I've never been so scared," Delilah says when we're out.

"I need a new pair of pants," Aiden whines.

Delilah laughs at Aiden, who is still covering the wet spot.

Tonight ended up being so much fun. Even though I was kind of scared in the haunted house, it was really great. I'm starting to feel like I may belong here and that Aiden and Delilah might actually think of me as more than just the guy who lives down the street.

Chapter Seventeen

DELILAH

The school day seems to be passing slower than usual. If that's even possible, considering how much each day drags on. I watch the time pass slowly, each second feeling like a minute. I scribble down the notes on the board, waiting for the lunch bell to ring. I don't hate school, but I don't necessarily like it. I just have a an overall dislike of every class, so school is average for me.

Finally, the bell rings, and I grab my things. I wait by my locker for Aiden, like I do every day.

"Are you all right?" he asks me when he sees me. "You look stressed."

I shrug. "We got a huge writing assignment in English. We have to interview someone and write about their life experiences. It's so stupid because it has to be someone our age. I don't know anyone interesting enough to do it on," I groan.

I could ask Levi, but I highly doubt he'd ever agree to it. I can't imagine he would willingly let me interview him for a school project.

"Um, hello, I'm interesting," Aiden says.

I roll my eyes. "I already know everything about you."

"Not everything," he whines.

I look at him from the corner of my eye as we walk down the hall. "You'd be surprised what Hunter tells me about you when you're not home."

Aiden's cheeks blush. "Oh, shut up!"

We get to the cafeteria and sit with our usual group of friends. There's myself, Aiden, Ally, Tyler, and Alex.

"Delilah thinks I'm not interesting enough to do her English project on," Aiden says the second we sit down.

"I never said that!" I tell him as I take out my lunch.

"What's your English assignment?" Ally asks.

I explain it to everyone, and we all try to think of people I could interview.

"What about that math genius who sits behind me in chem?" Alex says.

"I'm not in your chem class, I don't know who you're talking about," I tell him.

"What about Levi?" Aiden blurts out.

"I thought of him, but I don't think he'd agree," I tell him.

"Who's Levi?" Tyler asks.

"This kid who moved into our neighborhood from Australia. He doesn't talk. His dad is Anthony Harrison, the soccer coach at the middle school," Aiden says with his mouth full.

I roll my eyes. "He's more than just some kid," I say.

"Oh?" Ally says, laughing.

"That's not what I mean!" I say, blushing. "I just mean that he's, like, complicated. He doesn't talk, he doesn't go to school, and he's just so *different*."

"Why doesn't he talk?" Alex asks.

I shrug. "We don't really know. I don't know much about him." I do know he stopped talking when his girlfriend died, but I'm not sure *why* he decided to stop.

"Seems interesting enough to interview," Tyler says.

"You think so?" I ask.

Levi could be someone to interview. I'm just not sure if he'll give me the answers I need.

———

After school, I head straight to Levi's house. I knock on the door, and Anthony opens it.

"Hey, Delilah! Looking for Levi?" he asks.

"Uh, yeah," I tell him. I'm nervous to tell Levi about the English assignment. I'm afraid he'll get angry or upset. He probably won't want to do it anyway.

"Okay, he's in his room," Anthony says.

I head to Levi's room, and the door is partially closed. I knock, and after a few seconds, Levi opens the door. He steps back to let me in. Each time I come, I feel extremely awkward. I never know what to do or what to say. I always end up standing in the center of the room, looking around, but not really seeing what I'm looking at.

I clear my throat. "Hey."

Levi nods and rocks back on his heels. I've noticed that he does that a lot when he waits for someone to say something.

"So, uh, I got an English assignment today, and I was wondering if you'd want to maybe help me with it." I say it more like a question than a statement.

He shrugs and types in his phone. "What's it about?"

"Well, uh, I have to interview someone my age and learn about their experiences and what they've gone through. I thought that maybe I could do it on you since I don't know much about you, and I thought you might be a good person to interview. But if you don't want to do it, I understand. I just thought I'd ask." I talk very fast, and I'm out of breath by the time I'm done because I'm so nervous.

He sits on his bed and rests his chin on his hand. He types something in his phone. "What kind of stuff would you want to know about?"

"Um, maybe life in Australia, and how it felt moving here. You could tell me about your childhood or something. If you don't want me to know certain things, I understand." I don't mention his girlfriend because I don't want to intrude. I know he likes to keep that to himself.

He thinks for a few seconds. "Why did you pick me?"

111

"You seem interesting to learn about, I guess." I don't really know how to answer. Why did I pick him?

"I'm not interesting, trust me."

I don't say anything because again I don't know how to respond. I just hope he'll agree to let me interview him.

He types more onto his phone. His fingers hesitate as he writes whatever he wants to tell me. "I guess I'll let you do your project on me. I'll only answer the questions I want, and I can't promise that you'll like the answers I give you."

It takes a second for his answer to sink in. I thought for sure he'd automatically say no. I can't believe he actually agreed. Now that he's actually said yes, I feel a whole new set of nerves.

"Really?" I say.

He nods and types something. "When do you wanna start?"

"Can you do Saturday? We can go to the coffee place downtown if you want." I have a flashback to the time when he threw his coffee on the ground. Hopefully that won't happen again.

He nods.

"Okay, I'll see you then," I tell him.

As I turn to leave, I look back and say, "Hey, Levi . . . thanks!"

Oddly enough, I also notice that he is smiling.

———

Saturday comes quickly, and I'm sitting at a table, waiting for Levi to show up. A part of me feels like he isn't going to come, that maybe he's changed his mind. I wouldn't be shocked if that happened.

I see Levi walk in, and he looks around. I wave, and he sits down across from me. He takes off his black jacket and replaces his snapback on his head.

"Do you want something to eat or drink?" I ask him.

He nods, and we both get up to order our coffees. Well, I order both of them so Levi won't have to write his order down. When I order my coffee, he flinches a little. I guess he doesn't like the kind I like.

We sit back down at the table and get started. I wrote down all the questions on a piece of paper and left room for Levi to write a response. I hand him the paper and give him time to answer the questions. After a few minutes, he hands the paper back to me. While reading his answers, I notice that he has surprisingly good grammar and spelling for someone who doesn't talk.

1. When's your birthday?

July 25

2. Who is your best friend?

I met my best friend Caleb in Year 6. He has this obsession with music. He's always playing his guitar, and he stays up for hours writing songs. He's like a lyrical genius. Caleb's been there for me whenever I need him. I've been a pretty horrible person to him the past few months, but he hasn't given up on me like everyone else seems to have.

3. What was it like growing up in Australia?

I lived in the Western Sydney suburbs, which is just a vast area of lots of plants. It's basically a giant farmland with these little brick houses. It's a lot hotter there than it is here. And I look like I can surf, but I can't, so you better not have asked me that question.

4. What was it like moving here?

Moving to Maine was like moving to a whole other planet. The accents are different, the food is different, everything is different. I'm still not

really used to the time zone. I sometimes wake
up at awkward hours, and I can't fall back asleep.
I also don't know anyone but you and Aiden.
Everyone back home knew about me. They knew
my whole life story. Being in a small town, everyone
knew what happened to each other. After the
incident, I was looked at as a delicate, fragile
person. No one treated me the same. Some of my
friends stopped talking to me. I got sympathetic
looks everywhere I went. They all knew me as a boy
who got messed up because his girlfriend died. No
one here knows that.

I started with only four questions, and I decided to work off
of them. I ask Levi a few more questions afterward. Some of his
answers surprise me. I didn't expect him to share too much, but he
seems to be telling me a lot. I'm getting a whole different perspective on him.

I asked simple questions, like what his old school was like or any
hobbies he has. He told me he *had* hobbies, but doesn't anymore.

I also asked him three words that he would describe himself
with, and his response was interesting. He wrote down "destructive,
empty, depressed." When I told him he's depressed, and depression
isn't him, he smiled a little. He crossed out his answer and changed
it to "lost." I'm not sure which answer was better. Neither are too
positive. I get the feeling he doesn't think very highly of himself.

The last question I ask him is what his favorite thing to do is.
It takes him awhile to answer that one. He stares down at the paper
and twirls the pen with his fingers for a long time. He looks up at
me every so often.

"You don't need to answer it," I tell him.

He shakes his head and taps the pen on the table. After a few
more moments, he scribbles down an answer. He slides the paper
across the table and smiles shyly.

I like watching the rain and listening to the sound of it falling.

I wasn't expecting that as an answer. I can imagine him liking the rain though. He definitely doesn't seem like someone that would love sunshine. His answer somehow fits perfectly with him the more I think about it.

Once we're done with the questions, we decide to walk around outside a little. There's a beach right next to us, and even though it's November, we're walking along the sand. It's dark out, and I can barely see anything.

"Did you go to the beach a lot?" I ask Levi.

He shakes his head no.

I cold breeze blows by, and I wrap my arms around myself. I notice Levi start to take off his jacket.

"No, Levi, I'm fine," I tell him, even though I'm shivering despite my heavy sweater.

He shakes his head and hands me his jacket. I put it on, and I can smell a faint hint of smoke and cologne. I put my hands in the pocket and feel a pack of cigarettes.

"Why do you smoke?" I ask him. Once I say it, I realize what a stupid question it is.

He shrugs and types something in his phone. "It relaxes me. I'm trying to stop, though."

In the other pocket, there's a bag of Skittles. I smile and show them to Levi.

He quickly types something. "I bought those earlier for us. That's why I was late."

His cheeks turn slightly red, and he looks down at the sand. I smile and open up the bag, handing some to Levi. He eats all the red ones first, and I do too.

A wave crashes at our feet, and Levi bends down and splashes me. I splash him back, and he shields his eyes. We continue splashing each other until I run away from the water. He smiles widely, the first real smile I've ever seen him have. I notice how straight his teeth are, and how big his dimple really is.

I stick out my tongue, and he runs over to me. I throw some Skittles at him, and he manages to catch one in his mouth.

I throw another one, and it hits him right in the forehead. He rubs the spot like it hurt, and I laugh.

He rolls his eyes and reaches into his jacket pocket, which I'm still wearing, for some more Skittles. We end up reaching in at the same time, and he grabs my hand, most likely on accident. He holds on to it for a few seconds before reaching away. Even in the dark, I can tell that he's blushing. I think I am too.

I laugh and give him some Skittles. "Don't be embarrassed," I tell him.

He waves his hand and tosses all the Skittles in his mouth. When I'm not looking, he throws one at me.

"Taste the rainbow," he mouths.

Chapter Eighteen

LEVI

I miss her.

I miss her.

I really, really miss her.

It's the sixth of November. It's been 221 days.

I'm afraid that with every day that passes, I'll forget more about Delia. I'm starting to forget the way she said certain things, or the exact color of her hair. I don't want to ever forget. I want to always remember.

Today's one of those days where I just want her here. I've been thinking all day long about everything happening in my life. I miss doing nothing yet everything, all at once, with her. Maybe today we would've been sitting on the couch watching a movie. Or maybe we would've gone out for pizza and people-watched together.

I remember when I was little, I would draw happy faces on everything. I was surrounded by people with happy faces. But now, I'm just a sad person surrounded by sad faces.

I hate it.

She wouldn't have let me be sad like this. She would've made me happy, no matter what. She would've been the one happy face in the sea of sadness.

And when the one person who could make you happy is gone, it feels like the end of the world.

It's weird how fast things can change. One minute, you can be perfectly happy, and then the next you can be sad.

Sad, sad, sad.

It doesn't even sound like a word anymore.

You know what else is weird? Life. No one is promised life. But we are promised death. That's one thing in life that's guaranteed. Everyone is going to die at some point. The one thing that most people don't want is the one thing that is bound to happen at some point.

Sometimes I wonder how long Delia would've lived. If we'd still be together. What she would've done when we graduated. But I'll never know.

I'll also never know what would've happened to me if she was still alive. I wouldn't be here, for one thing. I would be talking right now. I wouldn't be writing in some notebook to get my feelings out. I would be telling them to someone, most likely Delia.

She would've listened.

She would've listened to how sorry I am. How much I hate my life. How I've messed up everything.

She would've known just what to say. She always did.

And here I am, not saying anything.

I'm sorry.

I quickly wipe the tears that are spilling down my cheeks and close the notebook. I shut my eyes tightly and put my head in my hands. I shake my head quickly as I try not to cry.

I hate this.

I rub my nose and take a deep breath.

Something Delia will never be able to do again.

I hate thinking about stuff like that. It just makes me sadder. All my thoughts just attack me all the time. I never get a break from my own mind. Whether it's my thoughts, or memories, or forgetting something, my mind is always doing something that makes me sad.

I think about Delilah and her project. How she chose to do it on me. She probably only chose me for the obvious reasons, like how I don't talk, and all my emotions. She didn't pick me because I'm "interesting." I'm messed up, that's what I am.

She didn't even ask interesting questions. It was just background info on me. Maybe she didn't want to ask me personal things because she thinks I won't tell her.

I probably wouldn't have told her a few weeks ago. But now I'm not so sure.

When I first met Delilah, I wanted nothing to do with her. I didn't want to see her, hear her, or do anything that involved her. I hated her so much. It's strange how quickly that changed. I don't hate her anymore; I'm not sure if I like her, though. I'm still slightly uncomfortable around her, yet I'm comfortable at the same time. It confuses me so much. She is so much like Delia, I can barely stand it.

I don't understand myself at all. Everything is all scrambled in my mind today, and I feel like I'm thinking of a thousand things at once. I'm thinking about Delia, Delilah, myself, everyone, and everything. It's exhausting.

I look out the window at the rain that is quickly falling. The sky is dark with clouds, and there are puddles all over the street. I trace my finger down the windowsill, leaving a small smudge.

I rub my eyes and throw on a shirt that's on the floor. I find my dad watching television.

I sit down beside him, and he looks up at me.

"Are you okay?" he asks, quickly shutting off the TV.

I bite my lip, tears threatening to spill out of my eyes again just because of his simple question. I shake my head no, immediately starting to cry again. I hate being so emotional all the time. It's like the sadness erupts within me and comes out instantly.

"What happened?" my dad asks.

I shrug. I don't really know why I'm upset. It's always about Delia or something involving her, but it comes at random times without warning.

"Uh, um—I, we—Do you wanna do something maybe?" he asks, unsure of what to say.

I shake my head no.

"Do you wanna talk about it?"

I shake my head no again. I thought I could just come out here and sit with him. I didn't mean to start crying like this.

I take some deep breaths and calm down. We sit in silence for a few minutes. My dad isn't really good at this stuff.

"We can go see Candace if you want," he says. "Are you that upset?"

I shake my head and stand up from the couch. I write down that I'm going for a walk, and I'll be right back. He looks concerned when he reads it, but lets me go anyway.

I know exactly who to go to. I know how to get rid of all these confusing thoughts in my mind.

It's still raining as I walk outside. I head down the street, keeping my head down as the rain falls. I'm quickly soaked because of all the rain, but I don't mind. It feels nice on my skin. It also will make it look like I haven't been crying.

I get to the house I'm looking for. I hesitantly walk up the driveway and stand at the bottom step below the doorway.

I pull my phone out of my pocket and shield it from the rain as best as I can. I scroll through my contacts and text Delilah.

Come outside. There's something I need to tell you.

Chapter Nineteen

DELILAH

Levi: Come outside. There's something I need to tell you.

I look out my window and see Levi standing on my front steps. He's soaked and standing there with his feet turned in, and he's biting on his bottom lip.

What does he want to tell me?

I grab a sweatshirt, pull it on, and head downstairs, taking the steps two at a time. I pull on my hood and open the door.

The rain is bouncing off the pavement, and Levi looks like he is freezing. His shirt is sticking to his skin, and he's completely drenched.

"Levi, come inside," I tell him.

He shakes his head and pulls out a folded piece of paper from his pocket. He hands it to me, and I slowly unfold it. The paper is already slightly damp.

"C'mon. Just come inside."

Levi looks at me with pleading eyes.

I feel like he doesn't want to come inside because of my family. He must not want to meet them for some reason. I can understand that, since he doesn't seem to like meeting new people.

"No one is home. It's just me," I yell over the loud rain and wind.

He slowly comes inside and looks around when he first steps in. He runs his hand through his wet hair, which is sticking to his forehead. He's dripping wet.

"I'll get you some dry clothes," I tell him.

He shakes his head, but I go into my brother's room anyway. He's at college right now, but some of his clothes are still here. I grab a shirt, sweatpants, and towel for Levi.

He's moved up to the kitchen, and he's standing awkwardly in the entrance. There's a small puddle around him because he is so wet.

"Here. The bathroom's right there. I'll read this once you're out, okay?"

He nods and heads into the bathroom to change. He comes out a few minutes later. The shirt is a little short, and I can see the lining of his underwear since the pants are a little small too. I try not to laugh at him.

I walk into my room and sit on my bed. Levi stays standing, so I pat the spot beside me. He hesitantly sits down.

I unfold the paper again and read it out loud.

"I have to let this out, so I'm telling you. You know, for your project, I guess . . . And because I need to tell you this. But, anyway. My girlfriend, her name was Delia, did you already know that? I can't remember if I told you that. It's a lot like your name . . . She died in May. It was a car accident. It was nighttime, and they say she was on the phone sending someone a text and I think it was to me. She went off the road and died instantly. She would've turned 17 a week later. Just like that, she was gone."

I look over at Levi, and he looks like he's trying not to cry. He's biting his nails, and his eyes are watery. I look back at the note and keep reading.

"And everywhere I go, things remind me of her. Especially you. And that scares me. I don't think I can do any more for your project, it hurts too much. So I'm telling you this so you have enough information to finish it. I don't think I can do anything with you anymore.

I think I have to be alone, not with you or Aiden or anyone. I don't like how I'm feeling lately, and I don't want to get attached to anyone here. I think I just need to figure things out on my own. And I don't even know if we're considered friends, but I just need to be alone. I hope you understand, and I hope this is enough for your project. I hope we can all just pretend like we never met each other because it's too much for me to handle right now. I'm sorry."

I look at Levi again, and he won't look me in the eyes. I don't say anything for a while. I don't know what to say. What do you say when someone tells you that?

Levi doesn't want me or Aiden or anyone in his life.

"Levi, I understand, but—"

He shakes his head quickly and covers his ears. I put my hands over his and slowly bring his hands down.

"Just listen, please. It's okay to be afraid of how you're feeling. I don't know how you feel, and I won't try to figure it out. But Aiden and I are here for you if you ever need us. I hope you know that. If you have to be alone, you can do that. But I can't pretend like I never met you."

Levi finally looks at me, and he starts to cry. He quickly wipes under his eyes. He then reaches out and hugs me, which I didn't expect. His wet hair rubs against my cheek as he pulls away.

He slowly stands up from the bed and grabs his wet clothes from the floor. He waves and heads out of my room, leaving me sitting alone.

I'm kind of stunned and confused by what just happened. I didn't expect that at all. I feel like Levi is constantly leaving me confused.

I feel sad too. I thought we were becoming friends, maybe.

I fold and unfold the paper. I read it again and run my fingers over the words Levi has written.

And everywhere I go, things remind me of her. Especially you.

For some reason, I remind him of Delia. I don't know if it's just because of the names or if there's more.

"Levi, wait!" I yell, quickly running out of my room. I can't just let him leave like that.

I stop short in the hallway because Levi is standing there, his hair dripping, his eyes red, and his cheeks stained with tears.

He drops his clothes on the ground and pulls out his phone to type something.

"I didn't make it very far. I forgot my socks."

"Oh, um, all right," I say awkwardly.

He gets his socks and stands in the doorway.

"I guess this is good-bye for now," I tell him from the top of the steps. He opens the door and leaves. I watch him walk down the street until I can't see him anymore.

Just like that, he's gone.

Chapter Twenty

LEVI

I walk into the waiting room for a therapy session, and of course Delilah is behind the front desk. It's been almost a week since I last saw her, and I've been doing pretty well avoiding her until now.

"Hi, Levi," she says quietly when I walk past the desk.

I don't do anything in response. I sit in the farthest possible seat from Delilah.

I can't help but notice that she's wearing a shirt Delia had.

"That song is horrible, Caleb. How do you—Levi! You just spilled your water all over my shirt!" Delia shrieks.

I bite my lip to try not to laugh. "Oops, sorry!"

"You're so clumsy. You're lucky it's just water."

"Want my shirt?" I offer.

"Please, say no," Caleb says.

"It's fine," she says, laughing. "It'll dry."

"Sorry," I say, snickering.

"I hate you," Delia mumbles as she leans her head on my shoulder.

"I hate you more," I whisper.

"I hate you guys the most," Caleb says.

"Shut up," we say in unison.

"I'm just saying, this is my house. You guys come in here and eat my food and curl up together on the couch. It's my house. You're supposed to do things with me."

"We're not going to do things with you," I say, laughing.

Delia slaps my shoulder, but I can tell she's trying not to laugh.

"I hate you so much, Levi," Caleb says, rolling his eyes.

I get off the couch and run over to Caleb, who's sitting in a beanbag chair. I wrap my arms around him and nearly crush him.

"Caleb needs a cuddle," I say in a childlike voice.

"I do not," he says, shoving me off of him. "Go back to your girlfriend."

I lay on the floor and poke Caleb in the cheek. "C'mon. Smile!"

He pushes my hand away. "No."

"You're no fun," I say. I hug in my knees and rest my head on top of them. I smile cheesily at Caleb, and he looks up at Delia.

"Your boyfriend is a weirdo," he says.

"When will you stop referring to us as boyfriend and girlfriend? We have names," Delia says.

"When you break up."

"Who says we'll break up?" Delia and I say in unison. Again.

Caleb laughs. "It's creepy how you always say the same thing."

"You're just jealous," I tell him.

Delia leaves for a second to go get something to eat, leaving Caleb and me alone.

"Have you told her that you love her yet?" Caleb asks quietly.

Caleb knows everything about me, and vice versa. We tell each other everything—he's like a brother to me.

I look down at my hands. "No."

"You need to tell her."

"Tell me what?" Delia asks, returning quicker than expected.

"I, um, there's a, uh— That I'm really hungry," I say, reaching over for some of the pretzels she brought.

She rolls her eyes. "You could've told me before. I would've brought more."

"Levi?" I hear Delilah say. I look up and see Candace standing in the waiting room.

"I called you a few times, Levi," Candace says, smiling widely. She's way too happy all the time.

126

I stand up and walk past Delilah without looking at her. I sit on the same couch I always sit on, and Candace sits across from me.

"So, how are you feeling today?" Candace asks.

Anxious. Upset. Tired. What else is new?

I shrug.

"How's everything going with your dad? You haven't been in to see me for little over a month."

I give her a thumbs up. I kept cancelling appointments because I didn't want to come.

"That's good. You don't want to write on the board today?"

I shake my head no.

"All right. Hmm . . . Have you met any other people yet? Made any friends?"

I think about Aiden and Delilah.

I shake my head no.

"Maybe you could try one of the support groups again. I know you did one a few months ago in Australia, but maybe now you'll like it more. You'll get to meet some people."

I glare at her and raise my eyebrows. I am not going to another support group. You're supposed to talk at those, which is something I clearly don't do.

I know that Candace is trying to be helpful, but today she's annoying me. I want to leave; I don't feel like being here today. I just want to go to sleep.

I look up at the whanda painting. I still haven't determined if it's a whale or panda. It could be neither.

"I know Delilah lives in your neighborhood. Have you met her?"

I look at Candace, a little shocked from the mention of Delilah's name. I shake my head yes slowly.

"See! You have met people!" she says happily.

I roll my eyes.

I've barely thought about Delilah since I last saw her. Now Candace has to bring her up, which is making me think about her.

I wonder what Delilah wanted to tell me when she ran out into the hall before I left. She looked so upset and sad.

I hadn't really forgotten my socks. I was standing there debating whether or not to leave. I almost walked back into her room.

But I couldn't. I trudged home in the rain, feeling horrible and strangely upset. I thought I would feel better knowing that I wouldn't have Delilah in my life.

Even though, in a way, I feel better when I'm with her.

No, I don't. I can't.

I need to stop thinking about her.

Candace asks a few more questions in hopes of getting some responses from me. She asks I've been taking my pills, which I nod in response to. I'm getting better and try to take them every day.

The visit with Candace finally ends, and thankfully, when I leave, Delilah isn't anywhere to be seen. The car ride home is silent like it usually is.

When we get home, Aiden is outside. He waves when we get out of the car.

"Hey!" he yells, walking over.

I guess Delilah didn't tell him.

"Hi, Aiden!" my dad says, shutting his car door.

I force myself to smile a little. I'm not really in the mood to see Aiden right now.

"I haven't seen you in a while," Aiden says, smiling. "Thought you went back to Australia or something!"

I shake my head no and roll my eyes. Not in the rude way, though.

I yawn and walk inside, leaving my dad and Aiden outside.

I go into my room and find a shipping box has tumbled off my desk. I still haven't unpacked a lot of my things, and I don't think I will since most of my stuff was sent over after I got here. I bend down and pick up the box, but most of the things fall out.

Everything inside is old pictures, newspaper clippings, awards, stuff like that.

As I move the box, a picture of Delia and me lands on top of my foot.

I put the box down and grab the picture, holding it tightly in my hand. I run my finger gently over the edges.

I've tried not to look at pictures since she died. I didn't even know that I still had a box full of them. My mum must have packed it without me knowing. I used to have a lot of pictures, especially of Delia.

The photo is of us outside. Both of us are laughing. I don't remember what was so funny, but we're in our school uniforms. It looks like it was taken a few months before she died. Her nose is crinkled, which always happened when she laughed too hard.

I quickly put the photo into the box before I start crying. I decide not to look at the rest of the pictures; I'll save those for another day, when I'm ready. If I ever am. I doubt I will be.

I quickly pick up the rest of the things that fell out of the box and put them back inside. It will probably be months before the box is opened again.

After looking at the picture, I can't help but notice that Delilah scrunches her nose like that when she laughs too.

They have so many similarities. I'm not sure if I'm imagining them, or if they really are alike. It seems impossible for two girls to be almost exact replicas of one another. Even their names are alike. Maybe it's all in my mind. They do act somewhat differently, though. Delia was outgoing and loud, while Delilah is a little quieter. Maybe she's only quiet around me, because with Aiden she seems more comfortable, which is understandable. I haven't been so great to her since I met her.

I really do mess everything up, don't I?

Suddenly, Aiden barges into my room.

"Hey, haven't seen you in awhile!" he says happily, sitting down on my bed. "So, what's up?"

I type quickly in my phone, "I take it Delilah didn't tell you?"

129

"Tell me what?" he asks, tilting his head to the side.

I sigh. I didn't want to have to go through this again, as it was hard enough the first time.

I search through my desk drawer for the letter I have for Aiden. I wrote one for him too just in case this happened. I was hoping I wouldn't have to do this.

I hand him the letter. It's almost exactly what I told Delilah, except I didn't include the things about Delia. I just told him I needed some time alone to think about things.

Aiden hesitantly opens the letter and reads it. Once he's done, he looks up at me with sad eyes.

"So, basically, you don't wanna hang out with us or anything at all anymore?" Aiden asks.

I nod slowly.

"All right."

I've never seen him at a loss for words. Neither of us do anything. We won't even look at each other.

Finally, Aiden stands up and starts leaving my room.

"Well," he mumbles, "I'm right down the street if you ever need anything or just wanna play FIFA again."

I nod.

"See ya around, I guess," he says quietly.

Chapter Twenty-One

Levi

It's been 241 days.

It's been almost four weeks since I last saw anyone but my dad or Candace. I haven't gone anywhere or done anything remotely interesting.

Aiden hasn't stopped by since I told him. I don't think he really knew how to handle it since he's, well, he's Aiden. He likes being happy and being around people. I think he thought I would warm up to him. And I was starting to, which is something I didn't want.

When I told him, he seemed heartbroken. He read the letter and stayed quiet for a while afterward. He left like the first day I met him, sad and quiet. The total opposite of how he usually is. He said bye, and I haven't seen him since.

I've avoided Delilah as best I can. I see her in the neighborhood or at therapy sometimes. She's given up on saying hi or smiling, or even communicating at all. It's like she doesn't know who I am.

But I guess that's my own fault. I told her to forget me.

I've gone back to my old ways. I stay alone, mostly in my room. I don't do much. I've gone back to that numb feeling. I feel anxious and dull and tired. I feel like nothing at all.

There are no more Skittles in my pill container.

I haven't written in this notebook for a long time, but today it was necessary. I just need someone, I guess, and this is the closest I have. I guess I'm simply writing about everything that's happened the past month because I've been holding it all in. I need to let it all out, and here's a place to do that.

Delilah left me a letter a while ago. It's her finished project. She wrote on the envelope that she thought I might like to read it. I can't bring myself to look at it, though. I don't want to see what she has to say about me. I've contemplated every day whether or not to open it, but I can't get the courage to tear open the envelope. I'm too nervous about what's inside.

Most days I try to remember, but not think too much, about Delia. I find that my memories of her are slowly fading away. I don't remember them quite as vividly as I used to, and that scares me. My flashbacks still come, but parts are missing. Some of them are getting jumbled with newer memories, and I can't tell what happened when. I hate it.

I think my dad is more worried about me than he used to be. He sighs more often, and he looks tired. I feel like I'm wearing him out, just like I did to my mum. I wear everyone out. Even myself. The whole reason I started writing today is because of tomorrow. Tomorrow is this big holiday called Thanksgiving. I didn't even know what that was until a few hours ago. I guess Americans eat food to celebrate settling on some rock. I don't get what eating turkey has to do with that, but whatever.

The problem is, we're going over to Delilah's. Apparently my dad has celebrated with them since he moved here. We're not even American, so I don't see why we're celebrating. He told me this morning. I didn't handle it very well. I may or may not have punched the wall.

And my hand may or may not be bruised and hurting right now.

I'm debating even going. It'll be extremely awkward for everyone, not just Delilah and me. And I don't want to be surrounded by a bunch of people I don't know. That's way too many people to be confused as to why I don't talk, and why I'm me.

I'm really nervous. What if Delilah hates me? Wait, I know she does—why wouldn't she?

How am I supposed to celebrate some weird holiday with strangers and someone I told I never wanted to see again? I can already feel my anxiety coming.

I can't go. I won't go. I'll say I'm sick. This is so stressful, I hate this. Why did I ever have to move here in the first place? I wouldn't have

Suddenly, something falls off my bedside table and onto my lap. It's Delilah's project.

I put it inside my drawer and leave my room.

My dad is eating dinner without me, which is what usually happens. I'm often not hungry or I just have cereal. I don't really like eating with my dad anyway. It's extremely awkward because all I hear is our chewing.

But today, I sit across from him. He looks up at me and grins.

"What's up, bud?" he says with his mouth full. He still calls me bud even though I'm seventeen, and I wish he'd stop.

I shrug.

"Something's wrong, I can tell," he says, putting his fork down.

I type quickly in my phone. "I don't feel well. I think I'm sick. I can't go tomorrow."

He tilts his head to the side and squints at me. "You look okay . . . You sure you just don't want to go?"

I nod and hold my stomach as if I'm queasy.

"I know about you and Delilah and Aiden. And I know you're not sick. You think I don't know why you punched the wall this morning? I wasn't born yesterday."

Of course he knows.

"You're going to go tomorrow. It'll be good for you. You need to get out of the house. You've been in here for months. You barely do anything, and it's not healthy."

I glare at him and leave the table. I shove my chair in as I leave, causing it to crash into the table.

"Levi!" my dad yells.

I continue walking until I'm back in my room, and I slam the door shut, causing some things in my room to shake.

I plop down on my bed and look up at the ceiling. I count to one hundred to try to relax myself, but it doesn't work.

I wish I could just disappear right now. No one would notice, or even care. I wouldn't have to celebrate some stupid American holiday with stupid American people I don't know. I wouldn't be having anxiety over all of this if I could disappear.

I could disappear, *just like that.*

Chapter Twenty-Two

DELILAH

"Delilah, can you go check on the turkey?" my mom asks for the hundredth time. I exhale heavily and quickly look in the oven. The turkey looks the same as it did last time.

I head into the living room and sit on the couch next to my brother, Noah. He's home from college for the next few days.

"Look at Elmo!" my younger sister, Lucy, screams as she points to the balloon on TV. She's been watching the Thanksgiving Day Parade for a while, screaming every time a character she likes comes on.

"Yeah, cool," I mumble, seeing a car pull into the driveway. "Mom, the Harrisons are here!"

I've been dreading seeing Levi again. I know it's going to be weird to have to sit through a whole meal with him when I haven't talked to him in a month.

"Can you get the door?" my mom asks.

"No!" I yell, not wanting to be the person to greet them.

"So I finally get to meet your boyfriend?" Noah asks.

"He's not my boyfriend," I mumble, rolling my eyes.

"Not from what Mom's told me."

"She doesn't even know anything. We're not even friends."

Noah talks in a girly voice and says, *"Delilah met this new boy, Levi. Delilah's been hanging out with Levi. Delilah did her English project on Levi, oh my goodness, it's just so adorable!"*

"Shut up!" I say, nudging into his shoulder.

Just then, the doorbell rings. I instantly become more nervous at the thought of seeing Levi again. I don't know how I'm going to eat dinner with him. He's willfully ignored me for a month, and I am sure he will ignore me today. I'm surprised he's even coming.

Noah doesn't get up to get the door, and neither do I. I refuse.

"You go," Noah says.

"No."

"Yes."

"No."

"Lucy, go answer the door," Noah says.

"Noah, she's three! She can't even reach the doorknob," I tell him. I reluctantly get off the couch and head toward the door. My hand stays on the knob for a few seconds before finally opening the door.

"Hi, Delilah!" Mr. Harrison says, handing me a pie.

"Happy Thanksgiving! Come on in!" I say with as much happiness as I can. I don't want Levi to know how nervous I am.

I look over to Levi, who is behind his dad. He's looking at the ground, and his feet are turned in as he shifts his weight from side to side. He quickly looks up at me before looking back down, his cheeks turning slightly red.

"Hi, Levi," I say quietly as he walks past me and up the stairs, following his dad.

He doesn't even look up at me, but I swear I saw him flinch a little.

"Who are you?" I hear Lucy ask when Levi gets into the living room.

"That's Levi," I tell her. She's has to tilt her head far back in order to look up at him. Levi waves a little to her, and she waves back.

"I'm Lucy, I'm three, and I like to play Barbies. Do you like Barbies?" she asks Levi.

He shakes his head and smiles a little.

"Levi, that's my brother, Noah," I say quietly. I figure I should introduce them since Levi obviously isn't going to introduce himself.

Levi doesn't even look at me when I talk. I feel like I'm invisible to him.

Do I really cause him so much pain that he won't even look at me?

"Hey," Noah says, reaching out to do that weird handshake boys do. Levi looks down awkwardly at Noah's hand and raises his eyebrows. "Dude, it's daps," Noah mumbles.

Levi makes a confused expression and shrugs.

"Let's just forget that happened," Noah says. I can tell he's trying not to laugh; I am too. This is already so awkward.

Next, my mom and stepdad come out to introduce themselves to Levi. I already told my family about how Levi is, but I don't think they actually realized what I meant, or understood how someone just doesn't talk. My mom asks Levi a ton of questions. I think she thought he would give a response, but all he does is shrug or shake his head.

We all sit down at the table a few minutes later. Of course, Levi is sitting across from me. He stares down at his empty plate and moves his fork side to side until the food is ready.

It's going to be a long day.

Levi picks a small piece of turkey and piles a bunch of mashed potatoes onto his plate. He doesn't take anything else but those two. I wonder if he doesn't understand the point of Thanksgiving or if he just doesn't like the food.

"So, Levi, how do you like it here so far?" my stepdad, Cory, asks.

Levi shrugs and pushes his potatoes around his plate.

"You're quiet," Lucy says.

Levi nods, and I can tell he's holding back a smile. At least he likes someone at the table.

Everyone else continues like this is a normal family dinner. Levi continues to not acknowledge my existence, and I stay pretty quiet. I feel extremely awkward, and I don't know what to say or do. I just listen to everyone else talk, and I sometimes add to the conversation, but not much. Every now and again, I catch Levi looking up at me, and he blushes every time.

After dinner, Noah, Cory, and Mr. Harrison go watch the football game. I help my mom clean the dishes since I have nothing better to do. Lucy wanted to show Levi her room, which he surprisingly agreed to do.

"Levi is interesting," my mom says.

"Yeah, I guess so."

"What happened with you guys?"

I stop drying the plate and put it down on the counter. "What?"

"Well, for a while you two hung out. And today you will barely look at each other. Is there something I should know about?"

"No."

"Delilah, you don't have to be embarrassed to tell me about your relationships."

I widen my eyes. "Mom! Do you think I dated Levi or something?"

"Well, yes, I mean—"

"Mom, no. We were friends, if even that. Whatever it was is over."

"If you say so. But I see the way you look at each other when you think the other isn't watching."

"Mom, stop! I'm done with this conversation. Good-bye," I say jokingly, leaving the kitchen. I can hear Lucy in the living room, and when I walk out into the hall, I see her sitting with Levi. They're both cross-legged on the floor. Levi looks so large compared to Lucy, it's cute. I stand there quietly and watch.

"How old are you?" Lucy asks.

Levi holds up one finger, and then seven.

"You're seven?"

Levi shakes his head and does it again.

"Seventeen?"

Levi nods.

"You're old. I'm three. Did you know that?"

It's about the tenth time she's told him how old she is.

I like how Levi is acting with Lucy. It's cute how he's willing to sit with her, and she's the only person he's actually smiled at today.

"Wanna hear a story?" Lucy asks, reaching out and grabbing Levi's hands. "I can tell you're a good listener because you don't talk." She puts her palms face down on Levi's hands, and they're barely big enough to cover half. Levi doesn't pull away like I thought he would; he just looks at Lucy with a smile on his face. His expression is relaxed, and he looks *happy*.

"Come on, lean close. It's a secret story," Lucy whispers, but it's loud enough for me to hear. Levi leans closer to her, and she puts her hands around his ear. She whispers something that I can't make out.

Levi smiles widely, and he laughs.

Levi *laughs*.

He quickly puts his hand over his mouth, and it's like everything is frozen. He stops moving, and his eyes widen. His eyebrows furrow together, and I can sense his panic.

I can't believe he actually laughed. I don't think he believes it either.

He finally notices me standing in the hallway, and he stares at me with wide, shocked eyes. I smile meekly and walk into the room.

"Hi," I whisper, sitting down beside him and Lucy.

"I told Levi a secret," Lucy says. She looks over at Levi and says, "Shhh."

He nods and looks over at me. Levi looks like he's about to cry, but he starts to smile.

Then, he laughs a little again. We both start to laugh, until we're laughing for no reason at all.

I like the sound of Levi's laugh. It's light and quick. It's weird to hear him making an actual sound, but I like it. His dimples are deeper than they've ever been, and his eyes squeeze shut as he laughs.

Levi wipes at the corners of his eyes once he's done laughing. He shrugs like it was no big deal, but it was.

He doesn't stop smiling for a long time.

He takes his phone out of his pocket and quickly types something. He passes his phone over to me, and I read what he's written.

"I'm sorry."

I look up at him. "It's okay."

He smiles a little and tilts his head to the side. He reaches out to shake my hand.

It's like we're starting all over.

I feel like things between us are going to get better now. I wonder what Lucy said to him.

Chapter Twenty-Three

DELILAH

"What are we gonna do today?" Lucy asks. She's sitting on the windowsill, tapping her finger on the glass panes.

"Noah wants to go see a movie. Do you wanna do that?"

"Can it be *Frozen*?"

"I already told you, it's not at the movies anymore."

"But I wanna see Olaf!"

"I'm sorry, Lucy, but he's not at the movies right now."

"Why not?"

"Because."

"Cause why?"

"Because it's summer?" I say more like a question. It's fall, but hopefully she won't realize it.

"It's not summer, silly," she says, giggling.

I sigh, knowing I'm not going to get anywhere with this. I pick Lucy up off the windowsill and set her down beside me on the couch.

"What about going to the park?" I ask her.

She tilts her head and thinks for a second. "Okay!" she says excitedly. "Let's go to the park! Let's go to the park!" she says, jumping up and down.

After a few minutes of getting Lucy into her jacket (she just *had* to zipper it herself), we're finally ready. It's kind of cold out, so I'm hoping she won't want to stay long. Noah decides to stay home.

"Can we ask Lev-ee to come?" Lucy asks.

"His name is Levi. And no, he's busy," I lie. She's asked about Levi every day since Thanksgiving.

She pouts and looks up at me. "No, it should be Lev-ee. It sounds like Lucy."

I laugh and decide not to correct her again. "What did you say to Levi the other day?" I ask, still wondering how she made him laugh.

"When?"

"Thanksgiving."

"When was that?"

Lucy always forgets things, or at least she says she does. I don't believe her half the time.

"It was a few days ago," I tell her.

She shrugs, putting one hand in the air. "I dunno."

"Are you sure?"

"It might've been about a green bean, I don't really know. Was I eating a green bean when I said it?"

"No," I say, trying not to laugh.

"Oh . . ." she says, losing focus and looking around. As we walk, she holds tightly to my hand, swaying our arms back and forth.

When we're almost to the park, Lucy lets go of my hand and starts running down the sidewalk. I'm about to yell at her until I recognize what, or who, she's running to.

"Levi!" she shrieks, running toward Levi. He's standing at his front door with his hands in his pockets. Lucy wraps her arms around him, or more so his legs, and hugs him tightly. He slowly puts his arm around her as best he can since she's so much smaller.

She looks up at him, still holding tightly to his knees. "Will you come to the park? Puh-leaseeeee?" she says, drawing the word into two long syllables.

Levi smiles and looks down at Lucy, then up at me. I don't say anything.

He nods.

"Yay! He said he'll come!" Lucy reaches up to grab Levi's hand, and she opens and closes her hand until Levi notices. He holds her small hand inside his and walks over to me.

"Sorry about that," I tell him quietly.

He shrugs and *smiles*.

We all walk down to the park, with Lucy in between us, holding both of our hands.

Lucy runs over to the swing set, waiting for someone to help her up onto one. Levi surprisingly lifts her up onto the swing and starts pushing her lightly.

It's cute to see this side of Levi.

"Do you have a younger sibling?" I ask Levi as he pushes Lucy.

He shakes his head no.

"Higher!" Lucy shrieks.

She continues to giggle as she swings back and forth. Levi grins as Lucy shrieks every time she goes higher. She's not going too high, but to her it probably feels like it.

"Okay, I can stop now," Lucy says abruptly. She gets bored easily with things.

Levi quickly grabs the swing to stop her. She jumps off and stands between Levi and me.

"Can I go on the tire swing?" she asks.

"You don't have to ask," I tell her.

"With Levi?"

I look over at Levi. He bites on his lip ring and slowly shrugs, then grabs Lucy's hand and walks over to the swing. He picks her up and puts her onto the tire, then sits across from her. His legs are too long, and he has to lean far back to keep them off the ground. Lucy laughs uncontrollably as they spin.

After about thirty minutes of going from the swings to the slide to the see-saw, Lucy gets bored. She wraps her arms around herself and runs over to me.

"I'm frozen!" she pouts.

I know where this is going ...

"It's not that cold," I tell her.

"I said, I'm frozen!" She pretends to shiver.

Levi grabs the beanie off his head and puts it on Lucy. It's probably bigger than her whole head. It slides down a little bit onto her forehead and she giggles. He runs his hand through his flat hair to try to fix it.

"I'm still frozen," she says, tugging at Levi's hat. "Let's go watch *Frozen*!"

"Lucy, please," I beg. "We watched it a few days ago."

"Anna needs me, though."

"Oh, really?"

"She wants to build a snowman."

"Fine. C'mon, let's go," I say.

"Let it go, let it go, I can hold it in the back no more," Lucy sings. She always sings the wrong lyrics, but no one has told her yet.

"Pick me up, please," she asks.

"I don't really want to," I tell her. I honestly hate carrying her.

She sticks out her bottom lip and looks up at me. Levi bends down and swiftly picks her up. She wraps her arms around his neck and leans her head on his shoulder.

"Levi is nice. You're not," Lucy tells me.

I shrug. "Sorry."

It's strange seeing Levi being so nice. He cares so much for Lucy; I've never seen him be like this with anyone.

I want to know what Lucy told him so badly. It had to be something important. Otherwise, I don't get why he's being like this with her.

"Wanna just walk slowly around the neighborhood for a little? She'll fall asleep. Would you mind?" I whisper to Levi.

He shakes his head, and we walk slowly. After a few minutes, Lucy's eyes shut until she falls asleep. She can fall asleep anywhere.

We get back to my house, Levi still carrying Lucy. He puts her in bed, and thankfully, she doesn't wake up.

"Thanks for coming," I say, when we're out of the room. "She really likes you."

He waves his hand as if to say, "No problem," and we awkwardly stand in the hallway. He puts his hands in his pockets and rocks back on his heels like he always does.

I break the silence with the first thing that comes to mind. "Do you want some Skittles?"

Chapter Twenty-Four

LEVI

Delilah looks around her whole house searching for Skittles. They must keep a secret stash at all times or something, because she always has them.

I'm sitting on the couch, waiting for her to come back. I look around the room, even though I was here a few days ago. I notice things I hadn't paid attention to last time, like the family photo on the wall and the scribbled drawing made by Lucy that's on the coffee table.

Wait, on top of the drawing, it says Levi. The "e" is backward. I feel the corner of my mouth tilt up.

I pick it up and look at it. She's made my hair very tall, and my legs very long. All my clothes are black, but there's a rainbow behind me and a crown on my head. There's a tiny yellow sun in the corner, and it has a big smile and sunglasses.

I think I'm smiling wider than the sun is while I look at the drawing.

I hear the door open and put the picture back down on the table.

"Delilah, I meant to tell you earlier that I'm leaving tomorrow, but I—You're not Delilah," Noah says when he sees me sitting on the couch.

I shake my head.

"Where is she?" he asks.

I shrug and point down the hall.

Noah shrugs his shoulders too, and he sits beside me on the couch.

"So, how's it going?" he asks.

I shrug.

He points to the picture. "Did you see what Lucy made you? I think she has a crush on you," he says, laughing.

I nod and smile.

"I think she likes you more than Delilah does," he says.

I look at him with wide eyes, confused as to what he just said.

"Crap, I hope Delilah didn't just hear me say that," he says, putting his hand to his head.

I tilt my head to the side, still shocked.

"Don't act like you don't know," Noah says.

I scrunch my face in confusion.

"You seriously don't know? Are you really that oblivious? Before she even said anything, I could tell she liked you when you came over!"

She said something? About me?

"Do you like her?" he asks quietly.

Delilah walks in just then, happily holding a bag of Skittles. "I found some!" she says excitedly. She notices Noah beside me, who is still looking at me to answer him.

I don't answer.

"When'd you get home?" she asks him.

"Just now. And now I'm going to go," he says. He nudges my shoulder a little and gives a small thumbs-up before leaving the room.

What is *that* supposed to mean?

Maybe Delilah said something that was *about* me, not necessarily about liking me. I don't think she could possibly like me. If anything, she pities me.

She plops down beside me and smiles widely. She pours some Skittles into her hand and then gives some to me.

"Sorry about Noah and Lucy, if they bug you," she says quietly. I shrug and chew on the Skittles in my mouth.

I can't focus. All I can think about is what Noah said. She doesn't like me. Or maybe she does. Why would she like me? How can she like someone if she's never heard the sound of their voice? It seems impossible.

I look at Delilah as she digs through the Skittles bag for the red ones, like she always does. She eats all the red first, then she eats the green and orange at the same time. She notices me watching her, and stops chewing.

"What?" she asks, raising one eyebrow.

I shake my head. I take a Skittle out of my hand, which is now rainbow, and throw it at her. It hits her on the nose, and she scrunches her face when it hits her. She throws one back, but I catch it in my mouth.

"You always do that, and I can't do it," she says, sticking out her bottom lip.

I shrug and smile.

We hear Lucy wake up and walk down the hall.

"Why can't I be an only child?" Delilah mumbles when Lucy walks into the room.

Lucy yawns and rubs her eyes. "Did you watch *Frozen* without me?"

"No, we didn't watch it. Don't worry," Delilah tells her.

"Good," Lucy says quietly. She slowly gets herself onto the couch, and squishes between Delilah and me. I look over at Delilah, who is looking down at her hands, which are rainbow like mine.

She looks upset. I reach behind Lucy and poke Delilah's shoulder. She looks up, and I smile widely to get her to smile.

She grins back, and her cheeks blush a little.

Lucy pokes my cheek. "Can a Skittle fit in that?"

I'm guessing she's referring to my dimple. She quickly reaches for a Skittle that's in my hand and shoves it onto my cheek.

"Stop movin' your head," she mumbles, sticking her tongue out while she concentrates. She puts one of her little hands on my forehead while she tries to get the Skittle to stay on my cheek. It stays there for a second until I start laughing hysterically. Delilah laughs too.

This is the second time she's made me laugh. Out of all people, it's a three-year-old.

"Lucy, you are unbelievable," Delilah says, out of breath as she laughs.

"What's so funny?" Lucy asks, laughing just because we are.

"I can't believe you just did that," Delilah says while wiping her eyes.

I was kind of upset at myself for laughing the first time, but it feels so good to finally do it again. But at the same time, it feels like I'm breaking a piece of myself that I wanted to stay strong. Right now, though, the happy feeling inside me overpowers the guilt of being happy.

Once we stop laughing, Lucy crosses her arms across her chest. "Now can we watch *Frozen*?"

We end up watching *Frozen*, and halfway through Lucy falls asleep again. It amazes me that she can fall asleep so quickly, especially when she wouldn't stop talking about the movie.

It's a pretty cute film, if you're into that kind of stuff.

I may or may not be into this kind of stuff . . .

Lucy ended up falling asleep on top of me. Her head is in my lap, and I've been trying hard not to move and wake her up. Every once in a while, she'll move slightly. It's cute.

Lucy suddenly squirms and grabs lightly onto my hand, hugging it closer to her while she sleeps.

I wonder if she's actually asleep.

Every now and then, I can see Delilah turn and look at me, or maybe she's looking at Lucy. I notice that Delilah looks over at us more than she looks at the TV.

Maybe Noah's right. Maybe she does like me. Or maybe she's just checking on Lucy.

I see her watching me out of the corner of my eye, and I turn to look at her too.

I mouth the word "stop," but I'm smiling when I do it.

"Sorry. But cute things deserve to be looked at."

Chapter Twenty-Five

LEVI

Sorry. *But cute things deserve to be looked at," Delilah says. Her cheeks blush and she quickly starts talking again. "I mean, it's cute how Lucy is, uh—How she fell asleep . . ." She turns her attention back to the movie.*

I groan internally, thinking back to a few nights ago. I'm still confused as to what Noah told me and what Delilah said to me.

Did she really mean Lucy was cute? Or did she mean me? I can't stop thinking about it. I'm not sure why it's bothering me so much.

I decide to go to the person who knows Delilah best. Aiden.

I walk to his house, and even though it's not too far, I'm extremely cold. I don't think I'll ever be used to the weather here.

I hesitantly knock on his door and shove my hands into my pockets. I can hear footsteps running toward the door, and Hunter opens it.

"Aiden," Hunter yells, "Levi's here!"

Hunter runs away, leaving me standing in front of the open door. Aiden slowly walks toward me with a confused expression on his face.

It's been weeks since I last saw him. I've still been ignoring him. I'm not really sure why, as I wish I hadn't.

"Hey, Levi." He says it more like a question. "What are you doing here?"

He leans against the doorframe and crosses his arms. I awkwardly scratch the back of my neck and look down at my feet.

I quickly type in my phone. I'm not really sure what to write, so I go with what my fingers tap out. "I'm sorry about the past few weeks. I was having a rough time. But I need to talk to you."

"What about? Here, come in," Aiden says, sounding concerned. I follow him up to his room. It feels like only a few days ago, I was over here playing FIFA.

I thought Aiden would be mad at me and not be willing to talk. Though Aiden has never been rude to me, no matter how many times I'm awful to him.

"So," Aiden says, "what do you wanna talk about?"

Aiden sits down on his bed, and I crouch into the small beanbag on the floor. Aiden rests his chin on his hand while he waits for me to stop typing on my phone.

"Does Delilah like me?" the voice says.

He scratches his chin and takes a deep breath. "Do you like her?"

I roll my eyes. I type a response quickly. "No." I feel my cheeks blush.

Aiden sighs and lightly laughs. "Have you read her project from a few weeks ago?"

I shake my head no. I haven't looked at it since I shoved it into one of my drawers.

"That'll probably explain everything you need to know," he says with a slight smirk. "I think I actually have it somewhere in my email. She sent it to me to proofread, to see if what she wrote about you was okay, I guess."

He opens up his laptop and types quickly on his keyboard.

"Got it!" he says, passing the laptop over to me.

I push it away. I don't know if I want to know what she wrote.

"If you don't read it, I'll read it to you," Aiden says, laughing.

I roll my eyes and take the laptop, not wanting Aiden to read it. I guess I have to read it at some point, anyway.

I read the first sentence, and my hands start shaking. I'm so nervous. I shouldn't be this nervous to see what she has to say about me.

> I recently met a boy named Levi. I don't know much about him other than the fact that he's Australian, and he loves Skittles. I also know that he doesn't talk. Levi has gone through a tough time in his life, full of mourning and sadness. His way of dealing with it is not speaking—or at least that's what I think. He's a giant mystery to everyone.
>
> When I first met him, he threw his coffee when he saw me. I'm still not sure why. He was rude, and he always rolled his eyes. He rarely looked at me, and when he did, he glared.
>
> Most girls would leave, but I stayed. I stayed through his anxiety, his anger, his sadness, and now, I'm staying while he's ignoring me.

I forgot that she had been writing this while I was ignoring her. She's probably written about how much she hates me. I continue reading, afraid of what I'll see. I don't want her to hate me.

> After doing this project, Levi expressed the fact that he didn't want to be around me. He told me to pretend I'd never met him. I'm rereading the note he wrote me as I write this.
>
> I can't forget Levi, because it would be impossible. I won't forget how his blue eyes get brighter when he's happy (which isn't often, but they're like the color of a clear blue sky), or the way his jacket smells of cologne and smoke. I won't forget the time he opened up to me about his loss, which I'm choosing not to write about here. I especially will always remember the last day we spent together on the beach, throwing Skittles at each other.

Levi isn't like any boys that I've met, or any person I've ever known. He's unique and mysterious and is constantly confusing me. But that's what makes him so special.

I genuinely do believe that Levi is a fantastic person. When he wants to be, he is kind and gentle. I'm glad I've seen that side of him, even if only for a little bit. He has made a huge impact on me the past few weeks, whether he knows it or not.

Throughout the rest of her project, she explains the things she learned about me. She writes about the simple things like my birthday, and the more complex things that she's noticed, like the way I rock on my heels or the way I rub my nose. She's noticed things I didn't even know about myself.

But the last sentence is what changes everything.

As strange as this may seem, I think I'm falling for him.

I look up at Aiden, who is smiling widely. I shake my head quickly and scrunch my eyebrows in confusion.

This can't be real. She can't really like me, can she?

"Does that give you your answer?" he asks, still smiling.

I nod slowly, and then, out of nowhere, I start crying. It starts slowly at first, but quickly speeds up.

Aiden jumps off his bed and sits beside me on the floor. I hate how I'm always crying now—I can't seem to stop.

"Do you wanna go see her?" Aiden asks quietly.

I shake my head no.

"What's wrong then?" he asks worriedly.

I point to myself over and over, but Aiden just looks at me with a confused expression.

I reach for my phone and quickly type, even though my vision is blurred from all these tears. I pass him the phone, and he reads what I wrote.

154

"Levi, it's okay to feel that way," Aiden tells me after a long pause.

I shake my head no.

He awkwardly puts his arm around me. "I understand. But I promise, it's okay. It's okay to feel that way," he says again.

What Aiden says makes me cry even more. I hate that I'm sitting here on an old beanbag chair, with Aiden's arm around me, and tears streaming down my face.

I hate that I'm feeling this way.

I don't like it. I don't like any of this.

I wish I could just remember to forget.

Chapter Twenty-Six

DELILAH

I wake up to my phone ringing loudly, and I sleepily reach for it with my eyes shut. I squint as I look at my phone to see Aiden's name.

"Hello?" I say groggily.

"Where are you?" he asks.

"I'm in bed?" I say.

"Do you realize it's a Monday? And we should've left for school five minutes ago?"

I bolt upright in bed and look at the clock on my bedside table. Aiden's right. I must have slept through my alarm. "Just leave without me," I mumble, getting out of bed quickly. "I'll see you at school."

"Wait, but I—"

I hang up before Aiden can finish what he's saying. Whatever it is, he can tell me at school.

I get ready as fast as I can and text Aiden to cover for me if I'm late for first period. I somehow manage to get to school before the bell rings. Aiden is already at my locker when I get there.

"Delilah, we need to talk," Aiden says, leaning against the other lockers as I do my combination. He says it very seriously, which is unusual. I'm kind of nervous for what we have to talk about now. But knowing Aiden, it could just be about what the cafeteria is having for lunch today.

"About what?" I ask him, putting some things in my bag.

He looks around the crowded hallway. "In private."

"Okay?" I'm very confused about this, and why Aiden is being so weird this morning. I don't get why we have to talk in private. I don't see what there could be to talk about that's so serious.

Aiden waits for me to get all my things, and the second after I shut my locker, he starts walking through the halls. I quickly follow behind him.

"Is everything okay?" I ask.

"Yeah."

"Then what's happening?"

"We just need to talk."

Aiden is making such a big deal out of this, it's worrying me. What if he has bad news? Millions of terrible scenarios race through my mind as we weave through the crowded halls.

He brings me into one of the science labs, which is empty. He turns on the light, and we sit at one of the tables.

"So what's happening?" I ask him nervously. I bounce my leg anxiously on the stool.

"Levi came over to my house yesterday," he says.

"And? Did something happen?" With Levi, it could be anything. I never know what to expect with him.

Aiden nods. "He read your project."

I knew Levi had my project, so this shouldn't be such a big surprise to me. But for some reason, it is. My heart starts racing a little after Aiden tells me.

"What'd he think about it?" I ask quietly.

"Well, he, uh, he cried," Aiden says awkwardly.

"He cried?" I honestly didn't expect Levi to cry over it. There wasn't anything that fantastic about it, it was just stuff he had told me and some things I've noticed about him.

"Yeah, the last sentence really got to him, I guess."

"Wait—Aiden, what last sentence?"

"You know, the one about you falling for him."

I feel my cheeks heat up, and my stomach flips. "I didn't give him that version, Aiden. How did he get it?"

"You emailed it to me? To proofread?"

"This can't be happening," I say, putting my head in my hands.

"What? Was there something wrong with it?"

"Yes, there was something wrong with it!" I yell louder than I should. "That was the wrong version! That was the one I thought I deleted! I must have sent you the wrong one without realizing it. Did you really think I would turn that in for a school project? I'm not gonna confess my crush to a teacher! My real project didn't have any of the lovey stuff. I only did that for myself, just to get it all out because I didn't want to tell anyone!"

I nervously bite my nails. No one was supposed to read that, especially Levi. I can't believe I didn't realize I sent Aiden the wrong one.

"So what you're saying is that you emailed me a project, which I showed Levi, which is different from the one you gave to Levi and turned in to your teacher, and now Levi knows that you liked him, which isn't something you wanted?" Aiden says.

"Yeah, sure, let's go with that," I say quickly.

"Oh, well, this is awkward," Aiden whispers after a long time.

"You think? He knows I like him," I mumble into my hands. "This is a mess."

I can only imagine what will happen now. Levi will ignore me *again*, and at this point I'll probably never have him as a friend. He probably hates me now, if he didn't already before. Levi doesn't handle things very well; I doubt he's handling the fact that I like him. He's still getting over Delia. He definitely doesn't want anyone, especially me, liking him.

I hear the bell ring, and stand up, not wanting to talk about this anymore.

"I'm going to class," I say quietly.

"Wait, Delilah, there's more I have to tell you," I hear Aiden say as I leave.

"Just tell me later," I say quickly, walking out the door.

The school day lasts longer than usual, and all I think about is Levi. I'm so worried about how he reacted. Aiden and I didn't talk about it at lunch because I didn't want to. I think Aiden feels bad about this whole thing, but it's not like it's his fault. It's my own fault for being stupid enough to send Aiden the wrong version.

I messed everything up.

Even at work, I can't stop thinking about Levi.

Then I think I see him walk in, even though I know he doesn't have an appointment today. I do a double take, because I thought I was just imagining it. But he is in fact here.

He shyly waves to me, which surprises me. I wave back, and he smiles a little. He crashes into a boy with purple hair, and I can't help but laugh. He nervously bites his lip and walks over to me.

He types something on his phone and passes it across the counter for me to read. He's asking if he can see Candace.

"I don't think she's with anyone right now, I'll go check," I tell him. As I expected, Candace is just sitting at her desk doing paperwork.

"Hi, Delilah. What can I help you with?" she asks in her cheery tone.

"Levi Harrison is here. He wants to know if he can see you."

"Sure, I don't see why not," she says.

I get Levi, and he walks into the room. I wonder if he's here to talk about my project.

I doubt it. That would be extremely awkward if he was.

Levi probably doesn't even think about me like I think about him. He definitely doesn't.

While I'm lost in thought, the boy with purple hair comes up to the counter, anxiously tapping his hand against his leg.

"Can you— Where's the-the bathroom?" he says, stuttering.

"Right down the hall," I tell him, smiling.

"Th-thank you," he whispers, running in the direction of the bathroom.

I recognize him from school; he's new. I've definitely seen him before—it'd be hard to forget someone with hair that color. I don't notice him much though, since he's pretty quiet.

He's gone for a long time, and I wonder if he got lost. But he comes back, and is called in to his appointment. I find out his name is Mitchell.

To keep my mind off Levi, I think of what Mitchell's actual hair color might be.

About forty-five minutes later, Levi comes out of Candace's room. I notice that his eyes are red and his face is blotchy. He's definitely been crying.

"Levi, are you okay?" I whisper. There's no one in the waiting room but us right now.

He quickly shakes his head. He doesn't look me in the eyes, like he always does when he's nervous. He rubs his eyes, which makes them even redder than they already are.

"Do you need anything?" I ask him, even though I'm not sure what he'd even need.

He shakes his head and starts to leave. I debate making sure he'll be all right, but I know he will. He's Levi. He'll be fine without me, like he's made clear multiple times.

For the rest of the night, Levi's sad expression replays over and over in my mind. I can't help but think he really might have needed me.

Chapter Twenty-Seven

LEVI

For the past three days, I've barely done anything but sleep. When I'm awake, I'm just overcome with sadness and confusion. By sleeping, I don't feel.

I keep thinking about the past few days and all the stuff that's happened. I feel like everything is slowly getting more confusing for me as time goes on. I feel so conflicted about what has happened in my life. I don't know what to think about anything anymore.

Everything is a mess.

I check my phone for the time, and I look at the phone icon, which shows one new voice mail. Except it's not new. It's been there for eight months.

I've never listened to it.

The last time I saw Candace, she told me I should listen to it. She said it might make me feel better. I haven't been able to press play. I'm scared of what it is.

I think I'm scared of moving on too. I feel like if I listen to it, it will feel like I'm losing the last piece of Delia that I have.

I don't want to lose her.

The voice mail is from the night of the incident.

Delia didn't actually die instantly. I just tell people that so I don't have to think about the fact she was alive for a while after the accident.

So I don't have to feel so guilty.

She called me before surgery.

The time on the voice mail says 11:33 pm. She died at 5:04 am.

Her contact name still has emojis after it. Her contact picture is still the same.

It's possibly the only thing in my life that hasn't changed.

One simple voice mail can hold a lot of meaning.

I try not to think about the day of the accident too much, but now that I am, the whole day comes flooding back into my mind. I remember every detail vividly. Sometimes I think that if I don't remember it, maybe it's not true. Maybe it didn't actually happen. But I know that's impossible, and I can't reverse time.

It's the one thing I wish I could forget the most, but I can't.

"You need to move on," Caleb tells me.

"I don't want to," I mumble.

"Clearly, she's moved on. She doesn't seem fazed by the breakup at all."

"That makes me feel so much better," I groan.

"Well, it's been two weeks ..."

"It's been two weeks of an almost year-long relationship!"

My phone vibrates, and it's a text from Delia.

I'm on my way to your house. I need to talk to you.

"She's on her way over!" I tell Caleb, jumping off the couch. "Do I look okay? I haven't showered!"

"You need to chill. It's Delia. If she liked you last year, she'll like you now."

"What do you think she wants to tell me? You don't think she wants to get back together, do you?"

Caleb shrugs. "I dunno. Maybe she just wants to tell you that you need to stop obsessing over her."

"I'm not obsessed."

"Yes, you are, actually. You've liked her since the day you first saw her."

A few minutes pass of me anxiously waiting, and Caleb continuously telling me not to get my hopes up. Delia doesn't show up even though she lives close by. We figure she's stuck in traffic. A half hour goes by. We hear sirens, lots of them.

"Something bad must have happened," Caleb says, going to look out the window. "It's somewhere down there," he says, pointing to his right.

I start to get nervous. "That's the way Delia would have come," I say quietly.

"It's definitely not her, don't worry. Whatever happened is probably keeping her from coming down the street."

"Right, that makes sense." But something doesn't feel right. Delia would have texted to tell me she's stuck in traffic.

Or, she would have when we were together. Now, I'm not so sure.

Caleb goes home after an hour. I stay awake. I figure Delia decided not to come. What she had to tell me probably wasn't that important. I fall asleep shortly after.

I'm woken up by my mum shaking my shoulders gently.

"Levi," she whispers.

"What time is it?" I murmur.

"It's midnight. Delia's been in an accident."

It takes a few seconds for my mum's words to sink in. At first, I think I heard her wrong. But then I remember the sirens.

"What? Where? We need to go to the hospital, I have to see her," I yell, getting out of bed.

"She's in surgery right now. We can go and wait, if you want."

"I want to. I need to see her," I say.

I run out of my room, not bothering to change out of my pajamas. I grab things that I know Delia would like, to make her happy when she sees me. Even though she probably doesn't want to see me, I want to see her. All my anger and sadness over the breakup turns into nervousness in wondering what happened to her.

The drive to the hospital feels like it takes forever. Every minute that passes feels like an hour. I nervously tap the window and watch the rain fall.

When we get there, my mum goes up to the counter to ask where Delia is. I see Delia's parents in the waiting room and run over to them.

"Is she okay?" I ask the second I get there.

"We don't know," her dad says. Both of them have been crying, and they look exhausted.

"Where is she right now?" I ask.

"She's still in surgery. She has some head trauma and internal bleeding."

I'm shocked by the news; I definitely wasn't expecting that. I thought maybe a few cuts and bruises, not something so major.

"When will she be out?" I ask frantically.

Her mum shrugs. "We didn't even know she was out driving," she chokes out.

I'm hit with the realization that she snuck out to come see me. She was driving to see me. This is because of me.

I don't tell them that she was on her way to my house.

I sit in one of the chairs, overcome with anxiety. Nobody talks much, we all just sit there. My mum tries to calm me down, but I can't relax.

Another hour goes by before a doctor comes out. Delia's parents stand up abruptly.

"Her surgery is over. There were some minor complications, but as far as we can tell she will heal well, and you have nothing to be concerned over. She is still coming out of anesthesia, but we anticipate she should be conscious soon," the doctor tells us.

"Can we see her?" I ask quietly.

"Family only."

The doctors bring Delia's parents to her room. I watch them walk down the hall and turn down the corridor. I wish I was down there too.

"Why don't we go home and come back in the morning? Get some rest, maybe," my mum tells me.

"I want to stay here. I want to be here when she wakes up. I can't leave her."

I'm trying not to cry. I need to see her. I can't stand waiting. I bounce my leg anxiously and bite my nails.

"She'll be fine, I promise," my mum says.

"But how do you know?"

My mum says nothing.

Delia's dad comes out when police officers show up. They explain that they were investigating the accident. I overhear them saying they looked at Delia's phone, suspecting that could have been a cause of the accident, as it is for a lot of people. The screen had a text that said "be there in" but it was never finished.

It was addressed to a boy named Levi.

"No, no, no, no," I whisper once I hear my name. I break down sobbing in the middle of the waiting room. A doctor comes over and asks if I'm all right.

My mum answers for me and says I'm fine.

But I'm not fine.

I'm the reason Delia got in an accident. I'm the reason she's in this hospital.

She shouldn't have even been driving alone. She wasn't fully licensed; she wouldn't be for a year. We lived so close, Delia probably thought it would be okay. But it wasn't.

"I can't be here right now," I tell my mum, leaving the waiting room quickly.

She follows me down the hall, calling my name. She reaches out for me, but I push her away.

"Just get away!" I scream. "I need to be alone right now."

I walk through the silent corridors of the hospital and pass by rooms with sleeping patients. I've always hated hospitals. I hate the sanitary smell, I hate the depressing colors, I hate the pictures that line the walls.

I end up sitting down in the middle of the hallway, crying uncontrollably. I can't seem to stop.

"Excuse me, is everything okay?" I hear someone ask.

"I'm fine," I manage to say.

I hear the person walk away.

At some point, my mum finds me. Everything seems to be going by in a blur. I don't know how much time has passed.

"They're moving her to ICU," my mum tells me, sitting down beside me on the floor.

"Why?" I say in a barely audible whisper. I can't look her in the eyes.

"Her condition is worsening."

"Can I see her yet?" I beg.

My mum shakes her head no. It looks like she's been crying too.

I can't remember the last time I cried this much. I feel like I've been crying for years. I feel like my whole world is crashing down around me.

We head back to the waiting room, which seems even quieter than before. A nurse walks over to us, and I get hopeful that I can finally see Delia.

"Are you Levi?" she asks me.

I nod quickly.

"I was with Delia before her surgery. She asked if she could make one call, I think it was to you."

"What?" I ask, confused. She chose me to call? I don't know how to respond. "Did you hear what she said? I don't have my phone, I left it at home," I say. I can't believe I left it at home.

She shakes her head. "I think you need to hear it for yourself. I'm sorry."

All I keep hearing tonight is "I'm sorry."

She walks away, leaving me wondering. I debate going home just to get my phone, but I don't. I can't leave. I have to stay here.

Delia's parents come and go between the waiting room and Delia's room. They're sent out whenever something happens. They've been in the waiting room for a while with no signs of any doctors, which is starting to worry me.

After a blur of chaos, a doctor comes out. Delia's parents, my mum, and I all stand up expectantly.

"I'm sorry," he starts off.

I feel my stomach drop.

"Delia's head injury was more severe than we thought. She suffered major swelling, which can happen a few hours after an accident."

"Is she okay?" I whisper, even though I know the answer.

The doctor shakes his head. "I'm sorry. We tried. But she didn't make it."

Delia's parents hug each other, and both of them are crying. I run out of the waiting room in the direction of the exit. Again.

"Levi!" my mum calls.

"She's not dead. She's not dead." I repeat, over and over.

My mum grabs my wrist, causing me to stop walking. I whip around to face her, tears staining my cheeks.

"She's NOT dead!" I yell. I pull away from my mum's grasp. I'm breathing quickly, and my chest feels tight. I feel like I'm going to pass out.

"Levi, you heard the doctor. I'm sorry."

There it is again.

I shake my head over and over. My mum pulls me closer to her, and I can't stop crying.

"Do you want to see her?" my mum asks.

"Not unless she's alive," I say, a little more harshly than I should.

My mum tries to comfort me, but it's not working.

"She's dead. It's because of me. She was texting me," I choke out.

"It's not because of you, don't think that."

"But it is!"

"It'll be okay."

"How can you say that?!" I yell, pulling away from my mum.

She doesn't respond.

"The text was sent to me. I am the reason she looked away from the road," I whisper.

"It could've happened to anyone."

I turn around and keep walking toward the exit. It could've happened to anyone.

It happened to us.

"I never told her I loved her," I choke out. "And now I'll never get the chance."

Chapter Twenty-Eight

DELILAH

After much contemplating, I decide to go to Levi's to talk about everything that's happened over the past few days. The project, what Aiden told me, and basically everything else.

Whatever we even are, whether it's friends or just neighbors, I can't keep wondering anymore. I hate all the confusion involved with Levi. Whenever I think I have a piece of him figured out, it seems to be the complete opposite.

I hesitantly knock on his front door, and his dad answers.

"Hey!" he says cheerily, letting me inside.

"Is Levi here?"

"Yeah, in his room."

I walk slowly to Levi's room. I'm not sure what I'm going to say, or what it will even be about. I'm regretting coming here in the first place.

His door is slightly open, and as I'm about to knock, I hear someone talking.

"Hi, Levi, it's me."

It's a girl's voice. I stand outside the door, not wanting to interrupt the conversation. It sounds like a phone call, but through the crack from his open door, I can see Levi holding his phone in front of him. Maybe he's video chatting someone. He's sitting on the floor, leaning against the wall with his legs pulled close to his chest.

"I was on my way to your house, but I got in a little accident. I'm okay, though," the girl continues.

Who was coming over?

The sound is muffled, then I hear, "I, um, I just really wanted to talk to you and I—"

The girl stops talking, and I see Levi toss his phone onto the carpet. He puts his head in his hands, and I think I hear him crying.

That's when I realize who was talking. It wasn't a phone call, but a voice mail.

I think it's Delia.

I debate turning around and giving Levi some time alone, but he stands up and sees me in the hallway. He quickly wipes his eyes and slowly opens his bedroom door.

"Hi," I say quietly.

He nods slightly.

"I can go. I'm sorry, it probably isn't a good time right now, I just—" I stammer.

He grabs my wrist and pulls me into his room, shutting the door. He sits down on the floor and taps the spot beside him, gesturing for me to sit there, so I do. He twiddles his thumbs, and he won't look me in the eyes, like always.

"Was that from Delia?" I ask after a long silence.

He slowly nods his head.

"Have you listened to it before?"

He shakes his head no, which I expected.

"I can leave if you want to listen to it."

He shakes his head and reaches over to grab his phone. He puts it in my hands and points to the play button.

"You want me to play it? Are you sure? Don't you want to be alone?"

It seems unlike Levi to want me here when something like this is happening. Whenever Delia is brought up, he shuts down. I thought he'd be doing that right now too.

He keeps pointing to the play button, so I finally press it. It starts all over again.

"Hi, Levi, it's me." I really feel like I shouldn't be here now. Levi winces at the sound of her voice. Now that I can hear the recording more clearly, I notice it sounds like she is having trouble speaking and trying not to cry.

"I was on my way to your house, but I got in a little accident. I'm okay, though. I don't really remember getting into it—I just remember driving to your house, but not how I crashed. I, um, I just really wanted to talk to you, and I'm about to go into surgery. I wasn't supposed to call you, but a nice nurse is letting me." She tries to laugh, but it's quiet and sounds nervous. She talks slowly and gets her words mixed up sometimes. Some of the things she says are pronounced wrong. It's evident that she's suffering from the accident. "I wanted to get some things off my chest, in case it's a long time before we talk again. I am in a lot of pain and I heard the doctor say that I'm in rough shape. My head is hurting right now, but I'll try to get my thoughts out. I was coming to your house to say I'm sorry. These two weeks have been the worst two weeks. I miss talking to you and laughing at your stupid jokes." She laughs again. She coughs a little this time. This is almost too much for me to hear, I don't know how Levi is listening to this without breaking down. I didn't know Delia personally, and I'm getting upset over this.

There are long pauses between her sentences, and I can hear her continuously take deep breaths. "I made a huge mistake. I should have never broken up with you." There's muffled talking in the background; I assume it's doctors. I start to notice the faint beeping of machines. "The doctors are coming right now. I'll see you later. I hope this is a promise I can keep, Levi. I'm not gonna say good-bye, because I don't want to." Her voice cracks. "I'm scared, Levi." She coughs. "If I don't make it, I want to tell you I love you, Levi. All I want is for you to be happy. I hated seeing you so sad these past few weeks—it broke my heart. You should know that I was just as sad. If anything happens, please do that for me. Do what makes you happy. Don't be sad. I'll see you soon. Bye. I love you."

The voice mail ends, and I don't say anything. I look over at Levi to see how he handled it. He's staring straight ahead like a frozen statue. Tears are streaming down his cheeks. I reach over and put my hand on top of his in an attempt to comfort him. He looks over at me slowly, and his bottom lip is quivering.

He slowly shakes his head, still crying, and looks down at my hand on top of his. He puts his other hand on top of mine and brings it onto his lap. After a moment, he reaches into his pocket and pulls out a wrinkled piece of paper. He gently tucks it into the palm of my hand, then closes my fingers around it.

I open it up, and it's the picture Lucy drew of Levi. I wonder how long it's been in his pocket.

He flips the paper around, and on the back side, Lucy had written "Happy Prince Levi." She drew smiley faces, hearts, and flowers all around it. We both just look at it for a few minutes.

"We all want you to be happy," I tell him.

He bites his bottom lip, and it looks like he's on the verge of a whole new set of tears. He picks his phone up off the ground and types for what feels like forever. I've never seen him type so much. Whatever he has to say must be important. When he's done, he passes the phone over to me.

I read everything he wrote. He explained what really happened to Delia, and it looks like he didn't leave out any details. I start crying halfway through. I didn't realize this much had happened. He had told me she died instantly, but that's clearly not the case. Instead, it is the saddest thing, and not what I had expected at all.

He also wrote what he had gone through after the accident. He didn't immediately stop talking. It happened after the funeral. At first, it was just because he didn't want to talk to anyone. But then, after a few days, he didn't want to talk to people ever again. He felt guilty, and in a way he was punishing himself. He wrote, "Delia died because she was texting me. If Delia didn't get to talk, I didn't want to either." So he hasn't.

He went to multiple therapists; he had a new one every few weeks. Nothing helped. He was forced to go to group teen therapy sessions, which he hated, because he didn't talk, obviously. He had nothing to say, so it didn't help much. After three months, he was sent to a facility in Sydney that was guaranteed to help him. All it did was make him feel more different and alone. After almost a month there, he went back home. Nothing changed. He progressively got worse.

That's why they sent him here. It's apparently his last chance to improve. Doctors said there's nothing else they can do for him. Levi has to make his own choices for himself in order to get better. They wanted to separate Levi from everything that was making him upset and anxious. Moving here with his dad was one of his best options.

I didn't know Levi had gone through this much in such a short amount of time. His whole world just stopped. He lost someone who was clearly very important to him, and he's now living on the total opposite side of the world.

He's had to adjust to so many new things. I can't imagine what it's like for him.

As I take everything in, I'm shocked Levi's told me so much about what's happened to him. I guess at some point, everyone has to let out their emotions. They can't hold them in forever.

When I'm done reading, Levi lets out a shaky sigh. He wipes the tears from his cheeks, and he also wipes off mine. I laugh lightly, reaching up to dry my cheeks too.

"Look at us, we're both crying," I tell him. "We need to do something that makes us happy now."

He points to me.

I tilt my head to the side and look at him, puzzled.

He points to me again then to himself. He gives me a silly grin through his tears and points to his smile.

I make him happy.

Chapter Twenty-Nine

LEVI

I didn't expect Delia's message to be like that. I especially hadn't expected her to say she loves me. I never got to say it back, and I never thought I'd hear her say the words.

The message made me feel somewhat better, and somewhat worse. There were positive parts and negative parts. Overall, though, I feel very sad. Although, it's kind of like a weight has been lifted off my shoulders. For months, I've been dreading listening to that message, but I finally did it. I heard her voice again for the first time in months. Even though it didn't sound like the normal, happy Delia, it was still her. She said all that. In her last few hours, she wanted to talk to me. That means a lot. This whole time I had been thinking she might still hate me, but now I'm reassured that she really did love me like I loved, and still love, her.

After Delia died, I spent weeks in my room, barely ever getting out of bed. I physically couldn't bring myself to do anything. Getting out of bed became a struggle every day; it was like my body hurt to drag itself up. All day, my thoughts would be totally consumed by Delia. It came to the point where I wanted to stop myself from having any thoughts at all, which is practically impossible, because even when you're trying not to think, you're still thinking. I just needed everything to be quiet. I didn't want to speak, I didn't want to think, I didn't want to do anything. It was a vicious cycle of my mind attacking me and ruining me, followed by my mum trying to solve things.

I remember each day that followed Delia's death. Three days after she died, they held her funeral. I went with my mum and Caleb. I thought I would be able to not cry too much, but I was very wrong.

We sat in the front row of the church, which was possibly one of the biggest mistakes I made that day. The whole time, all I could look at was her casket and think that she was there, but she wasn't really *there*. I would never get to see her eyes again or hear her laugh or hold her small hand in mine. I cried the whole timel; I couldn't even focus on anything else. People kept coming over to me to ask if I was okay, and I would nod and tell them I was fine through all my tears. That was probably the worst day of my entire life because that was the day she truly left. That was the last day I would ever see her.

After the funeral, she was buried at the cemetery. I stayed in the car because I couldn't bear the thought of having to stand by her grave. I watched from afar, holding on to a white daisy because daisies were her favorite. With all my nerves and sadness, I ended up unintentionally plucking off all the petals. I waited until everyone left before I got out of the car. I got a new daisy and placed it on top of her casket. I didn't say good-bye; I told her I loved her.

Those were the last words I spoke for months.

My mum thought I wasn't speaking after the funeral because I was so sad. She was right. I don't think anyone suspected I would stop talking forever. They thought it was just a temporary effect of my grief. I did too, at first. But then it got to the point where I didn't want to talk to anyone about anything. I wanted to keep to myself and not have to answer anyone's questions. It was easier that way. Plus, if Delia wasn't there to talk to, I didn't see the point.

Once I hadn't spoken or left the house for three weeks, my mum decided it was best that I get a therapist, even though I refused. At this point, I was completely falling behind in school,

I hadn't seen anyone but my mum and Caleb, and I was sinking deeper and deeper into depression. There was nothing I could do to stop myself from getting so bad. I had lost control over my mind and believed the world was out to get me.

The first therapist I saw was Dr. Watson. She preferred to have me call her by her last name, and I never even found out her first name. I suspect it was something like Gretchen; that would have fit her well. She was at least sixty years old, with thin-rimmed glasses that always slid down her nose. Dr. Watson didn't help me cope much. She would just ask me questions; she wouldn't give me any solutions. I also wouldn't give her answers, so I'm partially to blame for that. But she's the one that diagnosed me with clinical depression and suggested I start taking medication. My mum was hesitant to sign off, because at the time I was only sixteen, and she didn't want me to be hooked on depression meds the rest of my life.

It took one week after I met Dr. Watson for Mum to sign the forms allowing me to be medicated.

That week I had my first bad panic attack. I remember it vividly. I was asleep and having a nightmare about Delia. I could see her getting into the car accident, except I was the one driving, and she was in the passenger seat. I saw her unconscious, but I was fine and left without any injuries. I couldn't help her, I couldn't even reach her. The EMT's were screaming at me, saying I killed her.

Then I woke up, drenched in sweat and with my heart was racing. I could barely breathe or feel any part of my body. I was completely numb and shaking uncontrollably. I had no idea what was happening, and it still felt like I was dreaming. I woke up from a nightmare to reality, which wasn't much better.

My mum was instantly at my bedside—apparently, I had been punching the wall while I slept. She rushed me to the emergency room, where I was carted off to an area of the hospital that was only separated by thin curtains.

I was there for a day. It was the first time in my life that I had ever had a panic attack, had to be connected to oxygen, and had to be admitted into the emergency room. None of that helped my situation at all; I think it just made it worse. That's when I realized how bad I really was, and I thought I was at the point of no return. At that moment, I was more afraid of living than I was of dying. That's what scared me the most.

I started Citalopram the day after I left the hospital. Dr. Watson explained to me how my brain needed help with the reuptake of some neurotransmitters and a bunch of stuff I didn't really care about. I didn't think the pills would help, but I took them, mostly because I was being told to. I didn't understand anything she told me anyway.

I also was forced to go to teen therapy sessions. I went to one every week for five weeks. It didn't help me at all. I had nothing to share since I didn't talk. There was no point in me being there. All it did was make me see how messed up I was. I didn't connect to anyone there like doctors said I would. I felt more alone than I ever had.

Surprisingly, Citalopram helped, and I've been on it ever since. When I would get better though, I would stop taking it, or sometimes I didn't want to be dependent on it anymore, so I just wouldn't take it for a few days. The longest was three weeks. That's when things got *really* bad.

When it got to that really bad place—and I mean, really bad—I was admitted to the psychiatric ward of a hospital that was three hours away. I was hardly sleeping, eating, or having any sort of communication with my mum. She was worried I would never want to speak again, which I didn't. She, as well as my therapist at the time—who I think was my third one—decided it would be best if I was sent there. They said I had selective mutism, meaning I chose not to speak. Most selective mutes only speak where they are comfortable, but of course I was the abnormal patient that spoke to absolutely no one. I don't like using that term, because it makes it seem like I made the choice to be like this. Which I did not. This all just crept up on me and turned me into a completely different person.

I stayed at the hospital for almost a month. I was on a constant schedule. They told me when I could eat, when to take my pills, when to sleep. I basically didn't have too much of a choice in anything. I spent most of the time in solitude, because who really wants to have a conversation with someone who won't respond?

Being there did help a little. Once Delia passed, I didn't communicate with anyone besides my mum. I would occasionally nod or shrug, but that was about it. I would carry a notepad around sometimes, but would only write notes when absolutely necessary. Then one of the doctors at the facility showed me how to use the speak setting on my phone. That became my way of communication. Slowly, I started conversing with others through my phone. I was finally feeling slightly better, like things were actually looking up. Not by much, but it was a start.

They even had a tutor for me at the hospital. I didn't pay attention to anything because I didn't really care. Education wasn't my top priority, not that I had any priorities. Shortly after, I decided it was best to drop out of school altogether. It was causing me more stress and not doing me any good. Looking back now, I kind of wish I'd stayed in school.

After I left the hospital, nothing changed. I was still depressed and angry all the time. The pills made it slightly more tolerable, but not by much. I was still miserable.

Now I'm here, halfway across the world. I never would have thought I'd be in this position. If someone told me months ago that I'd be living with my dad in Maine, actually speaking and having a solid group of friends, I would've thought they were joking.

But my reality is no longer a nightmare. I can breathe easy again, most of the time. It's like a spark was lit inside me and keeps glimmering even in my darkest moments when I think it's blown out.

I just told Delilah all of that. She knows almost everything there is to know. I have never opened up to anyone about most of those feelings and experiences. It feels nice to finally get it all out, as if a weight has been lifted off my shoulders. Now I don't have to hold it all inside me. It's out in the open now and is no longer tying me down. Writing it all down was almost like letting it go, like I don't have to keep all that a secret anymore from Delilah. She knows my full story now.

As we sit together after everything I revealed, it's clear Delilah isn't judging me for it, and it's not changing her perception of me. She's accepting it and understanding. Delilah isn't telling me how I should feel or not feel. She's just letting me be me. She's fine with me.

That's the best thing I could've asked for.

Chapter Thirty

LEVI

After an emotional rollercoaster, with crying and sadness and hugging, Delilah and I decide we should go do something. We need to be happier. I don't really want to, but I don't want to sit inside and wallow in my sadness either. We're about to go for a walk when I look out the window and see what's outside.

Snow.

In the past hour, at least four inches of snow has blanketed the ground.

I point outside continuously until Delilah looks over.

"What?" she asks, walking over to the window. "Oh, it's still snowing? It started a little when I came over," she says. She sounds unhappy about the snow. But this is the coolest thing I've ever seen!

I smile widely and run outside.

"Levi, you're gonna freeze! It's just snow!" Delilah says, laughing. She stands in the doorway with her arms wrapped around herself.

I stop in the middle of the driveway with my arms open wide and stick out my tongue. The snowflakes feel extremely cold against my skin. They melt within seconds. I try to see the shapes, but they're so tiny I can't.

I pick up a handful of snow and try to make a snowball like I've seen in movies, but it's a lot harder than it looks. My hands freeze within seconds. I didn't realize snow was this cold.

"You're acting like you've never seen snow before!" Delilah yells from inside. "Wait, this is the first time you've seen snow, isn't it?"

I nod quickly and run back inside. I put on my jacket, beanie, and gloves, despite the fact I'm already cold and somewhat wet. I grab Delilah's hand and try to bring her outside.

"All I have is a jacket to keep me warm!" she says.

I quickly go into my room to search for my other beanies and a pair of gloves. I throw each at Delilah, and she tries to catch but misses.

I wait impatiently while she puts everything on. Once she is ready, I run back outside.

"By the time it's Christmas, you're gonna hate the snow," Delilah tells me.

I shake my head and stick my tongue out at her. I could never hate the snow; this is amazing.

I try to make another snowball, and this time it comes out better. I throw it at Delilah, and she shrieks when it hits her.

"Hey!" she yells, making a snowball too. She tosses it at me, and I laugh.

This is so fun. I could stay out here forever. The snow is so cool, not just in the literal way.

I march through the snow, listening to it crunch under my feet. My feet sink deep with every step. I can feel snow soaking through my shoes, but I don't care. It looks so pretty and clean and white.

Delilah is far behind me, so I walk back over to her. She's kneeling in the snow, making what looks like a giant snowball. I look at her in confusion.

"You're kidding, right?" she asks.

I shake my head.

"You don't even know how to make a snowman?"

I widen my eyes in excitement and kneel down beside her. She rolls the snowball across the lawn, which makes it bigger. I'm amazed at how the snow just sticks together like that. I can't stop smiling.

The snow continues to fall quickly, and I'm freezing. I don't care, because I'm having so much fun. We lift the snowman's head onto the body, and it looks so cool. I never thought I'd make a snowman. I never thought I'd ever see snow. I feel like a little kid again.

I find two big sticks and use them for arms. We go inside in search for a carrot nose, but find nothing, which is upsetting. It can't be a snowman without a carrot nose. The first snowman I make has to be great. I only find one glove for the snowman, so I get an oven mitt for the other hand.

"I think Lucy has a snowman kit," Delilah says. "Wanna go get it?"

I nod enthusiastically and quickly go back outside. I walk through the snow as fast as possible to get to Delilah's house. When we go inside, Delilah's mom is pulling a boot onto Lucy's foot. She's wearing a snowsuit and thick gloves. She looks like a pink marshmallow.

"Levi!" she shrieks through the scarf that's wrapped around her face.

I wave, which feels weird since my hand is frozen.

"Are you two cold?" Delilah's mom asks in concern.

"We're fine," Delilah says, but I know she's chilled. She looks over at me and says, "I'm gonna go look for the snowman kit."

I follow her downstairs and help look. We find it behind a toolbox, and we both reach for it at the same time. She laughs and lets me take it.

"After we finish the snowman, should we make hot chocolate?" she asks while walking back upstairs.

I nod, even though she can't see me since she's in front. She turns around, however, to see my answer.

"You've had hot chocolate, right?" she asks.

I nod again. There's hot chocolate in Australia.

"Okay, good," she says, smiling.

"We're making a snowman?!" Lucy yells excitedly when she sees me holding the kit.

I nod.

"I knew you'd wanna come," Delilah says. "C'mon, let's go. Just promise you won't get too cold and make us go inside."

"I pinky promise. I never ever get too cold!"

"She gets cold within five minutes," Delilah whispers to me.

We walk back to my house, which takes forever since Lucy has trouble walking through the snow. Her legs can't move very well in her snowsuit, and the snow is deep for her since she's so short. I hold her hand to help her, or else she'd fall down.

On the way past Aiden's, he opens the door, with Hunter next to him. "Making a snowman?" Aiden asks.

"Yeah!" Lucy yells. "Hi, Aiden! Hi, Hunter!"

She waves her hand, even though her arm can only move up a few inches with her jacket on.

"We're going sledding!" Hunter yells.

"Have fun!" Delilah tells them.

Aiden rolls his eyes. "Oh, we will!"

We keep walking to my house, until Lucy starts to complain.

"It's . . . too . . . hard . . . to . . . walk!" Lucy yells. She says each word in time with a step.

"We're almost there," Delilah tells her.

"But the snow's not letting me go!" Lucy shrieks.

I laugh and keep walking with Lucy. She pouts and whines until she sees the snowman. She runs over to it in excitement.

"Can we name it, can we name it, can we name it?" she asks quickly, like it's one word.

"Name it whatever you want," Delilah tells her.

"I wanna name it . . . Olaf!"

"Of course you do."

"Olaf is my friend," she says, hugging the snowman. The head nearly tumbles down, but I manage to stop it. "Oopsies," Lucy says quietly.

I put the fake, plastic carrot nose onto Olaf's face. It's a little lopsided, but it looks okay. Lucy puts on the buttons, and Delilah wraps the scarf around it—or should I say him? The wind keeps blowing the hat off, so we decide not to use it.

When we're done, we take a step back and look at our creation. I can't believe I actually made it.

"I love Olaf!" Lucy shrieks.

I look at the snowman and start crying again. I can't seem to stop. The tears just keep coming. I sit down in the snow and sob. Lucy looks up at me with a worried expression.

"Levi is crying," she whispers to Delilah.

"Why don't you go try to build a little snowman so Olaf can have a friend?" Delilah tells her.

"Okay!" Lucy says, going over to another part of the yard.

Delilah comes and sits beside me. I can't stop thinking about Delia's message. She would have loved to see snow and build a snowman. We could have made hot chocolate afterward too. There's so much we could've done, but will never have the chance to experience together.

"I know you're thinking about Delia," she says. She always seems to know what I'm thinking. "You're probably thinking about the message. And you're probably thinking about how you and Delia could have done all this together."

I nod and wipe under my eyes, but end up getting a bunch of snow on my face. Delilah doesn't say anything for a while.

"I really am sorry. I hope one day you can find true happiness again. We'll work on it though, okay?" she whispers.

I nod and sniff.

"Do you want to go inside? It's okay if you do. I totally understand if you want to be by yourself," she says quietly.

I shake my head. I don't want to be by myself. I want to not think about Delia, and I know that if I go back into my room, I'll think about her even more and be sadder. I don't want to deal with the feeling of being alone right now.

I need someone.

Delilah smiles a little. "Are you sure?"

I nod.

We walk over to Lucy, who is struggling to build a snowman by herself.

"Are you okay now?" Lucy asks, taking her attention away from the pile of snow that is supposed to be a snowman.

I sniff and nod. I try to muster a smile.

"Good. I don't wanna see you sad!"

Delilah smiles and nudges my shoulder.

Lucy pokes my leg, so I bend down to her height.

"Look-it," she says, pointing into my backyard. I look over to where she's pointing, and there's a deer. I'm used to seeing kangaroos occasionally outside in Australia, but not deer.

I stare in amazement, and Delilah finally notices it too.

"Don't make any noise—not that you would," she says, smiling.

"It's Sven!" Lucy whispers excitedly. She starts running to it, but Delilah grabs her arm.

"Just watch Sven from over here," she says.

"Why? He's my friend," Lucy pouts.

"He's, uh, not in a friendly mood today?" Delilah says.

"Can I see him tomorrow?"

"Maybe."

Lucy turns around, but I can't stop watching the deer. It's so pretty and peaceful. I'm seeing so many new things today. Delia would have loved the deer too.

After making some snow angels, Lucy gets cold, as expected, but I am too. I'm worn out from all the crying as well. We head back to Delilah's house, but this time I carry Lucy so the walk is faster.

When we get there, Delilah's mom spends a few minutes getting Lucy out of all of her snow gear. While she does that, Delilah and I make hot chocolate. I don't really do much except stand in the kitchen wrapped in a blanket. I'm not used to being this cold. I didn't feel cold while we were outside, but now that we're inside, I feel like I have hypothermia.

"Can you go get the milk?" Delilah asks.

I head over to the fridge and grab the milk, which is very hard to do while wrapped in a blanket. Delilah laughs as she watches me struggle to hold the milk.

"You're such a dork," she says through giggles.

I scrunch my nose and feel my cheeks blush. I pull my blanket tighter around me.

Delilah finishes making the hot chocolate and pours two mugs. Lucy ended up falling asleep a few minutes after we got back.

We sit on the couch drinking the hot chocolate, and I'm finally warming up. I thought I'd never be warm again. I tug at the blanket so it covers my feet.

"I hope you like my blanket that you stole," Delilah says jokingly. "You're lucky I like you enough to let you have it."

I reach over and wrap my arms around her so she's inside the blanket too. Her laugh is muffled by my shoulder. We rearrange how we're sitting so we can both fit under the blanket comfortably. We could probably just find another blanket, but we don't.

Delilah looks over to me and smiles. I can feel her hands beside mine underneath the blanket.

For the first time in forever (yes, I'm quoting *Frozen*), I'm happy.

Chapter Thirty-One

LEVI

Once I got home from Delilah's the other day, reality sunk in and I was upset. But what else is new.

I had a great time with Delilah and Lucy when it snowed, but being that happy made me more upset. I feel guilty, even though Delia said that she wants me to be happy. It's just so hard. My sadness is a part of me now. I'm not automatically going to become happy. It's going to take a lot to do that. I'm not sure if I'll ever be fully happy without feeling slightly guilty.

The voice mail really messed with my emotions. It wasn't what I was expecting at all. I don't really know what I was expecting, but it definitely wasn't that. I'm not sure if it would have made things easier if she'd said she was mad at me, like I thought she was. I just wish I could have one more day with her and settle everything. But now I'll never know what could have, or would have, happened to us. I'll always wonder.

That night, I was awake for hours, just thinking about Delia. Nights will always be the hardest for me. I really am trying to get better, but it seems impossible sometimes.

So for the past few days, I've locked myself in my room like I usually do. Delilah's texted me a few times asking how I am, but I haven't responded. I just can't right now.

I've been thinking a lot about Delilah too. I'm really conflicted by everything about her. She makes me very happy, but she makes me sad too. It's so confusing. *She's* so confusing. I also haven't really wanted to see Delilah, but at the same time, I want to. Like I said, it's confusing.

When I was at her house, wrapped up in her blanket, I panicked. I don't know if it was because we were so close, or because I could smell her perfume, which reminded me of Delia even though it smelled nothing like Delia, or if it was just everything. I feel like I'm getting too attached. That's what always happens, and then something goes wrong.

I'm afraid of losing something, or someone, that means a lot to me again. I don't like how I'm becoming so close to Delilah; it scares me. So I had a small anxiety attack on the couch once I started thinking about Delilah, and Delia, and the voice mail and everything else that's happening. It all hit me at once, and I freaked out.

I've been avoiding her ever since. I feel bad that I always react that way when something happens, but it's just what I do. It's who I am.

Thankfully, Delilah isn't working when I go to my appointment with Candace. I don't know what I would have done if she was there. She makes me feel so many things all at once.

I *hate* it.

Candace is her usual chirpy self. I'm my usual depressed self.

"How are you today, Levi?" Candace asks.

That's when I break.

I tell her everything. Well, I write it on the whiteboard. It takes a really long time. I tell her how I listened to the voice mail and how I'm feeling about Delilah. I've been opening up a little more every visit. I think it's because I've been taking my pills continuously now. They've been making me do things that are so unlike me.

Or maybe I'm changing, I don't know.

Before I know it, I'm crying as usual. I blame the pills for crying so much too.

Candace always comforts me when I cry like this, and I find it extremely awkward. I don't even know why I cry half the time. It just happens. I'm constantly overcome with emotions. That's another thing I hate too. Whenever I cry, I try to stop myself. I end up breathing weirdly and getting the hiccups—it's awful.

Candace tells me that she's happy I listened to the voice mail. She asks if I've listened to it more than once, and I have.

I've listened to it every day, hoping to figure things out. I think it's just making things worse, though.

Candace says that probably isn't helping my situation. She says I need to live in the present, and try to not let the past hurt so much.

But the past is hurting me while making me happy too. Just like the present is.

"Levi," Candace says, once I'm done crying. I wipe my wet cheeks and look at her.

She gets up and hands me a small notepad. "I want you to make a list of things that make you happy. Keep this with you all week. When you find something that makes you happy, or smile or laugh, write it down. Bring it with you when you come next week, and we'll go through it. Does that sound like something you can do?"

I nod and take the notepad from her, sticking it in my pocket.

"Being happy isn't a bad thing, I promise."

I shrug and grab a tissue from the table.

"Now that you're becoming more open with things, I think it's time that you try a support group again too," she says, smiling kindly.

I shake my head quickly. She always tries to get me to go to a support group, but I refuse.

She sighs lightly. "I really think it would help. What about just one person?"

I shrug. One person would be better than a lot. If I have to, I guess.

"There's a new patient, Mitchell. You two have some similarities. I think you could really help each other."

I rest my head in my hand and sniff a little.

"Only if you want to, of course. I help him as well. I think he's here for speech therapy tonight," Candace says, standing up from her seat. She looks through a calendar and sits back down. "Actually, he's here right now. I think you two should meet. Want me to go get him?"

If I had my choice, I'd say no. I think I nod, though. Which is weird because my mind is saying no, but I'm nodding. I stop nodding, and I am feeling a bit confused as to what I just did. I roll my eyes at my stupidity.

Candace smiles and heads out to the waiting room. She comes back after a few minutes with whom I assume is Mitchell. He stands shyly behind Candace, looking down at his feet.

He's not what I expected at all. He has purple hair and a band shirt on. But he's wearing black jeans and Converse, so I guess he's okay. At least he dresses better than Aiden.

"Levi, this is Mitchell. Mitchell, that's Levi," Candace says, introducing us. I wave, and Mitchell waves back. He takes a small step forward.

I quickly rub my eyes, hoping it's not noticeable that I've been crying.

"You can sit right there," Candace tells Mitchell. He slowly sits across from me and avoids making eye contact. "Pretend I'm not here," Candace says, sitting in her chair.

I'm wondering if he doesn't talk either. Because how are we supposed to get anything accomplished if neither of us talk? Yes, two mutes sitting silently, having a wonderful time passing notes to one another. I'm dreading this already.

"Go ahead, Mitchell. Do what we've practiced," Candace whispers. Mitchell looks from Candace to me and hesitantly opens and closes his mouth a few times.

"H-Hi, I'm—I'm Mitchell," he finally says quietly. He blushes, then looks down and nervously bites his nails.

"Good, Mitchell, good job," Candace whispers happily.

I type into my phone, "Nice to meet you."

He smiles a little.

I type more into my phone. "My friend Caleb likes Green Day too. It's his favorite band." I point to his shirt, which has Green Day on it.

"Th-That's c-cool," Mitchell says, smiling for real this time.

I nod and type more. "I like their song 'Carpe Diem,' but that's it. I'm not really into music. Green Day I can tolerate, sometimes."

Mitchell laughs nervously and plays with the hem of his shirt. "I-I like a-all their s-songs."

We sit awkwardly, not knowing what else to say.

"Levi, tell him where you're from," Candace whispers to me, obviously trying to help the conversation.

"I'm from Australia," I type.

"Th-That's c-cool."

Mitchell says *cool* a lot.

I shrug. "I was kinda in the middle of nowhere, but yeah, I guess."

Mitchell points to my phone. "C-Can you t-talk?"

I feel my cheeks blush. I nod. "I just don't want to."

"Oh," Mitchell says, taking a deep breath. "Th-That's cool." He twiddles his thumbs, and finally looks up at me.

I wonder why Mitchell stutters. If it's something he's always had, or if it's nerves. But it's okay. After we talk for a while, I don't notice it as much. He says cool at least ten times, but that's okay too. I cry too much, he says cool too much. Everyone has their things. But the more we talk, the less he says cool and the less I feel like crying.

I actually kind of like "talking" to Mitchell. He's not so bad. Candace was right, it might help. We're sort of alike, I guess, in the talking area, anyways. He said he doesn't like Skittles, and I almost ended it right then and there, but I didn't. I'm not sure why.

I don't know what's happening to me. Old Levi would have never given Mitchell a chance.

"I-I'll see y-you around, Levi?" Mitchell says once we've been talking almost an hour. He says it more like a question, like he's unsure I'll want to see him again.

"Yeah," I type. "I'll see you later."

Chapter Thirty-Two

LEVI

I'm about to video chat my mum when Delilah shows up at my house. People always seem to show up whenever I video chat someone. I don't mind, though. Then my mum has someone to actually talk to.

I'm not avoiding Delilah anymore. Actually, we've been hanging out for the past few days. Candace, and Aiden too, helped me realize that avoiding her isn't going to help anything. I can't try to push away all the feelings I have when I'm around her; I have to try to figure them out.

I don't like trying to figure out my feelings, though. It's very confusing for me.

"Hey!" Delilah says, sitting beside me on my bed.

I smile at her and wave.

"I was thinking, since I probably won't have school again tomorrow, maybe we could go see a movie or something?" she asks, propping herself up on her elbow. She's been off from school the past two days due to the snow.

I nod. My laptop starts ringing.

"Oh, were you about to video chat Caleb or something? I can go," she says, getting up. I pull her back down beside me and accept my mum's call.

"Hi, Levi! Hi?" my mum says, seeming confused as to why there's an unfamiliar girl beside me on my bed. I can see why she looks concerned.

I look over at Delilah.

"Hi! I'm Delilah! I'm Levi's . . . friend!" Delilah says.

"Oh, I've heard about you! Nice to meet you!" my mum says.

Delilah's cheeks blush, and she looks at me from the corner of her eyes and smirks. "Oh?"

"How's the weather?" my mum asks in an attempt to change the subject.

"Snowy. Cold," Delilah says.

"It's pretty warm up here. Do you miss the warm weather, Levi?"

I shake my head. I like the snow.

"He likes the snow a lot," Delilah says, laughing, as if she can read my mind. "He just gets cold really quickly and steals all the blankets."

My mum laughs, and I can tell she's suspicious that something is going on between Delilah and me.

Which there isn't.

"Do you have plans for Christmas?" Delilah asks my mum.

Mum gets quiet. "I'm not sure. It'll be just me since Levi's not here. Caleb's family invited me over, so I may be with them."

I never even thought about the fact she'd be alone on Christmas. She's alone every day. I wonder what she does without me around. I wonder if she's constantly worried about me. Her time used to be spent caring for me, but now I'm not there for her to look after.

"Oh," Delilah says, not quite knowing how to respond. "I'm sure whatever you do will be great!"

"I hope so. Christmas won't be the same without Levi."

I bite down on my lip, suddenly missing my mum more than ever. It's been so long since I've seen her. I don't like thinking about the fact she'll be alone on Christmas. My being in Maine is probably harder on her than it is on me.

Not long into the video chat, Delilah's phone rings. She leaves the room and returns after a few minutes.

"That was work. I guess they need me to come in. Do you think you could watch Lucy for me? My parents are going out in an hour, and I was supposed to watch her," Delilah says quickly.

I'm not sure I can take care of Lucy on my own. It shouldn't be that hard, though. She's a pretty simple kid. I nod slowly.

"Really? You're the best. Okay, I'll be right back!" Delilah says.

When she leaves, my mom starts talking about her and asking me questions.

"Is she your girlfriend?" she asks.

I shake my head, feeling my cheeks heat up.

"Do you want her to be?"

I shrug and nervously chew on my bottom lip.

"It's okay if you do," Mum reassures me.

My mum knows about the voice mail. I played it for her the day after I listened to it because I needed advice. I was so upset, and I knew Mum would be able to talk me through it. I thought about asking my dad about it too, but decided against it. He didn't know Delia, so he probably wouldn't have been much help. My mum thought it was extremely sad, but said it should give me hope for the future. Those were her exact words.

I blankly stare at my mum through the computer.

"I like her. She's very nice," my mum says.

I nod slowly.

Delilah comes back a little later with Lucy, who is very excited to see me.

"Levi!" she shrieks, jumping up and down. I pull her up onto the bed, and she waves to my mum. "Are you Levi's mommy?"

"I am! And who are you?"

"I'm Lucy. I'm three." Lucy always introduces herself by telling her age. "I'll be four in, uh, Janwary?" She pronounces it wrong, but it's cute.

"It's in February," Delilah tells her, laughing.

"Febwary. I'll be four in Febwary!" Lucy says excitedly.

"That's great!" my mum says, sounding as excited as Lucy.

Delilah tries to hug Lucy before leaving, but she squirms away from her and clings to me. I put Lucy on my lap, and she leans against me.

"Bye-bye, Lila!" Lucy says as Delilah leaves. She has a hard time saying Delilah, so she calls her Lila sometimes. I like that nickname.

"Bye, Lucy! Be good for Levi, okay?"

"I will!"

Lucy grabs both my hands and puts them in front of her, and she holds tightly onto them. She moves them and claps them in front of her, giggling every few minutes as my mum talks.

"Whoaaaa," Lucy says, pressing my hand to her face. "It's as big as my head!" she shrieks, even though it's muffled by my hand.

I laugh and pull my hand away from her face. She continues to hold my hands as I video chat.

My mum tells me how Caleb is doing. It's summertime in Australia, so he's not in classes right now. By this time next year, he'll be done with school. I wonder where I'll be a year from now.

Once we're done video chatting, I say bye to my mum, and Lucy complains she's hungry.

"I want fruit snacks," she says as she follows me into the kitchen.

I have to lift Lucy up to set her in a chair while I search for fruit snacks in the kitchen. We don't have any, though. I knew we wouldn't—I don't think we've ever had fruit snacks.

Lucy ends up having cookies, and I'm afraid she'll choke from talking with so much food in her mouth. Thankfully, she doesn't. I don't know what I would've done if she had choked.

"Can we play hide and seek?" Lucy asks when she finishes her cookies.

I nod.

"I'll count first!" Lucy says, jumping off her chair and covering her eyes. "One, two, three . . ."

I quickly walk to the closest hiding spot I see, which is under the table. I almost hit my head, but I don't.

"Ten!" Lucy yells.

She turns around and runs down the hallway, oblivious to the fact that I was hiding right next to her.

I hear her footsteps run back to where I am a few minutes later. She looks behind the couch, as if I could possibly fit behind there, and then she finally finds me.

"I got you! I was super-duper fast. You gotta try to do better!" she yells, laughing. "Your turn to count!"

I count in my head, giving Lucy more time than she gave me. I wait until I can't hear her footsteps anymore, and then I search. It can't be that hard to find her.

I look under the table because I remember when I was little, I would always hide wherever someone else had. She's not under there. I check my room; she's not there either.

I start to get worried after a few minutes go by and I still haven't found her.

I check every single room in my house. She's so small, she could fit practically anywhere. But she's nowhere to be found.

I get even more worried when I realize the back door is open.

She couldn't have gone outside, could she?

I notice the tiny footprints in the snow.

She's definitely out there.

I quickly put on my jacket and shoes to go find Lucy. I can't believe she went outside. Isn't the first rule of hide and seek to not go outside? Are there even rules to hide and seek?

My heart starts pounding, and my hands start shaking. I can't get a panic attack now. Deep breaths, Levi. I focus on the footprints instead of my anxiety.

How have I lost Lucy when I've only been with her for less than two hours?

196

When I get to the trees in my backyard, I can't see any foot-prints. I check the obvious spots behind bushes and trees, but there's no Lucy.

This can't be happening. I debate texting Delilah or Aiden, but I don't want them to not trust me. The first job I have been given, and I mess up. I screw everything up.

Of course my dad is at work too. There's no one to help me.

If I were a three-year-old, where would I hide? She probably isn't too far. I walk through the woods that are connected to my backyard, listening for Lucy.

It's been over ten minutes. How far could she have gone?

After fifteen minutes of searching, I'm about to break down. I'm so scared I'll never find her. She could be anywhere. We never should have played hide and seek. Trying to find a three-year-old hiding in the snow is nearly impossible. There are so many differ-ent places she could be.

I notice a pink ribbon in the snow, the same pink ribbon Lucy had in her hair today. She has to be somewhere around here.

My breathing has been quickening, and I'm trying so hard not to hyperventilate. The freezing temperature outside isn't helping either.

I realize that in order to find Lucy, she's either going to have to be calling for me or I have to call for her.

But I can't call for her. I *can't.*

My heart rate increases even more, and it feels like my heart is about to burst through my chest. I open my mouth, but close it.

I can't. I don't even know if I *can* talk anymore.

I shake my head and shut my eyes tightly. Maybe this is all just a bad nightmare. I open my eyes, and I'm still standing amongst a hundred trees. I tug at the ends of my hair and crouch down in the snow. How could I have been this stupid? I rub my eyes to try to stop myself from crying and stand up as best as I can with my shaky legs. I feel like I'm about to pass out. Everything is getting blurry. I quickly blink and take some deep breaths.

I clear my throat and lick my lips. I take another deep breath and slowly let it out.

That's when I hear her call my name.

"Levi!" I hear someone say quietly.

I turn around to where I heard her voice, and see Lucy sitting down in the snow, tears streaming down her face. She's hugging her knees to her chest, and her cheeks are pink.

I run over to her and pick her up, wrapping her in my jacket to try to get her warmer.

"You didn't find me," she chokes out. "It took you so long, I got scared. I saw Sven, and—and, I wanted to give him a hug, so I went outside and he came out here and then I didn't know where I was and you weren't here and it's so cold out and I was so scared," she says in one long sentence through her sobs.

She wraps her arms around my neck, still crying.

I feel like the worst person in the whole world. She's so upset. I'm happy I found her, but I'm so mad at myself for losing her. I walk back to my house, my heart still racing. I can feel Lucy shivering.

"I'm so scared," she says again. "I thought you'd never find me."

I take a deep breath and ignore my racing heart. "You'll be okay," I whisper. "I'm sorry."

"You—You talked," Lucy says, picking her head up from my shoulder.

"Yeah," I whisper.

I forgot what my voice even sounded like. It's lower than I remember. I know that if I want to comfort Lucy, I'll have to talk. She's so frightened right now, I can't not talk to her.

"I thought you couldn't," she says quietly.

I shake my head.

"I just wanna go home," she says.

I take her back to my house and give her one of my sweatshirts to wear, even though it's longer than her whole body. I wrap her in two blankets and put her in front of the heater, worried that she'll never warm up.

I sit with her on the couch for a while because she's so scared. She cries for a very long time, which is expected. She was outside alone for over twenty minutes. I'd be scared too if I were her.

I text Delilah to tell her what happened. She responds, saying she'll be over soon.

"Levi," Lucy whispers while she's laying on top of me.

I raise my eyebrows.

"Tell me a happy story."

I clear my throat, unsure I want to talk again. But seeing Lucy so upset, I give in and tell her a story. I look up a book on my phone that my parents used to read to me when I was younger—*Oh, The Places You'll Go!* by Dr. Seuss. It seems kind of long, so I decide to only read a piece of it.

I take a deep breath and clear my throat. I start to read from the beginning of the book.

"I like the way you talk," Lucy says after I read the second page. "Keep going."

I laugh. "You have feet in your shoes."

"I'm not wearing shoes."

"Pretend you are."

"Okay."

I continue reading. "You can steer yourself any direction you choose."

"I won't follow Sven anymore."

"That's a good idea."

After I finish a few pages, I realize my heart rate has finally slowed down. I'm out of breath from the talking, though.

"What's a slump?" Lucy asks after a few minutes.

"Huh?"

"Read where it said *slump*."

I look for the part she's talking about. "And when you're in a slump, you're not in for much fun. Un-slumping yourself is not easily done."

"What does it mean?"

199

I take a second to think about it. "It means if you're feeling upset, it's hard to be happy again. But you can do it."

"Like you?"

I'm taken aback by her comment.

"Yeah," I say quietly.

"You can get un-slumped then, right?"

I nod slowly.

"Good," she says, cuddling closer to me. She shuts her eyes, probably exhausted by today's events.

I am too.

It's weird to be talking again. I forgot I even had a voice. I've become so used to not talking that now it's a struggle to say anything at all. It feels abnormal to speak, like it's not natural. I'm not sure I want to have anyone else know I talked. I don't think I'm ready for that just yet or if I ever will be. This may be a one-time thing.

Delilah comes after awhile, running inside.

"Is she okay? What happened? Levi, I'm so sorry. I shouldn't have left you alone … I'm so sorry."

I can tell that Delilah raced to get here. She's breathing quickly and her cheeks are bright red. She must have been so stressed and worried.

I take out my phone to type something, then decide not to. "It's okay," I tell her quietly, feeling my cheeks heat up.

"No, it's—Wait, did you just talk?" Delilah says.

"He talks now," Lucy says quietly.

"Yeah, I talk now."

Delilah runs over to me and hugs me tightly.

"I thought I'd never hear your voice," she whispers.

"I know. Me too."

Chapter Thirty-Three

DELILAH

I can't believe Levi actually *spoke* yesterday. It doesn't even seem real. Yesterday, when he talked, I thought I was imagining things. I hugged him for so long, I even started crying.

He made Lucy and me promise not to tell anyone, though. He's not ready to speak to anyone else, which is understandable. He went months without saying a word, so it's not like he's going to instantly switch and talk nonstop. It makes me happy that he's only talking to us right now. I guess I mean more to Levi than I thought.

I don't know what I expected Levi's voice to sound like, but it's better than I could have ever imagined. I almost forgot about the fact that he's Australian and would talk with an accent. I could listen to him talk all day. Right now, however, he talks in a whisper, and it's a little shaky and hesitant. He clears his throat a lot too, and it's like his voice is fragile and could break any second. I'm so afraid he'll stop talking again, and this will only last for a short time. I hope he never stops. With Levi, however, I can never be sure. He could never speak again.

All day I've been waiting to get home just so I can talk to Levi, and he can talk to me. As I'm walking out of the school, I notice someone in all black leaning against a tree. That someone could only be Levi.

I walk over to Levi, which is hard because the sidewalk is frozen over. I finally make it over to him, but slip on the ice that's in front of him. He reaches out quickly and catches me before I fall, tightly holding on to me.

"Thanks," I whisper, realizing how close his face is to mine.

"You literally just fell for me," he says, quietly laughing. I feel my cheeks heat up, and I quickly stand, regaining my balance.

"You did not just say that," I say, embarrassed.

"I did," he says, biting down on his bottom lip. "Is that okay?"

"Yeah, it's okay," I say, laughing. I decide to change the subject to avoid any more awkwardness. "So what are you doing here?"

"I wanted to see you," he tells me. Now his cheeks are turning red.

"Oh," I say, smiling.

"Did you want to see me?" he says quietly.

"Yeah, of course I did." I nudge his shoulder, and he scrunches his nose at me.

We head toward my car, which isn't too far. I'm guessing Levi's dad drove him here since Levi doesn't have his license. That's why we always walk everywhere, but now it's too cold to stay outside for very long.

We pass by Mitchell and Levi waves. I didn't know they knew each other.

"You've met him before?" I ask.

"Yeah. At therapy. He's cool."

"He says cool a lot."

He looks down at my hand and slowly reaches for it, entwining his fingers with mine. I get butterflies in my stomach, not expecting that at all.

"Is this okay?" he asks again.

"Yes, Levi, it's okay," I tell him. It's cute how he's so nervous and unsure.

"Your hands are cold," he says, pulling my hand into his jacket pocket. He's still holding onto my hand once it's inside, like he doesn't want to let go.

I notice that there's not a lighter or a pack of cigarettes. They're always in this pocket.

"No cigarettes?" I ask.

"No. I stopped a month ago."

"You did?"

"Yeah," he says, smiling a little. "I didn't need them anymore."

"Levi, that's great!"

He smiles and looks down at his feet.

"So that means the anxiety is getting better?" I ask.

He shrugs. "I figured smoking took a little off my life with each cigarette. I don't want that anymore."

I don't respond. I'm not sure what to say.

We walk the rest of the way to my car in silence. As I start driving us home, Levi turns down the radio.

"Why do you always turn it down?" I ask him.

"I don't like music," he says, looking out the window.

"Why?"

"Certain songs remind me of the things I want to forget the most."

"Levi . . ."

"Don't 'Levi' me," he says, turning toward me. He smirks and rolls his eyes.

"Someone's sassy when they talk."

"Australians are naturally sarcastic."

We drive the rest of the way home in a comfortable silence. Levi doesn't like to talk for long periods of time, which I totally understand. I don't want to force him into doing something he's not comfortable with.

I pull up in front of Levi's house, but neither of us get out of the car.

He looks over at me and sighs.

"What's wrong?" I ask him

"How long can you stay?"

"About an hour."

"Please stay for dinner. Please," he says, sticking out his bottom lip.

I put my hand in front of his face. "Don't look at me like that."

"Pleeeease," he whines, his voice muffled.

"Fine. But you have to help me with my homework."

"I'm a dropout!" he says, getting out of the car.

"That doesn't mean you can't do algebra."

"I failed it twice. I'm pretty sure that means I can't."

I laugh, waiting outside the front door for Levi.

"Have you talked to your dad yet?" I ask him.

He shakes his head.

"Okay. Then I'll act like you haven't talked to me yet."

He nods, already going back to silence.

I open the door, already hearing Anthony upstairs.

"It's Delilah and Levi!" I yell.

"Hi!" Anthony yells, coming to see us. "You guys look cold!"

"Because we are. It's freezing out."

Anthony laughs. "Want me to turn the heat up?"

Levi nods quickly, causing his dad to laugh.

"Your wish is my command," Anthony says, heading back down the hall.

We go to Levi's basement, since that's probably where we'll be able to actually talk without Anthony hearing us.

"Wanna watch a movie?" Levi asks, talking quieter than usual so his dad won't hear him.

"If you want to."

"Okay. You pick it out, I'll go get food," he tells me, already running up the stairs.

"Don't put chocolate on the popcorn like you did last time!" I yell.

He leans over the stairs. "It was good!"

"No, it was disgusting."

"Fine. I'll make a separate batch for you. You're welcome."

"Thanks, Levi!" I yell, laughing.

He rolls his eyes and heads upstairs, leaving me to pick out a movie.

I go through his Netflix account until I find a movie that looks slightly interesting. It only has two and a half stars. At least we can make fun of it if it's really stupid.

"I'm back," Levi whispers after a few minutes. He plops down on the couch beside me, tossing me my bag of popcorn. "Wait, I'll be right back," he says.

He runs back upstairs and returns with a bunch of sheets, pillows, and blankets.

"What are you doing?" I ask, laughing.

"We're gonna make a fort, duh. My dad questioned me, though, and I'm not sure he believes that's what we'll be using this for."

I laugh. "Lucy is rubbing off on you."

"Is not."

"Is too."

"Is not!"

"You're like a child."

"Am not," he says quietly. He looks over at me from the corner of his eyes, holding in his laughter.

I grab a pillow and toss it at his head.

It's nice to finally be able to talk to Levi. I feel like, now that he's talking, he seems a lot happier. Or maybe his pills are working, or therapy is helping.

Or maybe everything all together is making him less sad. Whatever it is, I like it.

"That was not nice," he pouts.

"You're so much more annoying now," I say jokingly.

"It's my specialty. Now just eat your popcorn with extra butter while I make this fort, and don't bother me."

I almost choke on my popcorn because of Levi's response, and I can't stop laughing. "You're a lot funnier too."

Today must be a really good day for Levi, because I've never seen him this happy. Seeing him so happy is making me happy too.

I watch Levi as he sets up the fort. He sticks his tongue out a little and bites his lip as he concentrates on keeping the sheets in place. He has to stand on his toes to put one of the sheet corners on the bookshelf.

Levi's dad comes downstairs, most likely to see if we really are making a fort. He laughs when he sees the basement with all the sheets.

Levi must have made a lot of forts in his seventeen years of life, because he makes ours extremely fast. I barely help, as every time I try, I mess up. Instead, I eat my popcorn like he told me, not bothering him. When he's done, he crawls through the opening and sits beside me on the couch. He somehow managed to make the fort above the couch and connect it over the TV. It's pretty impressive.

He snuggles up beside me and throws a piece of popcorn at me.

"What was that for?" I ask him.

"Press play."

"Oh."

He throws a piece of popcorn into his mouth and leans his head on my shoulder.

"Actually, don't press play yet," he tells me.

"Why not?"

"I haven't said thank you. So thanks."

"For what?"

He moves slightly, lifting his head back up. "Without you, I wouldn't be talking right now."

That makes me blush and sends chills up my spine. "Why me?"

"You helped," he says. "You made me feel like it was okay to talk again."

"I'm happy you're talking."

"I'm happy that you're happy," he says, chewing on his bottom lip and avoiding eye contact. "You can press play now."

So I do, and the movie starts. It's kind of boring. His dad brings us some pizza and Levi keeps throwing his chocolate-covered popcorn at me. He doesn't talk at all during the movie; I don't think he's even watching it. Most of the time he's eating or looking over at me.

Halfway through the movie, I see one of the sheets start to fall and then the whole fort collapses. We're stuck in a pile of sheets, and all I can hear is Levi laughing.

"Oops," he whispers.

I push all the sheets off me and pull them off of Levi too.

"That wasn't supposed to happen," he says.

"You're such a dork," I tell him.

"But I'm your dork." His cheeks turn red the second after he says this.

"That was even dorkier!"

We don't bother remaking the fort, and instead just sit on the couch. The movie ends at some point, but neither of us was really interested in it anyway. We've been lying down for the past hour, acting like we were watching the movie, but we really weren't. I know I was thinking about Levi, I just don't know if he was thinking about me too.

Levi's arms are around me, and his head is resting in the crook of my neck. I'm pretty sure he's going to fall asleep soon. His breaths are slowing down, and his heart is beating gently.

"Delilah," he whispers.

"Yeah?"

"Today was the best day ever," he says, yawning.

"We barely did anything and I never did my homework."

"I could do nothing with you and still have fun."

I smile and squeeze Levi's hand. I hadn't even realized how close we had actually gotten.

"We should do this again," I tell him.

"Tomorrow. And the day after. And every day after that."

I laugh, and Levi moves slightly to get more comfortable.

"I'm tired. All this talking has worn me out," he says, yawning.

"Goodnight, Levi," I say as I get up to leave.

"Goodnight, Delilah."

Chapter Thirty-Four

LEVI

The next few days go by quickly. Delilah goes to school, and then afterward we hang out for a little. Yesterday, while we were talking, I realized Christmas is a little over a week away, and I'm not prepared at all.

Dad and I don't even have a Christmas tree yet. I bet my mum put hers up weeks ago. It's our first time not decorating the tree together. It feels weird not being with her for Christmas, like Christmas can't happen without her.

I've been trying to get closer to my dad, but things are still not how they once were. It's getting better, however. It's definitely better than it was when I first got here. So, I thought I'd surprise him by getting a Christmas tree.

I call Delilah, even though it's nine o'clock in the morning on a Saturday. Hopefully she's awake. She picks up after a few rings.

"Levi, do you know what time it is?" she mumbles.

"Yes, I'm aware," I whisper, making sure it's quiet enough that my dad won't hear. I still haven't spoken to him.

"Why are you calling so early?"

"I just—I need a Christmas tree," I tell her, suddenly embarrassed that I woke her up to talk about this.

"Christmas is, like, a week away, and you still don't have one?"

"My dad's been super busy. I want to surprise him. He's leaving in an hour, and he'll be gone all day."

"That's so cute!" Delilah says loudly. She's much more enthusiastic now. I feel my cheeks blush.

"I need someone to drive me and help me get a tree."

"You're seriously only using me for a chauffeur?"

"No, no! I didn't mean it that way. I wanted you to come with me," I splutter.

"I don't know, Levi. I'm really busy and I—"

"Please."

"I'm just kidding. Of course I'll come," Delilah says, giggling.

"Really? Thank you, thank you, thank you!"

"You're welcome. Oh, and Levi?"

"Yeah?"

"Your voice sounds cute over the phone," she says quickly.

"Thanks?" It's a good thing Delilah can't see me right now, because I'm smiling widely and blushing a deep red.

"It's a compliment, accept it. I'll be ready in fifteen minutes."

I hear the doorbell ring a few minutes later. I'm getting dressed and only have on a shirt and boxers. I run to the door, even though I know Delilah has let herself in. I tug my shirt down as far as it can go.

"You said fifteen minutes!" I whisper-yell, so my dad won't hear from his room.

Delilah tries to hold in her laughter, but ends up laughing hysterically. "Are those pizzas?" she asks, referring to my boxers.

"I was getting dressed!"

"That doesn't answer my question!"

"Yes, it's pizza," I say, blushing.

"You're unbelievable. Go change—I'll wait out here," she tells me, still laughing.

"I hate you," I mumble as I head to my room. I quickly get dressed, still slightly mortified. I walk out of my room and find Delilah eating a bowl of cereal on the couch.

"I'm starving, and all you have is plain Cheerios. Not even honey nut. What kind of life do you and your dad live?" Delilah says with her mouth full.

I shrug and sit beside her, almost causing some of the milk to spill out of her cereal bowl.

"Can we go?" I whisper.

"Let me finish my cereal! You literally woke me up ten minutes ago, and I'm hungry!"

I put my hands up. "Whoa. Someone's not a morning person."

She quickly finishes her breakfast, while I anxiously wait. We lie to my dad—Delilah tells him that we're going to Aiden's for the day. He believes it, thankfully.

"So, where are we getting the tree?" Delilah asks once we start driving.

"I dunno. You're the one who's lived here all your life."

"You're so sarcastic now," she says, sighing heavily.

"Not speaking for months has given me time to think of great sarcastic responses."

"They're not that great, but whatever makes you happy."

"Hey!"

Delilah turns down multiple roads until I see acres of Christmas trees. She pulls into the parking lot, and I get out of the car quickly.

"Look at all the trees to pick from!" I say excitedly. I grab Delilah's hand and run toward the trees. She laughs and follows, although she has no choice since I'm tugging her behind me.

We walk through many trees, and I can't find any I like. I'm looking for a medium-sized one, but they're all either too big or too small.

"What about that one?" Delilah asks, pointing to a tree.

"Nope."

She sighs, and we continue walking. Half the time I forget to look at the trees because I'm too busy watching Delilah.

"Is that my beanie?" I ask.

"Yep," she says, blushing.

I smile widely. "It looks cute."

She pulls the hat farther past her ears and smiles.

Sometimes I wonder how Delilah and I have come to where we are now. When I first saw her, I didn't want anything to do with her. I never wanted to see her again. And now, I don't want to go a day without her. I hate feeling this way, but I like it too. I'm trying to be happier, not just for Delilah, but for everyone. For me too. But even when I'm happy, like right now, I still feel sad. I still feel incomplete, like something is missing, but I'm not sure what. I'm just trying not to show it as much.

"Everything okay?" Delilah asks, probably noticing that I've zoned out.

"Yeah, I'm fine. Let's keep looking."

Delilah links her arm through mine as we walk through the trees. After what feels like hours, I think I've found the perfect one.

"That's it!" I say excitedly.

"You sure?"

"It's perfect! We have to get it!"

We get the tree cut down (by a worker, of course, because I don't trust myself with something like that) and we nearly break the car trying to get it into the back.

The whole car ride home, I'm afraid the tree is going to smash through a window whenever we hit the slightest bump. Being in a vehicle without a tree in the back makes me nervous, and this is just adding to it. Thankfully, nothing goes wrong, and we get home safely.

"I think your dad will love this," Delilah tells me as we pull into the driveway.

"I hope so. Do you think Lucy would wanna help decorate?"

"She probably would, but she's at her friend's house today."

"Oh, all right. Tomorrow, do you wanna help me go Christmas shopping?"

"Maybe."

"I have to get something for my parents, Caleb, Aiden, you, Lucy, and Mitchell."

I was debating whether or not to get something for Mitchell, but I figured I would. He seems like he could use a friend.

"You don't have to get something for me."

"Of course I do!" I tell her, getting out of the car.

"I don't need anything."

"Sure you do. What do you want?"

"Nothing."

"But you're my best friend," I pout. I instantly regret saying it.

"I'm your best friend?" she asks quietly.

"Well, yeah," I say softly. I open up the back door and start to pull the tree out, trying not to scratch the car.

"You're mine too," she whispers, helping me pick up the tree. I feel butterflies in my stomach from knowing that I'm her best friend too.

We're able to get the tree into the house without damaging anything except for a lamp. Neither of us have any idea how to set up a tree on our own, so we have to look it up. It takes half an hour, but it's finally up and standing.

"Where are the ornaments?" Delilah asks.

"Ornaments? I didn't even think of that," I say, nervously rubbing the back of my neck.

"You're kidding me."

"Maybe the attic? Is there even an attic in this house?"

"Let's check downstairs," Delilah says, running into the basement. I follow after her, and we search through all the shelves. We can't find anything Christmas related. I'm starting to wonder if my dad ever did anything for Christmas.

"It's probably in the box marked 'Christmas Ornaments,'" I say after a few minutes, laughing and pointing to a box on the floor. I don't know how we didn't notice it sooner.

"That would make sense," Delilah says.

I bring the box upstairs, and, thankfully, I don't break or drop anything. I open up the box and take out every single ornament. Surprisingly, my dad has many nice ornaments and decorations.

"Wait! We need music!" Delilah yells, plugging her phone into the speakers. She starts to play Christmas music loudly and smiles widely. I roll my eyes, but I have to admit, it's putting me in the Christmas spirit.

I pick up an ornament and hand it to her. "Wanna put the first one on together?"

She nods and holds on to it with me. We put it in the center of the tree, and I watch it hang on the branch. It looks so small all alone on the big tree.

We continue to place the ornaments, trying to cover the whole tree. Delilah can't reach the top parts, so that's my job. I hum along to the music, quietly singing some of the songs.

"You sing well," Delilah says, looking at me from behind the tree.

I shake my head.

"And you say you don't like music," she whispers.

"I don't! I promise, this is the only time you'll ever hear me sing."

"Not if I have anything to do with it," she says, smirking.

One of the ornaments I'm holding slips out of my hand—lucky for me, it lands on the carpet, so it doesn't break. It bounces a little and rolls into the kitchen. I chase after it and put it on the tree.

Once we're out of space on the branches, it's time to put the star on the top.

"Here, you put it on," I tell Delilah.

"I need a chair to stand on."

"No, you don't." I pick Delilah up by her waist until she can reach the top of the tree. She puts the star on the top, and we both stare at it.

"It's beautiful," I whisper.

"Isn't it?"

I keep holding her in the air, despite the fact she's begging me to put her down. I squeeze her sides and lift her higher. She laughs and tells me to put her down, but I put her over my shoulder.

"Levi!" she yells "Put me down!"

"Nope."

"C'mon!" she yells, giggling. She gently hits my back and kicks her legs. I toss her onto the couch and sit beside her.

"It looks good, don't you think?" I ask her.

She nods. "It looks great! Your dad will love it."

"I hope so."

"Levi?" she whispers as we both look at the tree.

"Yeah?"

"It's nice to see you happy like this. It's nice to see you getting better."

I shrug, not really knowing how to respond. There's too much that I could say. For instance, that it won't last long, but I could be wrong. Maybe I actually am getting better.

We end up putting up Christmas lights and little snowmen around the house too. It's very Christmasy. It really feels like Christmas now.

It's also the first Christmas with snow outside, which makes it even better. It's strange having Christmas in the winter, since it's summer in Australia now.

I just try not to think about the fact it's the first Christmas ever without my mum.

I heat up some pizza for us while we wait for my dad to get home. I'm anxiously pacing the kitchen while Delilah sits on the counter.

"Relax; he's going to love it," Delilah tells me.

"I know. I just really wanna make him happy. I was so rude to him for months. This is kinda my way of apologizing, I guess. I just want him to like it."

Delilah hops off the counter and puts her hands on my shoulders. "Your dad will love you no matter what. He knows what you've been going through. He's your dad—he'll always forgive you."

I hug Delilah tightly, which is quickly ended by the oven beeping.

"The pizza's ready," Delilah mumbles into my shoulder.

"I know."

I take the pizza out, and while we're eating I hear the front door open. I anxiously stand up and run to the stairs. I wave to my dad while he's taking off his coat.

"It's cold out there! How was Aiden's? Did you—" My dad stops talking when he sees the tree, and his jaw drops. "Did you do this?" he asks quietly.

I nod and nervously rub my nose.

He hugs me tightly, and I feel like he's never going to let go. "It's beautiful, Levi. Thank you so much," he whispers. He walks over to the tree, gently touching some of the ornaments. "I haven't had a tree for two years," he says. His eyes fill up with tears, and I'm afraid he's going to start crying.

Delilah comes over and puts her arm around me. I know she can tell that I'm still nervous, even though I know my dad is happy. She knows what I'm going to do. She always seems to be one step ahead of me.

"This is the best surprise. I love it. Thank you so much," my dad says, wiping his eyes.

"Merry Christmas, Dad," I whisper, hugging him again.

I hear him start crying while we're still embraced.

"You talked. You're talking," he whispers.

"I know. I'm sorry for being so awful," I mumble.

"Don't be sorry, Levi. I love you. You have no idea how proud I am."

"I love you too, Dad."

"I never thought I'd hear you call me Dad again."

Chapter Thirty-Five

DELILAH

I found some extra Christmas decorations at my house, so I decided to bring them over to Levi's and see if he'd like them. He was so excited about the Christmas tree and decorations the other day, I figured he might want some more.

I go over to Levi's right after school. I ring the doorbell, but no one comes to answer it. After a minute, I walk inside since the door is unlocked and head down the hall to Levi's room. His dad must not be home, and I'm not sure if Levi is home either.

Before I even step inside Levi's bedroom, I see him sitting on the floor in front of his bed with a calendar in front of him. I put the bag of decorations down quietly.

"One hundred twenty-seven, one hundred twenty-eight ..." he's whispering to himself. He has tears streaming down his cheeks. He doesn't even notice me standing in the doorway because he's so focused on what he's doing.

"Levi, is everything okay? What are you doing?"

"One hundred thirty-two ..." he continues, completely ignoring me.

I sit down beside him on the floor.

"Levi?"

"One hundred thirty-six ..."

"What are you trying to do?" I ask, patting his hand to try to get his attention.

"I didn't count . . . One hundred forty . . ." he mumbles, wiping his teary eyes.

"Count what?"

He flips to the next month on the calendar and continues counting.

"I can help if you just tell me," I say, putting my hand on the calendar.

He pushes my hand away and shakes his head. "Just let me do it, okay? One hundred fifty—fifty-two? Or was it fifty-three? You made me lose track!" he says, raising his voice. He looks up at me, his eyes frantic and wide.

"Track of what? What is going on?" I ask.

He flips back through all the months in the calendar, seeming panic-stricken.

"Levi, just tell me what's wrong. Maybe I can help," I say again, calmly.

"You're the reason this happened!"

"What happened?" I ask, confused. How do I have anything to do with this?

"I've lost count of the amount of days since Delia died, okay! I stopped right here," he says, going to November and pointing to a day toward the end of the month. He forcefully jabs his finger onto the paper and looks at me. Every day has a blue X written across it, up until the twentieth. "I don't remember anymore. I forgot to keep count. I have to figure it out. I don't know how I didn't realize sooner." He's talking quickly and frantically, like he can't catch his breath. He looks back down at the calendar and starts again.

"One, two . . ."

"Levi . . ."

He continues to count and ignore me.

"You can't keep count of the days forever," I whisper.

217

He snaps his head and looks at me sternly. "Yes, I can. And I will. I need to. How else will she be remembered? I can't forget—I can't." He shakes his head and tugs at the ends of his hair.

"Just because you don't know the number of days since she left doesn't mean she won't be remembered," I tell him, reaching for his hands.

He pulls his hands away. "No. I have to! I need to know the days she's been gone!"

"Levi, just listen—" I reach for his hand again, but this time he pushes me away from him. He's not forceful, but it's enough to make me move away. I'm taken aback by the fact he's like this. I've never seen him so upset and frantic.

"Delilah, no. I won't listen. I want you to leave. I lost count because of you. *You* distracted me this whole time. I was too focused on you and didn't keep track. This is *your* fault." He starts sobbing and leans his head against the edge of the bed. "Just please leave. Please."

"I'm not leaving you home alone like this. You're not okay."

"I'm fine," he snaps, turning away from me. "I just need to count the days, and everything will be fine. It will be okay."

"Why is keeping count of the days so important?" I ask. I don't understand how knowing the amount of days since Delia died will make him feel better. If anything, I would've thought it would make him feel worse knowing how long it's been. I remember when he first got here, he ran away because it had been two hundred ten days since Delia died, and he was a mess. I thought after that, he might stop because it was making him so sad.

He doesn't turn around to look at me. "No reason."

"Then why do you have to know?"

"I just do," he mumbles. He sniffs a few times.

I don't say anything.

"Please leave. I need to get back to counting, and I can't do it with you here," he says harshly.

"Okay, fine."

I get up and walk toward the door. He doesn't stop me like I thought he would.

"C'mon, go!" he says loudly, still not turning to look at me.

I take a deep breath. "I can't leave you like this," I say once more.

"Yes, you can. I can handle this on my own. I don't need you every step of the way. Delilah, just go!"

His words sting. I remain standing in the doorway.

Levi stands up and walks over to me.

"I said *go*," he says, glaring at me. His cheeks are stained with tears and his eyes are red.

I shake my head.

He rolls his eyes and exhales a shaky breath. It's like when I first met him. He's trying so hard not to cry.

He clears his throat and won't make eye contact. "I don't want you here right now. I can figure this out on my own. I need you to leave." He grabs his door and leans against it like he's ready to shut the door in my face.

"I'm sorry, I can't do that," I tell him. I reach for his hand and bring it away from the door. "I'm not leaving you alone in this state. We can either count the days together and I will help, or you can step away from it. You need to let go."

He whips his head away from me and folds his arms across his chest. "I can't believe you just said that! I don't *need* to do anything! You're not in charge of me, Delilah!"

"I didn't mean it that way! I meant you *can* let go. You know what I was trying to say."

"No, I heard what you said, and I know exactly what it meant. You think this is stupid and pointless. I'm just wasting my time doing this. You're thinking exactly what everyone else has always said." He pounds his fist against the wall and then drops his hand to his side. I flinch and nervously bite my nails. I have no idea what he's capable of doing when he's so upset.

"Levi—"

"Leave! Look, I'll even put the calendar away," he says angrily, shoving the calendar into his desk drawer. "See? It's over with. You don't have to be concerned. I'm *fine*. Now go."

I shake my head and start to leave. I stop for a second and look over my shoulder. "I know you're going to pull that calendar back out the second I leave. Call me when you figure it out, and you're back to being the Levi I know. Enjoy the Christmas decorations I brought you."

Chapter Thirty-Six

LEVI

It's two o'clock in the morning. I've been trying to fall asleep since midnight but all I've been doing is crying and thinking and crying some more. This has been happening way too many times, and I can't stand when I do this.

Sometimes I feel like when things finally start going great for me, I overthink everything, and it all comes crashing down. Lying here alone in the darkness, I recall everything that's happened to me, whether it was yesterday or last week or last year or five years ago. I just keep thinking and thinking until I regret every single thing I've ever done and realize that my whole entire life is one big mess. I hate it. I feel so alone everywhere I go, especially at night.

Tonight, I'm thinking about Delilah and how rude I was to her earlier. I don't know what came over me. I realized I'd lost track of how long I'd been without Delia, and I was distraught. My mind became frantic, and it was like I couldn't control myself. For over an hour, I was back to how I felt when I first moved here. Delilah looked afraid and nervous, like I was some sort of monster. I *was* a monster. I would be scared of me too.

I've come to the conclusion that I have completely and utterly messed everything up with Delilah. I need to somehow mend things, because for a while, everything was going well.

I stumble out of bed and head to my dad's room, because I need someone to talk to. I slowly open his door, and he's sound asleep. I quietly walk over to his bed.

"Dad," I whisper, poking his foot. He doesn't move. "Hey, Dad."

He slowly moves, but then quickly sits upright.

"Levi? Is everything okay?" he says, sounding worried.

"Uh, I know we've never really done this. And, like, we've never really talked, like, actually had a conversation where I'm speaking, but, uh, I was kinda hoping you wouldn't mind helping me right now. I'm just really confused." I rub the back of my neck and awkwardly rub my feet together.

"Yeah, yeah, of course," he says frantically, turning on his bed-side lamp. He moves over on his bed and pats beside him. I slowly sit beside him, hugging my legs to my chest and resting my chin on my knees. "So, what's wrong?" he asks.

I don't really know how to have a conversation like this or say what I want to say. I'm kind of new to this whole saying-what-I'm-thinking thing.

I nervously clear my throat and take a deep breath. I have no idea how to put my thoughts into words. This was a stupid idea. I should've just stayed in bed. I don't even know why I came in here; it's pointless and awkward.

"I made a mistake," I mumble.

"With what?"

"Delilah." I slowly look over to my dad, who is smiling. "Stop looking at me like that."

He smiles wider. "What about Delilah?"

"I got mad at her for trying to help me with something," I start. I don't mention that it was because I lost track of the days since Delia died. Then he'd *really* think I'm insane. No one, besides Delilah, knows about the counting. "And I got really angry with her and told her to leave and she left and I didn't actually want her to but she did and—"

"Slow down. What were you mad about?"

"It was stupid, really." I sniff and rub my eyes.

Thankfully, he doesn't ask again. "Have you apologized?"

"No, should I?"

My dad nods. "If you were that mad, she's probably not feeling that great either. Call her up in the morning and talk to her about it. Tell her you're sorry for whatever you did."

"That'll work?"

"It should."

"Is that all?" my dad asks, tilting his head to the side.

"Yeah, that's it."

"Are you sure?"

"I think I like her," I blurt out. I should not be having a conversation at two in the morning. I'm clearly not in the right state of mind, because I wouldn't have told my dad that, *ever*. I feel my cheeks turn red, but thankfully it's somewhat dark where I'm sitting.

"That was kind of obvious," my dad says.

It feels like how things used to be with my dad years ago. Like suddenly, because we're talking while the sun hasn't even risen yet, everything is okay between us. Or maybe we're both just exhausted.

"It was?" I didn't think it was obvious at all.

"Yeah. Did your getting mad have anything to do with Delia?"

I nod slowly.

He takes a deep breath. "Levi, Delia was a part of your past. Sadly, she is no longer with us, and however sad that is, it is time to live in the present. It's okay, though. You're not leaving Delia, you're just moving on. She will always be a part of your life—nothing can change that." He takes a deep breath. "But I think Delilah makes you very happy, and I like that you've been happy and smiling. I think you need to do things and be with people who can help you get through a very tragic and sad part of your life, but they—we— can help you move on. You don't need to forget your wonderful memories with Delia, but it is okay to start making new memories with Delilah. Levi, it is okay to be happy."

"Just because I'm smiling doesn't mean I'm happy," I cut in.

"I think that's how it used to be for you. But I know you. I know what you're like when you're happy. And that's what you've been. It's okay to admit it. It's okay to feel it. I think you forgot how to actually be happy for a while, and now that you are, you're not sure how to handle it. And that's all right."

"I'm scared, though," I mumble.

"Don't be scared of being happy. I promise that it's not bad. It's okay to laugh and smile."

"But it's weird. I hadn't felt like this in months. And suddenly, I move here and everything changes again. But I'm not changing back to who I was."

"I think that's nearly impossible. Now you're figuring out who you really are, not who you were. You've grown up, Levi. You have been through more than most kids your age. Change isn't a bad thing."

"But I was happy . . . before. And now it's a different type of happy. I don't know how to explain it. Before it was like I felt excited and highly caffeinated all the time. But now I feel completely comfortable and safe. They're totally different kinds of happiness, if that's what happiness even feels like." I sigh and bite on my bottom lip.

"See, you just admitted to being happy."

"No, I didn't," I say quickly.

"Yes, you did. Say it."

"Say what?"

"That you're happy."

"But I'm not."

"Levi."

"Dad."

"Fine. I'm happy. Okay?" I say, throwing my hands in the air.

"Say it like you mean it."

I roll my eyes and sigh heavily.

"I'm happy. I'm feeling happy, despite constantly thinking about Delia. But for the first time in months, I don't feel like I'm carrying five thousand pounds on my shoulder, and I can finally breathe easily, and I don't feel trapped anymore, and I'm not always anxious, and I'm laughing and talking, and I'm happy," I say very quickly, and almost run out of breath. I inhale deeply and let the air out slowly. "But now I might have just pushed away the person who makes me happiest and ruined everything," I whisper. I wipe under my eyes before I start crying. I have absolutely no idea where all that came from.

My dad puts his arm around my shoulders and hugs me closer to him. "I'm proud of you, Lee. It'll all work out."

"I thought I outgrew that nickname years ago," I say, pulling away from my dad.

He laughs lightly. "You never will." He nudges my shoulder. "That was good dad advice, huh?"

"It wasn't *awful*."

Both of us smile and sit in a comfortable silence for a few minutes. I'm not sure when my dad suddenly became some wise father who is actually good at giving advice, but what he said actually helped. I feel a little better now. Maybe a lot better. We talk for a little longer about random stuff, and it's actually really nice. It feels good to be with him again, like how things once were. I start to yawn a lot and almost fall asleep midsentence.

"I'm gonna go to bed now," I tell my dad, slowly getting out of his room.

"Are you feeling better?"

I nod. "Yeah. Thanks."

"If you ever want to do this again, I'm always here."

"I know. I just wish I'd realized it sooner. You're not really that bad. I'm sorry."

"Don't be. Goodnight, Levi."

"Goodnight. Oh, and Dad?"

"Yeah?"

"Thanks for letting me move in with you and eat your food, and for not kicking me out for being such a jerk."

"That's what dads are for. You're not so bad yourself, Lee."

Chapter Thirty-Seven

DELILAH

I'm woken up at three in the morning by the sound of my phone ringing. I reach over and see that Levi is calling. I sigh and pick up the phone.

"Hello?" I whisper.

"Did I wake you up?" Levi asks.

"Yes."

"I'm sorry."

I don't say anything.

Levi speaks up after a few seconds. "I figured it out."

I sigh. "Okay," I respond. I knew he would go back to counting the second I left.

"What I figured out is that you're right. I don't need to know how many days it's been. I *can* let go. I need to live in the now. And that's with you. I'm sorry for yelling at you and getting so angry. I don't know what came over me. I can't help it sometimes. I promise I'll try not to have it happen again, because I don't want to lose you. I'm also sorry for calling while you were sleeping, but I needed to tell you now. I needed you to know. I get it if you don't accept my apology," he says.

"Levi—"

"Wait, I'm not done. I didn't count the days. I still don't know. When you left, I stood in my doorway for a really long time debating if I should go after you but then too much time had passed and I wanted to, I really did. But I wasn't mad at you, I was mad at myself. None of it is your fault."

He stops and takes a deep breath.

"Please say something," he whispers.

I smile a little. "Of course I forgive you. I get that you were upset. I understand. It's okay. I appreciate you calling me. I regretted not staying with you, and I was really worried. You weren't in a great state of mind; it happens to everyone sometimes. I'm happy you're okay now too. Thanks for calling," I tell him.

I hear him exhale slowly. "I was so worried you would be mad at me," he says quietly. He sounds like a little kid; the total opposite of earlier. He also sounds exhausted.

I wonder if he tried to continue counting the days, or if he didn't try again. Either way, I'm proud of him for making the right choice. It's healthier for him to not be keeping track; it probably just made him more depressed. I can't even imagine counting the days since someone's death.

"Go to sleep and we can talk later, okay? You sound like you haven't slept," I tell him, yawning. I need to sleep too.

He laughs quietly. "I haven't slept at all. Goodnight, Delilah."

"Goodnight, Levi."

Both of us wait a few seconds before hanging up the phone.

"See ya," he whispers, ending the call.

Chapter Thirty-Eight

LEVI

I walk over to Delilah's house the next morning. I want to make sure she really does forgive me, because I feel awful about how I treated her. I don't want her to be mad at me. Over the phone, I can't see her face and tell how she truly feels.

I ring her doorbell, and she answers it after a few seconds.

"Hi," she whispers.

"Hi." I should have thought about what I was going to say before I got here.

We both awkwardly stare at one another, not knowing what to say.

"I'm sorry," we both say in unison.

"Why are you sorry?" I ask, surprised.

"I should've just let you count the days. I know how important Delia is to you. I just hated seeing you so upset."

"No, no. You were right. I should've just listened to you from the start. It was just making me sadder. I actually feel kinda better not knowing how many days it's been."

Delilah smiles. "I'm happy to hear that."

I nervously run my hands through my hair. "So we're okay now?"

"Yes, don't worry."

"I can't help it." I don't know what I would do if Delilah was mad at me.

"Wanna come in?"

I nod. "So does this mean you forgive me?" I ask, stepping inside.

Delilah laughs. "I told you when you called that I forgave you, and I meant it."

"Okay, just making sure. It would suck if you didn't forgive me."

I follow Delilah into her room, waving to Lucy when we walk past her.

Lucy runs out of her room and grabs on to my leg.

"Lila said you were mad at her," Lucy says.

I look up at Delilah, and she's blushing.

"Lucy, no, I didn't."

"Yes, you did. I asked yesterday if Levi could come over and you said he was mad at you."

Delilah puts her head in her hands and I laugh.

"Are you still mad at her?" Lucy asks me.

"Nope."

"Why were you mad?"

"Just a silly reason."

Lucy laughs. "*Silly* is a funny word."

I smile.

"Lucy, why don't you go draw us some pictures, okay?" Delilah tells her.

"Okay! I'll bring them when I'm done!" Lucy says, running into her room.

"Sorry about that," Delilah says.

I shrug. "I wasn't mad at you."

"You so were!" she says, laughing.

"Only temporarily! Now I'm not," I tell her, hugging her tightly to annoy her.

She laughs and tries to squirm out of my hug.

"Okay, I get it! You can let me go now," Delilah says, hitting my chest.

I laugh and stop hugging her.

Everything feels back to normal. Yesterday was just a weird day for me, and I think Delilah realizes that. She doesn't seem to be holding anything against me, which is good.

I tell Delilah that I looked at all the decorations she brought over yesterday. I put some in my room, and some more around the house. It was really thoughtful of her to do that, and I was so rude to her. I didn't even notice the bag of decorations until today. Even though she told me about them when she left, I was so concerned about counting the days that I must have forgotten.

Delilah points outside. "It's starting to rain," she says, looking over at me and smiling.

I stand in front of the window, looking outside. "It's not gonna be too much."

"How do you know that?"

I shrug. "I was really interested in the rain when I was younger, I know all about the clouds. It's super embarrassing," I tell her, feeling my cheeks heat up.

"That's cute!"

"No, it isn't! It's weird!"

Delilah laughs. "It's interesting. I remember when I had the interview for school and you said that your favorite thing to do was watch the rain."

I roll my eyes. "I couldn't think of anything better."

"Wanna go outside?" she asks, looking out the window.

"In the rain?"

"Yeah."

"It's freezing out!"

"So what! Just go out for a little then come back. Like you said, it won't rain too much."

Before I can make any decision, Delilah throws on her rain jacket and starts heading out. I pull on the hood of my sweatshirt and follow her.

She stands outside in the driveway, smiling at me while I'm in the doorway.

"C'mon!" she yells, waving me over.

I laugh and run over to her.

"Why are we out here?" I ask. The rain is gently hitting the pavement, leaving small spots everywhere. There are some rain-drops on Delilah's coat, which is a little too big for her.

"Because you like the rain."

"That doesn't mean I want to be outside in the cold," I tell her, wrapping my arms around myself. "I'm not seven years old anymore."

"Pretend."

She jumps into a small puddle and laughs. Her hood falls off, but she doesn't bother pulling it back on.

It's cute how she's running around in the rain like a little kid. She's so excited for some reason. I watch her stand under a tree, trying to keep somewhat dry. Her cheeks are rosy and her hair is damp. Some of her mascara has started to run.

I have to admit that I still do like being out in the rain. For some reason, it relaxes me. I like feeling the water cool my skin. The steady sound of raindrops is calming. It's something familiar that I've always known.

"I'm cold!" she tells me.

"Told ya."

I reach my arms out and catch some rain in my hands. I splash some of the water at Delilah.

"See, I brought you out here and you're already happier."

"What are you talking about?"

"You were tense when you got here. Now you're not."

I shake my head. Even though she's right.

"Levi?" she whispers, walking close to me. We're both beneath the tree now.

"Yeah?"

"Why do you like the rain so much?"

"It reminds me that I'm still alive."

She smiles and runs a hand through her wet hair.

"If you would've asked me what my favorite thing is now, I would've had a different answer."

"Oh, really?"

"Yeah."

"What would it be?"

I feel my cheeks blush again. "Being with you."

I realize that I stopped searching for the end of the rainbow a long time ago, but I think I found one in Delilah.

Chapter Thirty-Nine

LEVI

H-Hi, L-Levi," Mitchell says. He's sitting across from me in Candace's office. We're doing our weekly session together. He's gotten a little more talkative lately.

I wave. I haven't spoken to Candace or Mitchell yet. I clear my throat and write on my whiteboard. *I have something to say.*

"Go ahead, Levi. Say whatever you want," Candace says.

I nervously rub my nose and clear my throat again. I wipe away some of the words on the whiteboard with my finger before I gain the courage to speak. "Hi, Mitchell. Hi, Candace." I smile. Candace stares at me, shocked.

"Is that the first time you've spoken?" Candace whispers, which is strange because she's always loud.

I shake my head. "No. I've been talking for a few weeks now."

"I'm so proud of you, Levi," Candace says. She gets out of her chair and hugs me tightly. Which is also really weird.

This whole time, everyone's been trying to get me to talk. Candace probably feels like I've experienced some psychiatric breakthrough, which I guess I have. She smiles widely at me, not saying anything.

"Y-You have a cool accent," Mitchell says, smiling widely. He plays with a loose string on the hem of his shirt.

"Thanks," I laugh.

We talk for awhile longer, until it's been an hour, which means it's time to go. Candace asks me more questions than usual because she knows that I can talk now to answer them. It still feels a little strange to actually be talking to people, but I'm getting more used to it. Sometimes I stop because I get tired or I just don't feel like talking anymore. Living almost a year in complete silence, not speaking became comfortable and easy for me. But now, I'm talking and I'm out of my comfort zone. It's not as bad as I thought it'd be, though.

"I-I did-didn't understand h-half the st-stuff you said," Mitchell tells me, laughing as we head outside.

"Because of my accent?" I ask him.

He nods. "W-What's a-a ch-cheese toastie?" It takes him awhile to say the words *cheese toastie*, like they're stuck on his tongue. That happens a lot. He has to think hard about what he's saying.

I laugh. Mitchell had been talking about some pizza place he went to, and I had said all I had for lunch was a cheese toastie. "It's what you call a grilled cheese."

"O-Oh. I like those."

We walk in silence for a little. Mitchell always seems sad; I wish I could see him a little happier. I know what it's like to be sad, and I don't want anyone else to go through that. I wonder if that's how people feel when they're around me. Or used to anyway, now that I'm getting better.

"Do you wanna come over to my house tonight? I'm hanging out with Aiden and Delilah—you know them, right?" I ask him.

He looks over at me with wide eyes and nods.

"So is that a yes?" I ask.

He takes a few seconds to think and then shrugs. "I-I'm not really g-good with new p-people."

"That's okay, they're nice. If you don't want to, I understand. I just thought I'd ask."

"I-I don't w-wanna intrude."

"You won't. We're probably just gonna have pizza and watch a movie or something. Even though you had pizza for lunch."

"I-I like p-pizza."

I wait for Mitchell to say whether or not he wants to come, because it looks like he's thinking.

"I-I guess I'll come. A-Are you sure th-they won't mind?"

"I'm positive."

"I-I'll come." He runs his hands through his now red hair and pulls a little at the ends.

"Great!"

My dad drives Mitchell and me home. He tries to talk to Mitchell, but I'm not sure my dad could understand a lot of what he said. It took me awhile to understand Mitchell, but now I don't even notice his stutter most of the time.

When we get home, Aiden and Delilah tell me they'll be a few minutes late. Mitchell and I sit on the couch and wait for them.

"I-I like the Ch-Christmas tree," Mitchell says, poking one of the ornaments.

"Thanks! Delilah and I decorated it a few days ago. I can't believe Christmas is in five days!"

"I kn-know. D-Do you h-have plans?"

I shrug. "I guess my dad and I will do something. What about you?"

Mitchell shrugs. "We don't do m-much on Christmas."

"Oh."

We talk for a little longer, until Delilah and Aiden show up.

"Hey! We're here!" Aiden yells, running up the stairs. "We have the pizzas!"

Aiden throws the pizza boxes onto the table and opens one up instantly. He takes out a slice and shoves it into his mouth.

"Did you know that— Hey, who's this?" Aiden says, talking with his mouth full.

"That's Mitchell. Remember him from school?" Delilah says, sitting down beside me.

Aiden shrugs. "I don't pay attention to school. I'm Aiden. You have cool hair, dude."

"Th-Thanks."

"Did you invite him here?" Delilah whispers to me.

I nod.

Her face lights up. "That was really nice of you!" She twines her fingers in mine and leans her head on my shoulder. I smile and feel instantly happier.

Aiden raises his eyebrows at me, and I roll my eyes.

"Watch this," I whisper to Delilah. "Aiden's gonna freak."

Delilah squeezes my hand and moves slightly on the couch.

"Aiden, wanna bring me over a slice of pizza?" I ask.

I haven't seen Aiden for a while, so this is the first thing I've said to him.

"What do I look like— Wait, what? Who just said that? Levi, that wasn't you, was it?"

"It was me," I say, laughing. Delilah and Mitchell laugh too.

"Since when do you talk?! Why has no one told me this? No one ever tells me anything! This is the greatest news I've heard in forever! It's a Christmas miracle!"

"Oh, shut up," Delilah says. "We tell you everything—you just don't pay attention."

"Don't say that," I whisper to Delilah.

"Say what?"

"You know . . ." I say, not wanting to actually say it.

"Shut up?"

I nod. "You wouldn't want him to actually stop talking."

She sobers. "I'm sorry, I didn't realize."

"It's fine."

After some more ranting on why no one told him I'm talking, Aiden finally brings us all some pizza. We chat about random stuff, but Mitchell stays pretty quiet. Aiden then goes on and on *again* about how he can't believe I'm finally talking and how my voice sounds. Delilah gets Mitchell into the conversation every once and awhile, but I can tell he's nervous. His stutter is a little worse than usual.

Last week, Mitchell explained to me why he stutters. He said it's genetic, which is pretty rare. Doctors think one of his relatives in an earlier generation probably stuttered. He said his nerves make it worse, but his stutter makes him nervous, so it's a vicious cycle for him. His brain doesn't process words the same way other people's do, which is what causes him to stutter. He's recently started speech therapy to help him. There's a small chance it will ever fully disappear, but he can work on making it better.

I feel bad for Mitchell, but he's a really nice guy. I want to help him as much as I can.

Delilah ends up laying her head down in my lap while we all talk, and I can see Aiden continuously staring down at her.

"Levi, can I talk to you?" he asks. I nod and Delilah sits back up, allowing me to stand. Aiden and I head into the kitchen.

"So, is there a thing going on between you guys now?" Aiden asks, wiggling his eyebrows.

"Not that I know of. We're just friends."

"But you told me you thought you liked her."

I shrug.

"Levi . . ."

"Okay, fine. I do like Delilah. But there's nothing going on between us."

Aiden rolls his eyes. "It's obvious that you both like each other. I just think you should start to like *yourself* more before you get into a relationship."

I did not expect Aiden to say something like that. I think for a few seconds before speaking.

"Delilah helps me like myself more," I whisper.

Chapter Forty

LEVI

"Tomorrow's your last day of school before break," I tell Delilah as she sits at her kitchen table, focusing on her homework. "I'll get to annoy you every day for two weeks!"

"I can't wait," she mumbles, erasing something on her paper. She's been struggling for the past few minutes. It's cute the way she sticks out her tongue when she concentrates. I move from the couch and sit down in one of the chairs beside her.

"Need help?" I ask, leaning my head on top of her shoulder so I can see her worksheet.

"No," she says, trying to nudge me off her shoulder.

"C'mon. Take a break—you're working too hard."

"I don't understand it."

"Well, the answer to the problem is seventy-two," I say, pointing to the maths problem that's been erased multiple times.

"How'd you know that?" she whispers, finally looking up from her homework.

I shrug. "My mum's a maths teacher."

"Math."

"No, maths. You Americans say weird things. It's plural. Mathsssss," I say, trying not to laugh.

"Says the person who was yelling Australian slang at their phone the other day."

238

"Okay, Siri wasn't understanding me."

Delilah laughs and scribbles down the answer after I explain how I figured it out.

"You said you failed math," she tells me.

"I lied. I just didn't want you to do your homework that day." I feel my cheeks heat up.

She slaps my arm. "Seriously, Levi?"

I rub my arm, pretending like it hurt.

Delilah's phone starts to ring, and it's a call from Aiden. She sighs and picks it up, tapping her pencil against the table while she talks.

"Yes, Aiden?" she says. "No, I'm not . . . Because I don't want to . . . No, he doesn't know . . . It's tomorrow, it's too late anyway . . ."

She rolls her eyes while she continues to talk, then finally hangs up.

"What was that about?" I ask.

"Snow Ball."

"Oh, cool . . . What's that?" I ask.

"A winter dance tomorrow night. It's no big deal."

"Why aren't you going?" I ask, scrunching my eyebrows in confusion.

She shrugs.

"You should go."

"But I have no one to go with."

"Oh."

I look down at my hands and awkwardly twiddle my thumbs.

"I mean, I wanna go with you, obviously. But you don't like that kind of stuff," Delilah whispers. "I didn't ask you because you don't like parties or crowded spaces. I thought you wouldn't wanna go," she says, twirling her pencil between her fingers.

She's right, I don't like that kind of stuff. But if Delilah's with me, I might not get as nervous.

"I'd go with you," I tell her, nudging her shoulder.

"You would?"

"Of course."

I nervously bite on my lip ring just thinking about it. I push the anxiety out of my mind, though.

"Are you serious?" she asks.

"Completely serious."

"I need a dress. You need something to wear!" she says, standing up from her chair. "It's too late. It's tomorrow. We don't have time."

"We can go right now," I tell her, grabbing her hand.

"But what about Lucy? My parents aren't home."

"She can come too. I'll go get her."

I run to Lucy's room, where she's playing with some dolls and talking quietly.

"We're going shopping," I tell her.

"For what?" she asks, tilting her head to the side.

"Delilah needs a dress."

"I don't wanna go," she pouts.

"You can bring Barbie."

"This is Kelly."

"All right, you can bring Kelly."

"I don't wanna bring Kelly."

"Then I'll buy you a cookie. How's that sound?"

She smiles widely and jumps up. "A cookie sounds good! Can it be a rainbow M&M one?"

"Whatever you want."

I help Lucy get on her shoes and jacket, which as usual takes a very long time. Delilah drives us all to the mall, which is extremely crowded because of Christmas shoppers. I cringe just thinking about the tightly packed stores and young kids running around everywhere.

"You sure you want to go?" Delilah asks before opening her door.

I nod. I slowly get out of the car and unbuckle Lucy from the backseat. Of course, she asks me to carry her, so I do. She continuously pokes the pom-pom on my beanie as we walk, almost causing it to fall off my head.

I follow Delilah to wherever the store is that we're going to, carefully weaving through all the people. Lucy points to things she sees in the store windows, like snowmen or giant nutcrackers.

We walk into the store, and I'm astounded by the multiple aisles of dresses. There are long ones and short ones and tight ones and puffy ones. There are way too many to choose from. I'm overwhelmed, and we just got here. I worry we'll be here for hours.

I walk over to the men's section while Delilah goes through all the dresses. I find a pair of pants and shirt that fit nicely. They aren't too fancy; they're just right.

"You like this one, Lucy?" I ask, standing in front of the giant mirrors.

Lucy nods quickly. She said she'd rather help me than Delilah, so she's sitting on the tiny chair while I stand in front of the mirror.

I see Delilah across the store and give her a thumbs-up to see if she likes any of the dresses in her hand. She smiles widely and gives a thumbs-up back to me, approving of my outfit choice

I move side to side, making sure I like everything. I feel somewhat awkward standing in front of this giant mirror dressed up so nicely. It doesn't look like me at all.

I decide I'll get the pants and shirt, as well as a tie, and go back to find Delilah. When I get to her, she has at least eight dresses in her arms. I'm surprised she can carry all that without dropping them.

"Want me to hold some?" I ask her.

"No, I'm gonna go try them on," she says, running into the dressing room. I sit in the chair in front of the giant mirror, and Lucy sits on my lap while she waits.

"I like that dress," Lucy says, pointing to a hideous orange one.

"You do?" I bounce my knee up and down, causing Lucy to laugh.

"Yep," she says in between her giggles.

Delilah comes out in the first dress, which is way too long.

"I don't like this one at all," she says, laughing.

I shake my head, and she heads back.

Five dresses later, Delilah slowly walks out of the dressing room.

"I like this one a lot," she says quietly, standing in front of the mirror. She smiles widely and sways side to side.

It's a red lace dress that ends above her knees.

"You're beautiful," I whisper. "I mean, the dress, it's beautiful," I say quickly. My cheeks are probably the same color as her dress.

"I love it!" Lucy shrieks, clapping her hands.

"Is this the one? Are you saying yes to the dress?" I ask jokingly. I had agreed to watch the *Say Yes to the Dress* marathon with her the other day, so it felt like the right thing to say.

Delilah laughs and spins in a little circle to face me. "I'll say yes to the dress, you goof."

"Aiden, are you sure my hair looks okay?" I ask for the hundredth time.

Aiden rolls his eyes. "Yes, Levi. I'm sure. It looks fine."

"I'm nervous," I whisper.

"You'll be fine. I'll be there, Delilah will be there, Mitchell will be there."

Mitchell smiles from where he's standing in my room. I somehow convinced him last night that he should come. It took a very long time for him to say yes, but he finally did. One of Delilah's friends even said they would go with him.

I take a deep breath. "Okay. I'm ready." I pull at the ends of my hair one last time, finally looking away from the small mirror in my room.

"Relax. It'll be fine," Aiden reassures me.

"Y-Yeah, we'll be o-okay," Mitchell says. I can tell Mitchell is nervous, but he's also very excited. He can't stop smiling. He's wearing a somewhat-fancy red flannel with his usual black jeans.

I nervously sit on the couch while I wait for Delilah, holding the corsage I bought her. A few minutes later, I hear the door open. Delilah and her friends are here, ready to go.

Delilah has her hair curled, and I honestly feel like I forget to breathe for a second.

"You look nice," she tells me, straightening my tie.

"You look better," I tell her quietly, smiling down at her. "Want me to put the corsage on your wrist? Is that what I'm supposed to do?"

Delilah laughs and nods her head. I nervously slip on the corsage. I can see Aiden taking some pictures of us on his phone. Mitchell quietly talks to his date for the night. He said her name was Ally, and they were in two of the same classes. According to Mitchell, she wears a Green Day shirt a lot, so she must be cool.

Aiden's date, whose name I don't know, seems slightly annoyed with everyone. Delilah said she's somewhat snobby, but Aiden really likes her, which I can't seem to understand. She didn't even say hello to any of us. Aiden is so nice, and she's so . . . not.

My dad takes some pictures, which just ends up with me almost falling over because Aiden can't stand still for a group photo.

After a few minutes, the limo Aiden rented comes to pick us all up. My school never had a Snow Ball, so I don't really know what to expect.

I have to admit that I'm nervous. This will be the first major thing I've gone to in a while. The last time Delilah brought me to something like this, when we first met, I had a panic attack. I'm going to try my best not to get nervous this time, though. I want to make this night memorable in a good way for Delilah, and me too. But sometimes I can't keep the anxiety away. I'm hoping nothing terrible happens tonight.

We pull up to the hall where the event is being held, which is much bigger than I expected. Delilah holds on to my hand as we walk in. I can hear the loud music from outside, which already makes my heart start to pound. I can't help but think of what happened at the party.

"Relax. It'll be fine. If you wanna leave, just let me know," Delilah whispers. She squeezes my hand as we walk into the room.

There's a DJ in the corner and bright, colorful lights illuminating the dark room. There are tables set up around a dance floor, where the majority of people are standing.

"Are you hungry?" Delilah asks.

I nod, and we all head over to an empty table. We talk and eat for a while, mostly trying to count how many people have fallen on the dance floor or tripped in their heels. Delilah introduces me to some of her friends, who seem very nice.

At some point, Aiden tries to see how many grapes he can shove into his mouth, which ends up being twenty-two. I'm surprised he didn't choke. His date does not seem amused with him. I, on the other hand, cannot stop laughing because one of the grapes shot out of his mouth and hit some guy in the forehead. He didn't seem amused either. Even Mitchell is laughing uncontrollably.

Delilah keeps pointing out people she knows, telling me what seems like their deepest secrets. I'm not sure if it's just a girl thing to know everything, or if she just knows everyone. I like listening to her stories, though. I could listen to her talk about anything.

A slow song comes on, and Delilah gently taps my hand.

"Wanna go dance?" she asks quietly.

My heart starts racing, and I can't seem to form words. I know this song, I know it really well. The air is suddenly becoming harder to breathe in.

"I'm not good at dancing," I choke out.

"I'm not either," she says, smiling.

I quickly stand up from my chair, heading to the doors. "I'll be back in a few minutes," I mumble, heading outside. But I'm not sure if I will.

Chapter Forty-One

LEVI

evi, wait," Delilah says, standing up from her chair and following me.

I shake my head over and over, ignoring her. I focus on the doors and try to get out as fast as possible.

The music continues to play, no matter how much I wish for it to stop.

I put my hands over my ears and walk faster toward the exit. I quickly get outside and get as far away as I can until I can no longer hear the music. I sit down on the ground and hug my knees tightly to my chest. I rock back and forth, focusing on my breathing. My lungs feel tight, and I'm on the verge of hyperventilating. I also can't stop crying.

Breathe, Levi.

I loosen my tie and take off my jacket, because I'm overcome with heat. I rest my head in my hands, trying everything possible to get my breathing back to normal.

My ears start ringing, and for a second, I think I might pass out. Everything is getting blurry and fading in and out. My vision is like a fuzzy television screen. I squeeze my eyes shut to try to make the feeling go away.

It's okay. It's okay. It's okay.

Tonight was supposed to be a great night. I wasn't supposed to get a panic attack like this. For once in my life, I want to be able to do normal teenage things without something going wrong. Why can't I be normal, just for one night? This was supposed to go smoothly. I was supposed to be getting better. I should've known that this would happen. I shouldn't have come.

"He's over here," I hear Aiden yell. I look up to see him, Delilah, and Mitchell walking toward me.

"G-Guys, don't c-crowd around him," I hear Mitchell say as they approach me. "It w-won't help him."

Mitchell quickly sits beside me, looking up at Aiden and Delilah as if to ask for some time alone. They understand and look at me for approval. I shake my head slightly, and they walk a few feet away from us.

"H-Here. I brought you some w-water," Mitchell tells me. He hands me a small water bottle, and I drink it slowly. I take deep breaths between each sip, and my breathing finally starts to get better.

Mitchell runs his hands through his hair and kicks the tip of his foot in the dirt.

"I-I'm not v-very good at the whole t-talking and giving a-advice thing. But I know w-what you're going through." He takes a deep breath and picks at one of the buttons on his flannel. "J-Just try to picture s-something that makes you happy. T-Try to remember every s-single detail. It'll keep your m-mind off th-things."

I nod and rub under my eyes to wipe away the tears.

I try to think of a happy place. I think of multiple things, actually. Most of the memories that automatically come to mind are recent ones, like when Delilah and I decorated the tree. It's easier to think of happy moments now.

I look over to Delilah, who is nervously watching me. She smiles a little and waves shyly. I motion for her to come over to me. Mitchell leaves, and Delilah and I walk over to an empty bench.

"Do you want to talk about it?" Delilah asks quietly.

I shake my head no.

"It was Delia's song," I finally whisper after a few seconds of silence. "It was her favorite song."

A tear slips out of my eye, and I quickly wipe it away. I bounce my leg nervously.

"There are so many memories attached to it. I hate when this happens," I mumble.

Delilah reaches over and gently puts her hand on top of mine. She rubs little circles on top of my hand with her thumb. "Levi, I want you to close your eyes really tightly."

I look at her and scrunch my eyebrows in confusion.

"Just close your eyes," she says, laughing lightly.

I shut my eyes tightly and wait for her to start talking again.

"What do you see?" she says.

"Black?" I whisper. Isn't it kind of obvious that when you shut your eyes you see blackness?

"Okay. Tell me when it changes."

"When what changes?"

"The color you see."

After a few seconds, I realize what she's talking about. "I see some green now."

"All right. Keep your eyes shut."

I wait a few seconds again. "Now it's yellow." After a few seconds, it changes again. "It's orange now."

"You can open your eyes," she says, giving my hand a squeeze.

"What was the point of that?" I ask her.

"Even though you had your eyes shut, the colors still changed. You can try to block out things in your life, but it's kind of impossible. Nothing is going to last forever, and nothing is always going to stay the same, no matter how much you try. In life, you'll get multiple different colors thrown your way, whether or not you want them. When you shut your eyes, the colors faded after a few seconds, and you didn't know what color would show up next, right?"

I nod.

"It's kinda like life, I guess. It's constantly changing, and you don't know what will happen next. You just have to be prepared for whatever life throws your way. But notice that the blackness always stayed there when you shut your eyes—it was the one thing that was constant. You will always have someone who will be with you through everything. I'm here, Aiden's here, Mitchell's here, your dad is here, and your mom is available by video chat. Caleb's back at home for you too. There are so many people you can go to, Levi. Don't let the memories overcome all the good things that are happening."

I start crying all over again, but this time they are happy tears. I hug Delilah tightly.

"I needed that so much," I murmur. "Thank you."

"I will always be here for you, Levi. I realize that you're still going through a lot of stuff right now, and I totally understand. I just want what's best for you."

"I think right now, you're what's best for me," I whisper.

Delilah smiles and leans her head on my shoulder.

"The second that song started playing, every single memory came flooding back. I couldn't help it. I thought I was going to pass out or something. I had been doing so well too. Mitchell said to think of something that makes me happy, and I thought of you. It used to be that everything you did made me think of Delia. But now everything leads back to you. You're who I think about the most. All you have to do is smile, and my heart starts fluttering. And sometimes, I'm not really sure how to handle it. And then you say things that make me beyond happy, and I feel like you're way too good for me, and all I do is get anxious or mad or annoying," I tell her.

"Levi, don't you ever say that you're not good enough, because you are. You have no idea how special you are."

"I just don't get it. Why me? You didn't have to be nice to me. You didn't even have to start talking to me. All I did was be rude to you."

"We don't have to talk about that. It was before we even knew each other."

I take a deep breath and lace my fingers with Delilah's. I can hear another slow song playing.

"I wanna go dance with you," I whisper, leaning my forehead against hers and smiling a little. Our faces are barely an inch apart.

"Are you sure? We can leave if—"

"I'm sure," I say, standing up and walking back inside, even though I'm still kind of shaky. I want to make this a good night for Delilah. Aiden and Mitchell notice us leave, so they come back inside too.

I walk over to the edge of the dance floor, trying to stay away from the other people dancing. I put my hands on Delilah's waist and pull her closer to me. She lightly leans her head against my chest.

"I thought you couldn't dance?" she asks quietly.

"I can't. But I will for you."

"Are you okay now?"

I shrug. "Almost."

She picks her head up from my chest. "We can leave."

I gently pull her closer to me again and bring her head back to where it had rested. "No, right here is fine for me."

"I can feel your heart beating."

"That's what hearts do. It's beating for you," I whisper. I hum along to the song quietly. I continue to hum along to the song until it's over.

"Can this be our song?" Delilah asks.

I nod and hug her closer to me. I rest my head on top of hers, and she giggles.

Tonight somehow went from extremely bad, to incredibly good. It's amazing how fast things can change.

Chapter Forty-Two

LEVI

Today is Christmas Eve, even though it doesn't feel like it. It's weird not being at home with my mum. In Australia, it's already Christmas Day. I've texted my mum and Caleb at least ten times since I woke up, but neither of them have responded. My mum promised she'd video chat tonight, but I don't think that will happen. It's already getting late in Australia. I wonder what she's doing. I wanted to actually *talk* to her tonight; it was going to be her Christmas present. She still doesn't know that I've started speaking.

To top things off, Delilah hasn't been answering my texts or phone calls either. It's Christmas Eve and no one is around. Delilah and Lucy were going to come over for a few hours today, but now I don't know if that will happen either.

I haven't seen Delilah since her Snow Ball. That night ended up going pretty well once my anxiety went away. I'm happy I went, even if I did have one of my moments.

My dad isn't home either. He said he had some last-minute Christmas shopping to do. Mum never would have left me on Christmas Eve.

My phone vibrates; hopefully someone has responded to my texts.

Delilah:-) *are you home right now?*

I respond, saying that I'm home. All alone. On Christmas Eve. I am not in the Christmas spirit.

Delilah:-) *ok:) i'll be over soon!*

At least someone didn't forget about me.

A few minutes later, the doorbell rings. I open the door to see Delilah standing there with a big smile on her face. Lucy waves to me excitedly.

"Hi, Levi!" Lucy shrieks. "Merry Christmas Eve!"

"Hi, Lucy!" I say, sounding equally as excited.

"Why are you so happy?" I ask, laughing at Delilah because she won't stop smiling.

She shrugs and doesn't say anything. Delilah moves aside and looks out to the driveway. All of a sudden, two people walk out of Delilah's car. Two very familiar people. It's my mum and Caleb.

"No way," I whisper. I feel my heart drop and butterflies erupt in my stomach.

"Merry Christmas!" Delilah says.

I run out of my house, which gets my socks all wet from the snow on the ground, and run to my mum and Caleb.

My mum instantly starts crying, and I hug her tightly.

"Hi, Levi," she says, not letting me go. "Are you still growing? How have you been? Is everything okay? I missed you so much!" she says quickly. I almost respond, but remember I can't just yet. I have to wait for the right moment.

I laugh and walk over to Caleb. He's standing with his hands in his coat pockets, and he looks freezing.

"Hey," he says, hugging me. "You have no idea how much it's sucked without you."

I smile widely, and the three of us just stare at each other. None of us can stop smiling.

"Yeah, all right, just leave all the bags to me! Don't worry about the poor guy in the background!" Aiden says, carrying four giant bags in his arms.

Delilah laughs and helps him get the rest. Caleb offers to help, but Aiden refuses to let him carry anything. My dad gets out of his car to help. I didn't even notice that his car was here too.

"You guys wanna go inside? You must be freezing!" Delilah says.

My mum and Caleb nod. They follow us all inside and awkwardly stand at the bottom of the stairs, unsure of where to go.

"You can follow me upstairs," my dad tells them.

Delilah pulls me away for a second. "You haven't spoken to them yet, right?"

"No, I was planning on doing it today."

"How do you want to tell them that you're talking?"

I shrug. "I have no idea. Did you do all this?"

She nods. "We can talk about it later though. You have to tell your mom and Caleb that you're talking. You have no idea how worried they've been about you. Do you wanna do it now or wait?"

"Now. I don't think I can wait." I hug Delilah tightly. "Thanks for all this."

I want to start talking to them as soon as possible. I don't want to have to wait a few hours, because we could be having lots of conversations in that time. I want to just announce it now and get it over with.

We walk back to where everyone else is. Aiden and my dad lead them to the couch, and are now asking them if they want anything to drink or eat. I sit in between my mum and Caleb. My mum smiles sweetly. Lucy reaches up to me, so I pick her up and put her on my lap. I bounce my knee, causing her to laugh.

"Are you Levi's mommy?" Lucy says, looking at my mum.

My mum nods. "You're Lucy, right?" My mum must remember her from video chatting.

Lucy nods. "That's me! You have a voice like Levi. Did you know that?"

"Huh?" my mum asks, looking as me, confused. I shrug and pretend I don't know what Lucy's talking about.

Lucy begins to stand on my legs and wraps her arms around my neck. She giggles as I try to get her to sit back down.

"That's a very cute Christmas tree!" my mum says.

I open my mouth to respond, but then shut it again. I nod and smile.

Delilah clears her throat. She eyes me conspiratorially, and I nod.

"So, uh, Levi has something he wants to tell you," Delilah says, smiling.

My mum scrunches her eyebrows in confusion. "Is everything okay?"

I put Lucy down for a second and stand up so I can look at my mum and Caleb. I clear my throat and nervously rub my nose. I can feel my heart beating a mile a minute. I have no idea what to say. "So, um, I'm talking now. Merry Christm—"

I'm cut off by my mum jumping up and hugging me tightly again. She starts crying all over again too. Lucy starts clapping, which causes Caleb to laugh.

"How long have you been talking?" she says, stretching her arms out so she can look at me.

I shrug. "A few weeks?"

"And you didn't tell me?" she says, laughing.

"It was gonna be your Christmas present! I wanted to surprise you."

She hugs me again. "I love you so much."

"I love you too, Mum," I say, laughing.

Caleb's smile almost stretches his entire face. "Man, I never thought I would ever hear your voice again. Someone went through puberty!"

I hit Caleb's shoulder. "Hey!"

He shrugs. "Well, you have to admit that I'm right!"

Delilah laughs, and we all sit back down. My mum holds my hand and won't stop looking at me. I think she doesn't want to ever let go, she's holding so tight.

We talk for over an hour. I tell them about Maine, and they tell me about what's been going on in Australia. It's really nice to have them around. I'm so happy they're here for Christmas. I'm surprised Caleb's parent's let him come over the holiday.

They're staying for the next two weeks. Delilah, Aiden, and my dad planned everything, which is pretty amazing. My mum is going to stay in the guest room, and Caleb will stay in my room. They debated getting a hotel, but my mum didn't want to have to leave me while she was here.

"How do you live with such cold weather?" Caleb asks, hugging his arms around himself.

Aiden laughs. "We're used to it."

"Levi's not used to it," Delilah laughs. "He usually just wraps himself in blankets."

"I do not!" I say.

"Yes, you do," Delilah says.

"Okay, maybe I do."

My mum and Caleb laugh, and I cover my face in embarrassment.

My dad calls from the kitchen. "You guys must be starving. We have all sorts of food in here if you're hungry!"

We all get up to eat, and because it's three o'clock I'm not sure if this counts as lunch or dinner. My dad didn't make any of it—he got it all at a restaurant because he is not a good cook. Wherever he got it, though, it's really good.

I sit next to Caleb and my mum while we eat. Delilah sits across from me, and I kick her under the table. She jumps and rolls her eyes once she realizes it was me. She sticks her tongue out at me, and Caleb eyes me suspiciously. I feel my cheeks heat up.

My mum asks the usual mother questions to catch up with me. Caleb asks random questions too. It's nice to actually be able to talk to them again. They probably never expected we'd have a conversation like this. I can tell how happy it's making them. It feels like I never even left them now that they're here.

Lucy pokes my arm to get my attention.

"Yeah, Lucy?" I say. She motions for me to lean closer, which is hard because she's not directly beside me.

"Who is that?" she whispers, pointing to Caleb.

"That's my friend Caleb."

"Oh, okay. He talks like you and your mommy."

"Yeah, he does."

"Except he doesn't look like you. He has a big nose."

I start laughing, and, thankfully, Caleb couldn't hear her. Delilah starts laughing too.

"Lucy, that's not very nice," Delilah whispers. She can't stop giggling.

"Well, it's true." Lucy shrugs. She continues eating, which ends the conversation about Caleb.

Once we're all finished eating, we sit around the Christmas tree to open presents. Since Delilah, Lucy, and Aiden will be with their families tomorrow, we decided we should give each other our presents today in case we don't see each other.

Mitchell is supposed to be here too. He texted me, saying he was on his way a few minutes ago. I knew his family doesn't do much for Christmas, so I invited him over.

The doorbell rings, and Mitchell walks in nervously. He waves shyly to everyone.

"Mitchell, that's my mum and my friend Caleb," I say, introducing them.

"H-Hi, nice to m-meet you," he says, shaking my mum's hand.

"Nice to meet you too!" my mum says.

"Cool hair, dude," Caleb tells him.

Mitchell smiles. "Thanks."

Mitchell sits next to Aiden and nervously bites his nails.

"Is everyone here?" Caleb asks.

I nod.

"Present time! I love presents!" Lucy shrieks. She's taken a position on my lap again.

Delilah passes Lucy a present, which is from me. Lucy quickly unwraps it, throwing the paper all over the place.

"It's a giant Olaf!" she yells. She hugs the huge Olaf stuffed animal I got her, and she can't stop smiling. "I love him, I love him, I love him! I will never ever let him melt!"

She moves so she's facing me and hugs me tightly while still holding on to Olaf. "Thanks, Levi!"

"You're welcome!"

"Can he open the present I got him?" Lucy asks.

Delilah nods and passes me a box. "You didn't have to get me something!" I tell Lucy.

"I made it very special, just for you!"

I open it and it's a picture of Lucy and me. I didn't even know this picture existed. It's from Thanksgiving, I think, when I first met her. She decorated the picture frame with stickers and glitter.

"I love it," I tell Lucy. "Thank you very much!"

"Yay! He likes it!"

Everyone laughs while Lucy beams. She stays quiet once she starts playing with the Olaf. She's whispering stuff, but I have no idea what she's saying. It's cute seeing how happy she is.

I give Aiden the present I got him. It's a giant banana pillow, since he's always eating bananas. I also found a signed picture from his favorite football player.

"This is so cool!" he says, holding it up so everyone can see. "Where'd you find this?"

"Online," I tell him.

"This is awesome. Thanks, Levi!"

I open Aiden's present, which is the newest FIFA game.

"Wait, you got him the new FIFA? That's sick!" Caleb says, straining his neck to look at it. "I don't even have that yet!"

Mitchell hands me a very badly-wrapped present, which causes me to laugh.

"I'm n-not very g-good at wr-wrapping gifts," Mitchell says, blushing.

"That's okay, me neither," I tell him.

I open it up, and it's a Modern Baseball T-shirt. I told him a while ago that it's one of the only bands I actually like. I thank him, and he opens up my gift to him.

He grins when he opens it. It's a movie all about bands and their stories. I thought he'd like that.

"Th-This is so c-cool!" he says. I can tell that he's really excited. He runs his fingers over the edge and reads the description.

"No way!" Caleb yells, walking over to Mitchell and looking at it. "Levi, where did you get this?"

"I found it online," I tell him.

Caleb points to me. "You better have gotten me something like that," he says, laughing.

I shrug and laugh.

Delilah and I decided not to exchange gifts today. We promised to see each other tomorrow. I thought bringing Caleb and my mum here was her and Aiden's gift to me, but apparently not. It's already the best Christmas I could've asked for.

"Who wants to sing some Christmas carols!" my mum says once we're done opening presents.

"Mummmm. We're not singing Christmas carols!" I say, putting my face in my hands.

"It's a Christmas tradition, so we have to!" she says, laughing. "Go play some songs for us, Levi."

I blush and shake my head. "I haven't played in months, Mum."

"C'mon," she says, pushing me toward the dusty piano that's in the corner of the room. It's always been there, I've just never played it.

"You play piano?" Delilah asks quietly.

I nod. "Not very well." I took lessons when I was younger, but it's not something I do a lot.

I sit down at the piano, even though I don't want to. Delilah sits beside me. I slowly place my fingers on the keys, trying to remember a song to play. I haven't played the piano in what feels like forever.

I start playing "Winter Wonderland," because it's the only one I can remember right now. Once I start playing, it feels like I never stopped, which is weird. I thought I would forget everything, but I don't.

"You're really good," Delilah tells me.

I shake my head. "Not really."

I continue playing a few more songs, only because everyone begs me to. Delilah leans her head on my shoulder as I play.

I thought this would be an awful day, but it's turning out to be one of the best ones yet. I have everyone here with me, and it finally feels like Christmas.

Chapter Forty-Three

LEVI

"M erry Christmas," my mum says quietly as she opens my bedroom door. I smile and sleepily rub my eyes to shield them
from the bright morning light.

"Merry Christmas," Caleb responds groggily, putting his face
in his pillow. "What time is it?"

"It's nine," my mum responds.

Caleb groans. "I barely slept all night. How am I supposed to
get used to the time zones?"

I laugh. "You'll get used to it." I slowly get out of bed and
quickly tug down my T-shirt, which went up slightly while I slept.

"Breakfast is ready when you are," Mum says, leaving my room.

I quickly try to make my hair a little more presentable, even
though it's going to be a mess no matter what. Caleb refuses to get
out of bed, and I'm pretty sure he fell back asleep, so I throw one
of my pillows at him.

"A few more minutes," Caleb mumbles, barely moving.

"C'mon, Caleb. I can smell pancakes and bacon. If you don't
get up, I'm going to eat it all."

Caleb slowly sits up. "Okay, fine." He runs his hands through
his hair and yawns. He follows me to the kitchen, and I can hear
him yawning every few seconds.

My mum tells us to sit at the table, so we do. She brings us our breakfast, which consists of eggs, pancakes, toast, and bacon. I don't remember the last time I actually had anything other than cereal for breakfast.

We both quickly eat, and my parents wait patiently for us to finish since they must have already eaten. My parents have always remained friendly, I think for my well-being, but it's always nice to see them having a normal conversation and not fighting.

It sort of feels like a dream, or maybe even a Christmas miracle, that both of my parents and Caleb are here. I thought it would just be my dad and me, and that Christmas would be really boring.

"Is Delilah coming over later?" Caleb asks with his mouth full. I nod.

Caleb smirks. "What'd you get her?"

I shrug. "It's not that great."

"Well, what is it?"

"I got her a necklace. It has, like, heartbeat lines on it connected to a heart. You know, like, the lines on a heart monitor," I tell him, feeling my cheeks heat up.

"Girls love stuff like that. Good choice."

"Are you boys ready yet?" my mum asks.

I nod and quickly finish the last of my breakfast. I sit down in front of the tree, and Caleb sits beside me. My parents sit on the couch.

"My presents for you guys were already shipped out," I tell my mum and Caleb.

My dad shakes his head. "Check under the tree. I didn't mail them."

"But what about Caleb's? How'd you—"

"Don't worry, I have it all under control," my dad tells me, laughing.

My dad helped me buy everything, since obviously I couldn't afford much. I had some money saved up, but not a lot. At some point, I guess I'm going to need a job.

I smile and search for presents marked with their names. I find Caleb's first, which isn't even under the tree, and give it to him.

He quickly unwraps the large box and opens it up.

"No way. You did not!" he yells.

I laugh. "I did."

I got Caleb a new guitar, because when I was still in Australia, his guitar was falling apart. He got his guitar when he was seven, and it was passed down to him, so it's pretty beat up now. He was always trying to get a new one, but his parents never would buy it, and he couldn't afford it himself.

He runs his hand over the neck and gently takes it out of the box. He quickly tunes it and plays some chords.

"This is perfect. I can't believe you got this for me!" He can't stop smiling or take his eyes off the guitar.

"Good luck getting it on the plane home," I tell him.

He shrugs and laughs, continuing to play.

He puts the guitar aside after a little, and we continue to open presents. Caleb brought me a bunch of stuff from Australia, which I really like. I've been getting really homesick lately, and he knows that. There's food, pictures, seashells, and it even kind of smells like Australia, which is weird. I never realized Australia had a distinct smell. He even got some of our old friends to write messages in a book. I honestly didn't think people would notice I was gone, but according to their messages, they do. I always just thought no one cared about me anymore. The majority of people that wrote messages haven't spoken to me in months.

I try not to cry because I'm overcome with emotions after opening Caleb's gift.

"Dude, you better not start bawling," Caleb says, laughing.

I quickly wipe my eyes. "I'm not," I tell him, laughing at myself.

I give my mum a homemade movie I made for her, which has videos and pictures I found from when I was younger. There are current ones in it too. My dad had secretly been taking videos and pictures of me, and so had Delilah. Little does she know that I did the same with her.

We finish opening presents an hour later. I gave my dad a book that my mum had sent here by accident when I moved, which had a lot of things from my childhood, like school projects and photos. My dad always says he wishes he paid more attention to the stuff I did when I was younger, so I thought he'd like it.

My parents got me two tickets so I can go home to Australia during the summer. I'm not sure if it's to go back for good, or just for a trip. I'm honestly torn between here and Australia, because they're both my home now. I don't want to think about that right now though.

After presents, we all just sit around and talk, which is really nice. It's been months since I've spoken to my mum and Caleb, so I think they want to talk about anything and everything.

Delilah texts me and tells me she'll come over sometime around noon to exchange presents. I am still nervous she might not like the necklace I got her.

Caleb and I go back to my room, because he wants to play the guitar. He sits down on the air mattress that's in my room and plays random chords on the guitar. He hums lightly as he plays.

He stops abruptly when my phone vibrates with a text from Delilah.

"Are you guys dating?" he asks, smirking mischievously.

I nearly choke, and my cheeks blush. "No."

"Sure seems like it."

"We're just friends."

"Friends don't kick each other under the table or give each other heart necklaces," Caleb says, using finger quotes around the word *friends*.

"Yes, they do."

"Not really. Are you blind, Levi? You obviously both like each other."

I shake my head and shrug. "Maybe we do. We're just not doing anything about it."

"Well, you should. I don't know what she's done, but I'm pretty sure she's the reason you've completely changed since I last saw you. Whatever's going on, it's working."

I roll my eyes and hear a knock at the door. Delilah walks in and smiles.

"Hey, guys," she says, standing in the doorway.

Caleb waves and smiles. "Merry Christmas!"

"Merry Christmas! Nice hair, Levi," she says, laughing.

"Okay, I know it's a mess, no need to tell me." I run my fingers through my hair to try to fix it.

"I'll be going now," Caleb says, picking up his guitar and leaving my room.

Delilah sits beside me on my bed and places a gift bag in my lap. "Merry Christmas," she whispers, smiling widely.

"You already brought Caleb and my mum here, you didn't have to get me something else," I tell her.

"It's nothing huge," she says, joining her fingers with mine.

"I can't open the gift if I'm holding your hand," I say awkwardly. She laughs. "Right."

I take out the tissue paper and pull out a beanie. More specifically, the beanie Delilah took and never gave back. There's also a sweatshirt she never returned to me.

"Figured you'd be wanting those at some point," she says.

I laugh. "I wondered where these went."

I take Delilah's hand in mine and place the small box in the palm of her hand.

She unwraps it slowly and gently opens the box to reveal the necklace.

"Levi, it's beautiful," she gasps.

"It's a heartbeat. I thought you'd like it. I thought of you when I saw it because you're the reason my heart continues to beat. Without you, I'm not sure where I'd be," I tell her nervously.

263

Delilah hugs me tightly. "This is the best gift ever, thank you. I love—I love all the thought you put into it."

I blush. "It's no big deal, really."

I help her put the necklace on, and she runs her finger across the zigzagged line.

"I don't ever want to take it off," she says.

"I was so worried you wouldn't like it."

"I love it. I couldn't ask for a better Christmas present from you."

I shrug. "Having you in my life is the best present I could have ever received."

Chapter Forty-Four

Levi

"Caleb?" I whisper. It's way past midnight, and I haven't been able to sleep for the past two hours.

"Yeah?" he mumbles.

"Are you awake?" I prop myself up on my elbow to try and see him, even though it's pitch black.

"Obviously, if I'm talking," he groans.

"Well, you sleep talk sometimes," I say, laughing.

"No, I don't."

"Yes, you do."

I hear him move on his air mattress, and the light from his phone illuminates his face.

"It's almost one in the morning. What's wrong?" he says.

"I can't sleep."

"And why's that?"

I shrug, even though he can't see me. "I can't stop thinking."

"About what?"

Caleb's always been like this. He's always concerned about me and asks questions to make sure I'm okay. Most of my "friends" back in Australia never bothered to see if I was really okay. Caleb never gets annoyed, though, no matter how awful I am.

"Delia. This happens a lot. And especially now that it's the first Christmas without her. I was trying to avoid being sad the past few days, but I can't help it, and it gets really bad at night, and I never know what to do because once I start thinking, it doesn't stop, and I just get wallowed up in my sadness, and I'm really trying not to let it happen, but sometimes I can't control it, and—"

"Levi, it's way too early in the morning to be speaking that fast. Breathe. Relax."

"I can't, though, because she's every single thought in my head right now, no matter how hard I try to stop it," I say, rubbing my eyes.

Caleb sighs. "I know this is hard, and it will probably always be a little difficult. There will be a lot of 'firsts' without Delia. It's okay though. You just need to cope with it, and it'll get easier as time goes on." Caleb yawns quietly. "Try to go to sleep, and we can talk more later."

"All right. Thanks, Caleb."

He yawns again. "Goodnight, Levi."

"Goodnight."

I stay awake for another hour. I try to fall asleep, but I can't. No matter how hard I try to calm my mind, my thoughts are going wild.

So many things have changed since last Christmas. Almost nothing is the same. Last Christmas, I was at my *home-home* in Australia. I had spent the morning with Delia, and we stayed up late that night talking on the phone. She gave me a bunch of really bad movies and candy for Christmas, promising that we would watch one movie every Friday and make fun of them. We only got through half of them. I haven't touched them since. They're sitting somewhere in the closet in my room back in Australia. I wonder what Delia would have wanted for Christmas. I wonder what we would have given each other. I can't help but think about what Christmas would have been like with her.

At some point, I must have fallen asleep, because I wake up in the morning to the bright sun shining through my window. I squint and look down at the floor to where Caleb is, and he's still asleep.

I quietly get out of bed and walk out of my room. Thankfully, I don't wake Caleb up. My mum is sitting on the couch, watching something on TV. I sit down beside her, and she smiles.

"Good morning," she says quietly. She's always quiet in the morning. Even when it's just her and me in our house, it's like she doesn't want to wake anyone up.

"Hi," I say, equally as quiet.

"You look tired," she tells me.

I rub my eyes. "Because I am."

She sighs. "Is everything okay?"

I nod. "Yeah, I was just thinking too much, I guess."

She puts her hand on top of mine. "Are you sure everything is okay? Did something happen?"

"No, no, everything's fine. I was just thinking a lot about Delia, but I'm good now. It happens every once in a while, I'm used to it."

"Have you been taking your pills?" she asks, concerned.

I nod. "Every day. I promise."

She smiles a little. "Good. You're getting much better."

"I know."

My mum gets up from the couch and leaves the room. She comes back with a large envelope with my name on it. "I wasn't sure when to give you this, but now seems like a good time. It's from Delia's parents."

I slowly take the envelope and debate whether or not I should open it. I'm afraid of what might be inside.

"They thought you would like it," my mum tells me.

I slowly rip open the envelope, and two pictures fall out. A piece of paper comes out too.

I look at the two pictures. One is of Delia and me at one of my games. We're talking through the fence, like we always did. Our fingers are slightly intertwined through the fence's wires, and she's smiling widely.

The second picture is Delia leaning her head on my shoulder with her eyes shut and a small smile is on her lips. I don't remember

267

this picture ever being taken, or even when it was taken. But I like it. I like to remember her smiling.

I try not to cry and take a deep breath.

"I haven't looked at pictures of her for a really, really long time," I whisper.

"I know," my mum says. Even without me telling her, my mum always seems to know things.

I open up the letter her parents wrote me and read it over a few times.

Levi,

Merry Christmas! We hope all is going well for you. We really do miss you. Your mum's been keeping us updated, it's like you never left!

We found these pictures in Delia's room and thought you might want them.

We want you to remember the happier times. You always made Delia very happy, and we know she did the same for you. She wouldn't want to see you sad or upset. All she ever wanted was for you to be happy.

Your mum has told us that things are getting better. You've made some good friends, which is fantastic! Please don't hold yourself back from them. We are sure they are all great, and you're making good memories with them. From what your mum has told us, they seem perfect for you! I'm sure Delia is looking down on you smiling. We know how hard it is to let go of someone who meant so much, but that's what Delia, and we, want. We want what will make you happy.

We hope you're having a great time in Maine, and we hope to see you soon. We don't want to end this on a sad note, so here's a picture of Delia and you. Delia loved these pictures! Look at your hair!

Be well.
Merry Christmas, Levi.

I smile, even though there are tears in my eyes. My mum hasn't stopped looking at me this whole time.

"They're right. We all want you to be happy, Levi. It's been so hard seeing you so sad. You have no idea how proud I am of how far you've come the past few months," my mum says, her voice slightly breaking.

"I love you, Mum," I whisper.

"I love you too. We all want what's best for you," she says, hugging me tightly.

We talk for a few minutes about Delia, but it doesn't make me sad like it usually does. It makes me strangely happy. My eyes are slightly watery, though.

Looking at the pictures, I notice differences instead of similarities between Delia and Delilah. I think about how Delilah bites her nails, and Delia didn't. Delilah's eyes are a little lighter, and her smile is a little wider. The more I look, the more I see.

I quickly wipe my eyes and stand up from the couch.

"I'm gonna go to Delilah's," I tell my mum. "I have to talk to her."

I grab my jacket and walk outside toward Delilah's. Hopefully she's awake.

I'm really thankful that Delia's parents wrote that letter and sent the pictures. I really needed it right now. It was nice to read what they had to say and see the old pictures. Although Delia and I didn't know each other when we were younger, we always compared pictures. It surprisingly didn't make me sad to read their letter or look at the pictures they sent. It made me happy, and I feel somewhat lighter. They told me what I needed to hear from them, which is that it's okay to move on. Many people have said that, but I guess what I needed was for Delia's own parents to say it. No one knew Delia better than them.

I call Delilah, and she picks up after a few rings.

"Yes, Levi?" she says.

"I'm outside your house," I tell her as I'm walking up her drive-way. I open up the front door that's always unlocked. "Okay, I'm inside your house now." I wave to Lucy while she's watching TV. "I'm coming to your room. And I'm here," I say, hanging up the phone and sitting down on Delilah's bed. She's standing in front of her closet, wearing her pajamas, and her hair's in a messy bun.

"What if I had already started getting dressed? You can't just barge in here," she tells me while pretending to be upset.

I shrug. "Too late. Nice pajamas." Her pants have smiling pen-guins on them.

"Not as bad as your pizza underwear," she tells me.

"Okay, you walked into my house *once* when I was getting changed, and you haven't let me live it down," I say, putting my head in my hands.

She sits beside me and laughs. "Why are you over here so early, anyway?" I notice that she's wearing the necklace I got her.

"I wanted to talk to you."

"About what?" She tilts her head to the side and scrunches her nose cutely.

"Well, Delia's parents sent me a letter, and it made me realize that I really like being with you, and you make me really happy, and you're the good thing I needed, and I know I say stuff like this all the time, but I'm really thankful to have you in my life, and I felt the need to come and tell you that right now because you never know when something might happen," I say very quickly. I feel my cheeks heat up.

"You're so cute, Levi," she says, smiling. "I'm thankful to have you in my life too."

"But I don't think you know how much you've done for me. You're the greatest thing that's ever happened to me, and you're making my life so much better. And it's weird to think that I lost someone who was that person to me, and I thought I would never be happy again. But I am, and it's because of you. I used to think that I could never find someone that would make me as happy as

Delia did, but you do. You make me happier than I've ever been. It's a different kind of happy than how Delia made me feel. It's a whole different set of emotions, and it scares me so much." I'm still talking really quickly. I barely take any breaths in between sentences.

She reaches out to hold my hand. "Don't be scared," she says quietly. She smiles lightly. "It's okay that someone other than Delia is making you happy. I'm happy that I'm that person for you."

"Everyone is saying that. But that's not what I'm scared about."

"Then what is it?"

"I like you, Delilah. A lot. All you have to do is smile, and my heart starts racing, and I hate it. I never thought I would ever feel this way about someone other than Delia," I blurt out.

She smiles and squeezes my hand. "Sometimes the best things aren't really what you were searching for."

She leans closer to me, and I can feel her light breaths. She smiles again and blinks slowly.

"Is this okay?" she whispers. It's like what I used to say to her.

I nod and smile, even though I'm extremely nervous. Our noses are almost touching.

Suddenly, Lucy comes running into the room. "I can't reach my sippy cup in the fridge!" she yells.

Delilah quickly scoots away from me and jumps off the bed. She rolls her eyes and walks over to Lucy.

"I, uh, I'll be right back," Delilah tells me as she goes into the kitchen.

I nervously rub my nose as I wait for Delilah to come back. What even happened? Is it going to be awkward when she comes back? Like, was that an almost kiss? I don't even know, I'm so confused, everything is so confusing. I don't know what just happened. Maybe it wasn't an almost kiss, and I just imagined it.

Delilah comes back shortly after and sits down next to me again. "Sorry about that," she says, looking down at her hands.

"It's okay."

"She ruins everything."

I shrug and rub the back of my neck. "I should get going. Caleb wanted to go see some new movie."

"Oh, okay. I, uh, I'll see you later then," she says quietly.

"Yeah."

"Oh, and Levi?"

"Yeah?"

She quickly kisses the tip of my nose and her cheeks turn pink. "You make me happy too."

Chapter Forty-Five

LEVI

W ait, what do you mean you had an 'almost kiss' with Delilah?"
Caleb asks me. He's sitting cross-legged on the air mattress
with his guitar beside him. I got home about an hour ago, and
Caleb has been helping me figure out what happened.

I pace my room slowly. "I don't know. Like, we were leaned
in and everything, and then Lucy came in and couldn't reach her
sippy cup, and Delilah left, and when she came back she kissed my
nose," I tell him, all in one breath. "Is that an almost kiss?"

"You literally had a girlfriend for over a year, and you're horrible
at relationships. Clearly it was an almost kiss!"

I pull at the ends of my hair and take a deep breath. "So what
does that mean now? Is it going to be awkward the next time I see
her? It's so going to be awkward, I know it will be. Am I supposed
to kiss her for real now? I don't know . . ."

"Stop answering your own questions," Caleb says, laughing
lightly. "You need to relax. Everything will work out. If you make
it awkward, it will be awkward."

"I won't make it awkward, then."

"You're one of the most awkward people I know," Caleb says.

I groan and sit down on my bed and put my head in my hands.

"Give me your phone," Caleb says, reaching his hand toward me.

"No, why?"

"Just give it to me."

I reluctantly pull my phone out of my pocket and toss it to Caleb.

He unlocks my phone quickly, and it's weird he still remembers my password. He quickly types something and puts the phone up to his ear.

"No, you're not doing what I think you're doing," I exclaim, trying to grab the phone from him.

He moves away from me so I can't reach my phone, and he keeps kicking me away.

"Hi, Delilah! It's Caleb!" he says cheerily.

"Hi?" I hear Delilah say. I have my head close to the phone so I can hear too.

"So, I was wondering, do you want to go ice skating with Levi and me tomorrow? Aiden and Mitchell can come too. I just thought it'd be fun for us to all go." Caleb smirks at me and raises his eyebrows. I shove him, and he kicks me away from him again.

Caleb continues to talk, but I can't hear Delilah anymore. "Okay . . . Sounds good . . . We'll ask Aiden and Mitchell too . . . See you then . . . Bye!"

Caleb gives me my phone and picks his guitar back up. He begins to play softly.

"Well, are you gonna tell me what that was about?" I ask.

"Oh, I mean, I could. If you really wanted me to."

"Do you want me to send you back home?" I say sarcastically.

He puts his hands up. "Jeez. We're all going to go ice skating tomorrow at one o'clock. Call Aiden and Mitchell to ask them."

"And why are we going ice skating?"

"Like I said, you are clueless in relationships. Ice skating is romantic, I am told. You can hold her hand and skate around and do whatever cute stuff people in relationships do."

"We're not in a relationship."

"Well, you're close enough. Buy her a hot chocolate and warm up her hands or something. Girls like that."

"You've never even been in a serious relationship. How do you know what girls like?"

"I'm Caleb Hopkins. I know *everything.*"

"I'm seriously going to put you on the earliest flight to Australia."

"I'm being helpful. I'm a great friend, and you'll be thanking me tomorrow—just wait and see."

"I'm nervous," I tell Caleb as we park in front of Delilah's house. Aiden is driving, and Mitchell's meeting us there. Caleb is in the passenger seat, and he turns around to look at me.

"It's Delilah. Don't be nervous," he says.

"But she *makes* me nervous!" I blurt out.

Aiden laughs and turns around too. "You've both admitted to liking each other, so stop being so panicky. Just go for it."

"But—" I say.

"Don't even say anything about Delia," Caleb mumbles, turning around. He always knows when I'm about to bring her up. "Delia was then. Delilah is now. It's okay, Levi. I promise."

Aiden smiles sympathetically.

"Okay," I say quietly, opening the car door. I'm not sure why I'm so anxious; I always hang out with Delilah. But that almost kiss has changed everything.

I'm afraid I'm going to mess everything up. Everything good in my life always turns bad, and I don't want that to happen with Delilah too. I'm trying my best to not mess things up.

I ring Delilah's doorbell and wait patiently on her front steps. The door opens shortly after, and Delilah stands there, smiling.

"Hey," she says, walking outside. "Nice mittens."

"Caleb has my gloves," I pout. I nervously fix my hair, which just makes it worse because I have mittens on. Delilah laughs and quickly reaches up to help me. "Thanks," I mumble.

She smiles and gets into the car.

"Hey, guys!" Delilah says.

"Hi!" Caleb and Aiden say in unison.

Delilah and I laugh. Delilah's hand is in the center of the seat, and I debate reaching for it, but I don't.

Aiden starts to drive to the skating rink, and we all talk about random stuff. Caleb and Aiden argue over which radio station to listen to, but they finally agree on listening to one of Aiden's CDs. I like how Caleb gets along so well with Aiden and Delilah. It's like we've all known each other our whole lives. Caleb fits in perfectly with us. I really don't want him to go back to Australia in a week.

We get to the rink, and Mitchell is sitting on a bench waiting for us. He waves excitedly when he sees us. He has a giant sweater on that goes way past his hands, so he continuously tugs the sleeves up.

The rest of us get some skates and sit on the bench to put them on.

Everyone else gets their skates on with ease, but I stare at them in confusion.

"Guys," I whisper.

"Yeah?" Delilah says, sounding concerned.

Caleb groans. "Levi, you better not say what I think you're going to say."

"I can't tie the skates tight enough," I mumble, struggling to tie the short laces.

Caleb starts laughing uncontrollably, to the point he's gasping for breath. I slap his arm.

"It's not funny!" I tell him.

"It kind of is," Aiden says, laughing too. He already has his skates on and is walking around. I don't get how he's able to walk on the blades.

Delilah smiles. "I'll help. You don't know how to skate, do you?"

I shake my head.

Delilah smiles and ties the laces on my skates with ease.

"Now how do I stand up?" I whisper to Delilah.

She laughs and stands up in front of me. She holds out her hands to me. "Just hold on tight and try to get balanced. It's not that difficult."

I grab tightly onto Delilah's hands and try to get up, but fall back onto the bench.

"Let me try again," I say, laughing.

I try again and manage to stand up. I hold on to Delilah's hand, and waddle awkwardly over to the edge of the ice so I can hold tightly to the ledge.

"Can we just go out there already before I fall?" I ask.

"Y-You're probably g-gonna fall on the i-ice," Mitchell says.

"But there's a wall to hold on to. I can do it."

Aiden, Caleb, and Mitchell step onto the ice and skate away from Delilah and me. Caleb looks back at us and gives me a thumbs-up.

Delilah steps into the rink and reaches her hands out toward me. "Just step slowly onto the ice."

"I'm gonna fall," I whine.

"I won't let you fall. C'mon," she says, smiling.

I reach for her hands and slowly step onto the frozen wasteland before me. I slip a little with my first step, but Delilah grabs tightly to my hands. I'm not sure how she stays balanced with me almost knocking her over.

"I don't like this," I say, laughing. "It's weird."

"You'll get used to it."

It's supposed to be the other way around. I should be teaching Delilah how to skate. It's embarrassing that I don't know how. I've never been skating before in my life. I've never even been able to roller skate.

Delilah starts skating slowly. I'm somehow able to skate slowly with her, although I lose my balance a lot. We're going very slowly so I don't fall, and she never lets go of my hand.

"Your hand is very hard to hold with a mitten on," Delilah tells me.

"Oh, well, I can fix it," I say. I fold off the top of the mittens, since they're the convertible kind.

"Much better," Delilah says, entwining her fingers with mine.

We pick up the pace as I get more comfortable with skating, and I'm actually not that bad. I thought I would constantly be falling, but I haven't yet. Caleb skates quickly by us. He used to always go to indoor skating rinks when he was younger.

"Hot chocolate," he whispers in my ear as he passes.

I roll my eyes.

"Do you want anything? Like hot chocolate?" I ask Delilah.

"Maybe in a little."

"Okay."

Suddenly, I completely lose my balance, and within a second I'm crashing onto the ice. I land flat on my butt, and Delilah falls down with me. We both sit on the ice, chuckling.

"I just saw my life flash before my eyes," I say.

"You're such a klutz," she laughs, standing up. She reaches down to help me, and I can barely stand back up. I keep slipping, and I can't straighten my legs.

"I think it's time for hot chocolate," I say, still sitting on the ice. I don't even bother to stand up, I just crawl to the exit. I can hear Delilah laughing behind me.

I get off the ice and sit down on the ground to take off my skates. Delilah sits beside me. I brush off some ice that's on my pants and try to warm myself up.

"You're a goof too," Delilah says, taking off her skates as well.

"You're the one who decided to sit on the floor with the goof, though," I tell her.

She rolls her eyes and smiles.

"I saw that," I hear Caleb say. I look up to see Caleb, Aiden, and Mitchell standing above us.

"You fell too," I say.

"At least I got myself back up."

"I'm h-hungry," Mitchell says abruptly.

"Me too. I want some nachos. Do you guys want anything?" Aiden asks.

"Two hot chocolates, please," I tell him.

Aiden and Mitchell go over to the concessions, and Caleb goes to the bathroom. Delilah and I find a table in the corner.

"Today was fun," I tell her. "Thanks for teaching me how to skate."

"You weren't too bad," she says, leaning her head on my shoulder. "You just have to figure out how to stand up after falling."

"That was pretty embarrassing, wasn't it?" I say, turning my head so it's almost hidden behind Delilah's.

"Kinda. It was cute though."

I laugh, and we sit in silence. It's a nice silence, though. She's breathing slowly while she's leaning against me. I take her hands inside mine and try to warm them up like Caleb advised me to. Her hands are pretty cold.

Caleb walks over and sits down across from us. "How cute," he says.

Delilah moves slightly, but doesn't pick her head up. I continue holding her hand inside both of mine and set them on my lap.

Aiden and Mitchell come over with the food and give us our hot chocolates. Neither of us move to drink it because we don't want to let go of each other's hands.

Delilah sighs and shifts closer to me.

"Are you tired?" I whisper.

"No. I just want to be closer to you."

Chapter Forty-Six

LEVI

After ice skating, we all went to Aiden's house. Each of us fell asleep while watching a movie, and I when I wake up on the couch, Caleb is lying on the floor, and Aiden is snoring in a chair. Mitchell is leaning against the stairs holding a stuffed animal, and I'm not really sure how or where he found it.

I look around for Delilah, but she's not anywhere in the room. Maybe she went home.

I quietly get off the couch and step around Mitchell to get upstairs. I don't know if anyone else in Aiden's family is awake right now, but I hope they're not.

I walk into the bathroom and almost scream when I see Delilah standing in there, putting her hair up.

"Levi, what are you doing?" she whispers, slapping my chest.

"Why didn't you lock the door?" I ask.

"No one else was awake! It's only seven in the morning! I thought you always woke up late!" she whisper-screams.

"I thought *you* would wake up late."

She rolls her eyes and laughs. She quickly finishes putting her hair up and turns to look at me. "Your hair really is messy in the morning."

"Stop it," I say. I quickly look in the mirror and try to fix it.

She ruffles my hair and messes it up even more. "Don't worry, it's cute."

"No, it's not. You're just saying that."

She laughs and shakes her head. She grabs my hand and pulls me out of the bathroom. We head into the kitchen and see Aiden standing in front of the fridge.

"Hey, guys! Want anything?" he asks.

I shake my head.

"There's not much here. Maybe we can all go out for breakfast," Delilah says while looking into the fridge as well.

"Yeah, that sounds good," Aiden responds.

"They probably won't be up for a while," Delilah tells us, walking into the living room.

"You usually wake up late. Why are you up early?" I ask her.

"How do you know when I wake up?" she says.

I shrug. "You always respond to my texts late."

"Okay, well, you're right. Aiden's snoring woke me up." She sits down on the couch, and I sit beside her.

"I do not snore!" Aiden defends himself.

I smile widely.

"Why are you smiling?" she asks, smiling now too.

"No reason. I'm just happy."

I've been in Maine for around five months now, and I never would have thought that this is how things would be. I thought I would be miserable and upset and hating everything still. But now I'm talking and sitting beside a girl I really like, and three of the best possible friends I could ask for are downstairs. It's amazing how things turn out.

"I'm gonna go try to wake them up," Aiden says, heading downstairs.

Delilah crosses her legs and reaches over to join her fingers with mine. I get butterflies every time she does this.

"Does Caleb always talk in his sleep?" Delilah asks me.

I laugh. "Sometimes, I don't really know."

"I've been meaning to ask you something," she says abruptly.

"What is it?"

I get slightly nervous, because I'm not sure what she's going to ask me.

"Remember Thanksgiving?" she asks.

I nod.

"What did Lucy tell you?"

"What?" I'm not sure what she's talking about. That was the first day I met Lucy, and she talked a lot.

"She said something that made you laugh. It was the first time I heard you make a sound, let alone *laugh*."

"Oh, I don't remember," I say quickly.

"C'mon, I know you do," she says while nudging my shoulder.

"It's really nothing important."

"Pleeease?"

She looks at me with wide eyes and sticks out her bottom lip.

"Um, she asked if she could be the flower girl when you and I get married," I mumble. I feel my cheeks heat up.

Delilah laughs. "She did not!"

"She did."

"That's so embarrassing!"

"It was cute."

"What'd you say to her?!"

"I said yes," I say, almost inaudibly. "Well, like, I nodded."

Delilah smiles.

We stop talking when we see Caleb walking upstairs, with Aiden just behind.

"I couldn't wake Mitchell up. He kept telling me to leave," Aiden tells us, laughing.

"Hello, lovebirds," Caleb says groggily.

"Good morning, Caleb," Delilah says.

"The floor is not comfortable," Caleb says, sitting down on the couch across from us.

"I slept nicely on the couch," I say.

"Lucky you."

"I slept up here because you all make too many noises in your sleep," Delilah says.

"I don't," I say defensively.

"You didn't. Caleb kept mumbling stuff, and Aiden and Mitchell snore."

Caleb runs his hand through his hair. "Why do I keep talking in my sleep? What do I say?"

Delilah shrugs. "I didn't understand anything you said. I don't think it was even English."

"I only speak English. I think you were dreaming," Caleb says.

My stomach grumbles really loudly, and both of them turn to look at me. Delilah starts laughing.

"Was that . . . your stomach?" she asks.

I nod. "I'm hungry!"

"Then let's go wake up Mitchell and go out for breakfast!" Delilah says.

"Yeah, I'm starving," Caleb says, standing up.

Caleb runs down the stairs and taps Mitchell on the shoulder.

Mitchell pushes Caleb's hand away. "L-Let me sl-sleep," he murmurs. He hugs the stuffed animal closer to him.

"We're going out for breakfast," Delilah says.

Mitchell sits up and looks at the stuffed animal in confusion. "Wh-What is this?"

"That's Hunter's. I don't know where you found it," Aiden says, laughing.

Mitchell shrugs and gently puts it down on the stairs.

"Where are we going for breakfast?" Aiden asks. He grabs his sweatshirt off a chair and pulls it over his head.

Delilah shrugs. "Wherever you guys want to go."

"I don't know what's around here," Caleb says, "but I want pancakes."

"I know the perfect place! Let's go!" Aiden says.

We all get our jackets and head to Aiden's car. Mitchell sits in the passenger seat, and Caleb, Delilah, and I squish into the back.

Aiden drives down a road that I'm kind of familiar with. I realize we're going to the little diner that Delilah and I went to a while ago.

"I remember this place," I whisper to her. For some reason, it makes me really happy that we're going here.

She nods. "That was the day we walked on the beach."

I nod quickly. I can't stop smiling. I like that she remembers too.

We go inside and sit at a table in the back corner. Delilah sits beside me in the booth, and I can't help but watch her while she looks at the menu. She looks cute when she's concentrating.

"Are you gonna look at the menu or just stare at her?" Caleb whispers. Thankfully, Delilah doesn't hear him.

I stare at him with wide eyes and mouth, "I am not staring at her!"

"Yeah, you kinda are. Man, you're whipped."

I open up my menu and put it in front of my face so Caleb can't see me. I quickly look over the top. "I am not," I say to Caleb, and go back to reading the menu.

I decide on chocolate chip waffles and home fries. I keep getting more and more hungry as we wait.

"Tell your stomach to quiet down," Delilah says, laughing.

"I can't help it!" I didn't think it was *that* loud.

Delilah giggles. She reaches into her jacket pocket and pulls out a bag of Skittles.

"I was saving these for later, but here you go," she says, handing them to me.

I smile widely. "Thanks." I open up the bag and take out a few red ones and give them to Delilah.

"So, tomorrow's New Year's Eve," Aiden says, taking a sip of his coffee.

"Yes, nice observation, Aiden," Delilah says.

He rolls his eyes. "I mean, we should all do something."

"L-Like w-what?" Mitchell asks.

Aiden shrugs. "I dunno. Just hang out. Watch the New Year's Eve show on TV. Go to a party."

"No parties, please," I say.

Delilah squeezes my hand. "Yeah, no parties."

"Right," Aiden says. "Sorry."

"It's fine. Why don't we all hang out at my house?" I say.

Caleb nods. "Can we get pizza?"

I laugh. "We can get whatever you want."

"Even a puppy?"

"I mean food."

"Oh. I'll still come."

"Well, you're staying at my house, so you kinda have to."

He shrugs. "You never know. I could go to some random person's party."

"You wouldn't, though. You love me too much."

Caleb's eyes dart over to Delilah quickly. "Eh, you're all right. Other people love you more, I think."

I glare at Caleb and kick his shin under the table.

The food comes out, and I reach over to grab a piece of bacon from Delilah's plate.

"Hey, that's mine!" she says.

"Too late," I say, biting into it.

"This is so hot!" Mitchell yells, spitting out the omelet he just bit into.

"Wait, you didn't stutter," Aiden says, turning to look at Mitchell.

We all go silent and stare at him.

He genuinely smiles and looks very happy. "Y-You're right," he says happily.

"Maybe because you screamed? Really loud, might I add," Caleb says. "Thanks for breaking my eardrum," he says sarcastically.

"S-Sorry. It's h-hot."

Aiden laughs.

I've noticed that Mitchell's stutter is slowly getting better. It's not as bad as when I first met him. I guess speech therapy is helping him.

I turn to say something to Caleb, and when I look back, I notice Delilah is eating some of my waffles.

"Hey!" I say, pulling my plate away from her.

She shrugs. "You took my bacon."

I take some of the whipped cream off the top of my waffles and flick it at Delilah's face.

"Hey!" she says, doing the same to me. She wipes it onto my cheek, and I quickly rub it off.

Delilah tries to clean the whipped cream off of her face, but doesn't get it all.

"There's some in your hair," I say, trying to get it out. I put the sleeve of my flannel down and wipe her cheek that has whipped cream splattered all over it.

"You guys are disgusting. Just kiss already," Caleb mumbles.

Delilah laughs, and I glare at him.

"We're all thinking it, Caleb just has the nerve to say it," Aiden says with his mouth full.

Mitchell nods and raises his eyebrows.

Delilah and I don't say anything; we both just smile at each other.

"You have whipped cream on your nose," I whisper. She really doesn't, but I quickly put some on it.

"And you have some right here," she says, pointing to my chest. I look down, and she flicks my nose.

"I can't believe I just fell for that," I mumble.

She laughs. "I can."

"You're as whipped as the cream," Caleb tells us.

Chapter Forty-Seven

LEVI

I'm freaking out for tonight. I don't even know why I'm nervous, but I am.

"What do people have at parties? Am I supposed to get balloons? Party hats? What about food? Do they have, like, brownies at these New Year's Eve things?" I ask Caleb as I frantically pace back and forth in my room.

"Well, not *that* kind of brownies."

I toss a pillow at him in frustration. "You know what I mean!"

He shrugs and laughs. "I never know with you!"

I sigh. "Why am I nervous? It's not like it's an actual party."

"Because you get nervous over everything."

"You're not helping."

"Look, if you want brownies, we can go get regular brownies. We could get a five-layer cake if you really wanted to. There are no rules to parties."

I run my hands through my hair and sit down on the edge of my bed. "I just want it to be fun. I don't want this year to end horribly."

"It will be great! Don't worry!" Caleb comes and sits down beside me. "We can go get stuff right now. Do you want to do that?"

I nod. "How are we gonna get there?" My parents went out shopping together, though I don't know what they're getting.

"I can drive. It can't be that much different than in Australia."

"It's a lot different. Plus, you can't even legally drive here."

He shrugs. "I can do it."

I shake my head. I'm always hesitant getting into cars. Caleb is a good driver in Australia, but I'm sure it's not legal for him to drive here. And everything is backward. It makes me too nervous. "I'll call Delilah and ask her to drive us."

"No, no. We have to plan tonight without her. Call Aiden."

"Okay?" I don't understand why Delilah can't come, but I call Aiden anyway. He excitedly agrees to go shopping with us and is at my house within the next five minutes.

Aiden continuously honks his car horn until we're outside.

"I call shotgun," Caleb yells as we walk out the door.

"We're not twelve-year-olds," I tell him, rolling my eyes.

He shrugs. "Too bad."

Even though we're walking to the car, Aiden continues to honk the horn.

"Chill," Caleb says bluntly when he gets in the car.

"You guys were walking too slowly," Aiden says, turning up the radio.

We first drive to the party supply store. Aiden insists on getting small fireworks to set off later. We also get party hats, a bunch of balloons, and sunglasses with the upcoming year on them. Aiden seems a little too excited about the sunglasses.

Afterward, we go to the grocery store and get way too much food. We pretty much grab everything off the shelves that looks good to us, which is a lot.

It takes almost two hours to get everything. Once we get back to my house, my dad is outside in the backyard, setting up a giant movie screen. That's what my parents went out to buy earlier. Apparently, he's going to set up a projector and make a bonfire so we can celebrate outside for part of the night, since it's too cold to stay outside the whole time. It's a little warmer than it's usually been, though. My dad says it'll be almost like we're in Times

Square. I highly doubt that, but I go along with it anyway. My mum stands behind my dad, telling him to raise the screen a little higher on the left to make it level.

It's nice seeing them doing normal stuff again, and getting along.

"So about tonight . . ." Caleb says once we're inside.

I look at him and raise my eyebrows. "What about it?"

"It's New Year's. You know what happens at midnight."

I feel my cheeks heat up. "I'd rather not talk about this."

"Well, do you have a plan?"

I shrug. "Not really."

"You need to have a plan, dude," Aiden says.

"Levi!" Caleb yells.

"Caleb!" I yell, mimicking him.

"You're so clueless. You can't go into tonight with no plan!"

"Stop being so judgmental about my love life! I can do what I want!"

"I'm just trying to help!"

We're not actually yelling at each other. Both of us are trying really hard not to laugh. This happens a lot with us, except it hasn't happened for a while, since I hadn't been talking until recently. It feels great to have things back to normal with Caleb, because for a long time things weren't like this. I'm so thankful he was able to come here for two weeks. It's great to have my best friend back.

Caleb starts laughing first, which causes me to laugh too. I hold on to my stomach after laughing for so long and quickly wipe under my eyes. Aiden laughs the most, like he usually does.

"I hate you," I tell Caleb once we've settled down

"You won't be hating me if you actually listen to me."

"I know what I'm doing," I tell them. Even though I'm not sure if I do.

Delilah gets to my house around five, right before the sun starts to set. Lucy came too, to bring me a cupcake she made especially for me. It has a giant blob of colorful frosting on top and a lot of sprinkles.

"I hope you like it!" Lucy says, hugging my leg.

"I'll have it later! It looks delicious!" I say, kneeling down to her height so I can actually hug her.

She gives me a huge smile. "My mommy said that today is New Year's Eve, and a giant ball is gonna drop from the sky. I'm gonna look out the window to see it!"

I laugh. "I hope you see it!" It's funny that she thinks it's going to fall from the actual sky. Delilah told me about New Year's Eve in New York, so I know what to expect.

Delilah's mom is standing in my driveway and calls Lucy so they can go back home.

"Bye, Levi!" Lucy yells, hugging me one more time.

"Bye!"

I shut the door and smile widely at Delilah. "Come see what we did!" I tell her excitedly. I grab her hand and run through the house. I stop in front of the back door and turn to Delilah. "Wait, close your eyes!"

"Why?" she pouts. She shuts her eyes tightly, though.

"Don't open them."

"I won't."

"Promise?"

"Promise," she says, laughing.

I slowly walk outside, still holding Delilah's hand. I stand her in front of what we've set up.

"Okay, open!" I tell her.

She quickly opens her eyes and smiles. "This is so cool!" she says, looking at the projector and screen. "How'd you think of this?"

"Actually, my dad did. It's pretty cool, though, right?"

She nods quickly and smiles even wider. "Isn't it too cold to be out here the whole time?"

"Yeah. We'll just stay out for a little."

"Oh, that sounds good."

She squeezes my hand lightly and walks over to Caleb and Aiden, who are inside.

"Hey, guys," she says, sitting next to them on the floor. She's still holding my hand, so I have to sit down too.

"Oh, hi!" Caleb says, as if he wasn't just whispering about us with Aiden. He thinks I don't know what he's doing, but I could hear him saying our names as we came in. Hopefully Delilah didn't hear anything.

I wrap my arms around Delilah's waist and rest my chin on her shoulder. She turns slightly to look at me and smiles.

Caleb smirks and raises his eyebrows.

"So what are you guys doing?" Delilah asks.

"Oh, uh, just setting up some stuff for later tonight," Aiden answers quickly.

"Oh, cool! I'm so excited. Are those fireworks?" Delilah asks, pointing to the the bag.

Aiden nods. "I convinced Levi we should buy them."

"As long as I'm not the one lighting them, it'll be fun."

"Isn't the snow going to stop them from lighting?" I ask.

"There's not too much snow, so we'll just clear a spot," Aiden says, shrugging.

I look out the window and see the sun is setting, which is painting the sky different tones of orange and pink.

I've seen plenty of sunsets before, but never one this bright.

"You're prettier than the sunset," I whisper in Delilah's ear, pointing outside.

"That was so cheesy," she mumbles, laughing.

"I know. That was the point."

"It was very sweet, though."

Caleb starts coughing hysterically, which I know is fake.

"Don't die," Aiden says, looking at Caleb weirdly.

"Sorry. Swallowed wrong or something. Jeez, I don't know *what* that could have been!" Caleb says. He punches his chest a few times.

I roll my eyes. "You're unbelievable," I mumble. I stand up and take Delilah's hand.

"I choked, and you don't even care!" Caleb says.

"We're gonna go get food," I say, pulling Delilah upstairs.

"Is Caleb okay?" she whispers.

I shrug. "That's just him."

I grab a bag of chips and bring it down to everyone. Mitchell texted me saying he's here, and he's already downstairs when I get there.

"Hey, Mitchell!" Delilah and I say in unison.

He waves excitedly. I also notice he brought Ally, the girl he went to the dance with. He was talking about maybe bringing her, but he wasn't sure. I'm happy he did.

We all sit around in my basement and eat the pizza Caleb wanted, or should I say, demanded.

"What are everyone's resolutions?" Caleb asks with his mouth full.

"D-Don't st-stutter," Mitchell says quietly. Ally smiles at Mitchell and reaches over to hold his hand.

"Get accepted to a college," Aiden says. "What about you, Caleb?"

"I'm pretty content with everything as it is," he says, shrugging his shoulders. "What about you guys?" he says to Delilah and me.

I shrug.

Delilah looks at me and smiles. "I'll just take whatever this year brings."

"Me too," I say, entwining my fingers with Delilah's. I play with her fingers nervously. There's so much more I want to say, but I'd rather keep it to myself. I'm afraid if I say it, it won't come true. I don't want to jinx myself.

For the upcoming year, I want to be truly, completely happy. I feel like it can happen—hopefully. Things have already improved so much in the past few months.

"So, who wants to play a game?" Caleb asks.

"No one," Delilah says.

"Well, okay then."

"I wanna watch a movie," Aiden says. Aiden goes over to the TV and starts searching for a movie.

We all set up pillows and blankets to lie on while we watch a movie. Everyone is sprawled out on the blankets, just talking about stuff. I'm sitting with Delilah, both of us huddled underneath some blankets. She's talking about her plans for the year, and she seems so hopeful and content. She smiles widely while she talks and moves her hands quickly because she's so excited.

She's telling me all about the colleges she's applying to and how excited she is for the summer. I could listen to her talk about anything. It's cute to see her so happy about everything.

She props herself up on her elbow and looks at me. "I was thinking, maybe, this summer we could go somewhere. Like a little vacation. I know summer is kinda far away and all, but I don't know. It's just a thought. So both of us can go somewhere." Even in the dark, I can see that her cheeks are slightly pink.

"Actually, about that. For Christmas, I got two tickets to Australia for the summer. And I was kinda hoping you'd wanna go."

"Really?"

"Yeah, if you want to go, of course."

"I'd love to go! That'd be so fun!"

"It's a plan, then. You and me take on Straya this summer."

"Please don't ever say that again," she says, laughing. She moves closer to me, and I wrap my arms around her.

"I'll just cuddle over here with myself," Aiden says, hugging himself.

"You're weird," Caleb tells him as he tries to figure out how to work the television. He's trying to get the TV to connect to the DVD player, but all that's showing up is static. He mumbles a bunch of stuff while he's figuring it out, and after a few minutes, it finally works.

Aiden picked out *Elf*, since apparently he hasn't watched it all year, so that's what we're watching.

The movie starts up, and I quietly hum the beginning song. I've seen the movie so many times.

Half the time the movie is playing, Delilah and I whisper the lines to each other.

"I'm here, with my dad, and we've never met," I sing along. Delilah laughs.

"And he wants me to sing him a song. And I was adopted, but you didn't know I was born," Delilah responds.

"So I'm here now, I found you, Daddy," we say in unison.

"Whoa, calm down over there!" Caleb says.

Delilah and I both erupt in laughter. I hide my face under the blanket because I can't stop laughing.

"We're so embarrassing," I mumble.

The movie ends a little after nine, so we have a few more hours to go. We decide to watch the New Year's Eve show in New York. I get bored with it after a while, as it's not as great as I thought it would be. I don't get why anyone would want to stand outside with thousands of strangers packed together. It does not seem enjoyable.

"Wanna go for a walk?" I ask Delilah.

"Where?"

I shrug. "I don't know. Anywhere."

"Um, okay. Sure. As long as we're back before midnight."

"We will be."

We tell everyone we'll be back soon, and we walk through the neighborhood with only the streetlights illuminating the street. It's nice and peaceful. Everyone's probably at a party or something right now. It feels like Delilah and I are the only ones in the world. Just her and me.

"Can we walk to the beach?" I ask. "*The* beach. It won't take too long."

She nods, and I smile.

"Should we see if everyone else wants to come?" she asks after a few minutes.

"If you want to. I'll call Caleb."

Everyone agrees to meet us at the beach. Aiden says he'll bring the fireworks, and we can celebrate the new year there.

I'm starting the next year at the place where it all began with the girl who started it all.

"You know what?" I say as we're walking. I'm swinging Delilah's hand back and forth as we walk.

"What?"

"I never would have thought that I'd be here with you. It's weird that I hated you at first since you reminded me of Delia, but now that I've gotten to really know you, you're a lot different. I wish I'd realized that sooner. I loved Delia, and I lo— I thought I could never find someone who would make me happy again. I don't know where I'm going with this, but I hope with this new year we can make more memories. Oh, and I promise not to throw any more of your coffees on the ground."

Delilah stops walking and hugs me tightly. "I'm so happy I met you this year," she says, her voice muffled as she hugs me. "You've changed me too, and I wouldn't want to be with anyone else right now but you."

I open my mouth to say something, but shut it. I don't want to ruin the moment.

We continue walking in a happy silence, still swinging our arms as we walk. We finally make it to the beach, and we have a few minutes to ourselves while we wait for everyone else. They're driving, but I told Caleb to wait a little. I wanted some alone time with Delilah.

"It's colder than it was last time," Delilah says, wrapping her arms around herself as we walk along the sand.

I hug her tightly from behind and sway side to side. "Warm now?"

She laughs. "Just a little squished."

"We should have brought Skittles," I say.

"For once, I don't have any."

"What a shame!"

I hear a car pull up, and soon after, everyone is walking down the beach.

"Hey, guys!" Caleb yells, running over to us. They brought blankets, food, and the fireworks. Aiden is even wearing the sunglasses.

We sit down on the blankets, away from the water so we don't get wet. Thankfully, the snow has mostly melted on the beach or gotten washed away by the waves. Aiden starts to line up the fireworks because it's almost midnight.

"H-Have you lit f-fireworks before?" Mitchell asks.

Aiden shakes his head. "There's always a first time for everything. I have ten more minutes!"

Caleb helps Aiden figure out how to use the fireworks. He reads the instructions, but both of them struggle to understand the correct way to light them.

"What about the projector your parents set up?" Caleb asks me while they're figuring out the fireworks.

"Oh, right. I guess we can just go back after midnight and watch it, right? Pretend it's the real thing."

Caleb laughs. "Sure, sounds good."

"Follow me," I tell Delilah once I realize it's almost midnight. I stand up, and Delilah follows behind me.

I walk away from everyone, but not too far. I dig my heel into the sand and write out something.

"Taste the rainbow," Delilah reads after I'm done.

She puts one arm around me and checks the time on her phone. "One minute," she whispers. She smiles and draws a heart in the sand.

I feel my heart start to race as I realize it's almost midnight. I take a deep breath and try to calm down.

"Twenty seconds!" I hear Aiden yell. I see him start to light the fireworks.

"Hey, what's that?" I ask, quickly pulling something out of my pocket and throwing it onto the sand.

"Is that mistletoe? Even though it's past Christmas?" Delilah says, giggling quietly.

"Ten seconds!" Aiden screams.

I shrug. "I don't know, but I definitely didn't put that there," I say, feeling my cheeks blush.

"It's supposed to be above us," she whispers, leaning closer to me.

"I had to improvise."

"Five!" Aiden says.

I wrap my arms around her and pull her closer to me.

"Four!"

I look from her eyes to her lips quickly.

"Three!" they all yell in unison.

Some of the fireworks shoot up and burst, causing Delilah to flinch slightly. I feel her smile against our almost-touching lips.

"Two!"

"Is this okay?" I whisper.

"One!"

She doesn't respond with words. She places her lips on mine and wraps her arms around my neck gently. Every single part of me that was nervous turns into happiness in the few seconds that we're kissing. After more fireworks erupt along with the butterflies in my stomach, we pull away from each other for a quick second.

"Happy New Year, Levi," Delilah whispers before pulling me closer and kissing me again.

For the first time in a long time, I'm focused on nothing but right now, and yes, it is a happy New Year.

Connect with Ashley Royer!

www.ashleyroyer.com

 @singsongash

 @RTFbook

 /aer98

 /callmeashley98